Arbiter Petronius, William Burnaby

The Satyricon of Petronius Arbiter

A Roman Knight, in Prose and Verse with the Fragments...

Arbiter Petronius, William Burnaby

The Satyricon of Petronius Arbiter
A Roman Knight, in Prose and Verse with the Fragments...

ISBN/EAN: 9783744771962

Printed in Europe, USA, Canada, Australia, Japan

Cover: Foto ©Andreas Hilbeck / pixelio.de

More available books at **www.hansebooks.com**

THE SATYRICON

400 Copies of this Edition have been printed.

No................

Feast
rimalchio

THE SATYRICON OF PETRONIUS ARBITER A
ROMAN KNIGHT IN PROSE AND VERSE WITH THE
FRAGMENTS RECOVER'D AT BELGRADE IN THE
YEAR 1698   MADE ENGLISH BY MR. WILSON OF
THE MIDDLE TEMPLE AND SEVERAL OTHERS
WITH A FRONTISPIECE IN PHOTOGRAVURE DE-
PICTING THE FEAST OF TRIMALCHIO

A VERBATIM REPRINT OF THE ORIGINAL EDITION
OF 1708 A.D. PRINTED AT LONDON FOR PRIVATE
CIRCULATION ONLY IN THE YEAR 1899 A.D.

THE CONTENTS

OF

Petronius Arbiter.

Translated by several Hands.

The principal Matters contain'd in the First Part.

The principal Matters contain'd in the Second Part of *Petronius*.

vii

ix

The Contents of the Third Part of *Petronius Arbiter*.

The End of *Petronius.*

THE
PREFACE.

*Oncerning the Difficulty of Trans-
lating this Author I shall say
nothing, tho' the* French *Translator
has bestow'd half his Preface to
enforce it, because if the Difficulty
was greater than the* Undertakers
*could well go through with, or vanquish with Reputa-
tion, the Infamy is not lessen'd, but their* Folly *much
magnify'd. Besides, this* Version *has already been
receiv'd with such success, that the Bookseller has
thought it worth his while to venture a new Impression, by several Hands : In short, both the Prose
and Verse is so much improv'd, that this may justly
be said to be wholly new ; besides a Third Part
never before made* English.

*Having said in few words all that was necessary
as to the Translation, I shall come to the main point
of this Præludium, which is, to remove some Reflections on the Original ; and to give some few
Remarks upon its Author.*

There are some People that are prepossess'd with a Prejudice against the Works of Petronius Arbiter, not from their own Reading, or Knowledge of the Matter, but from a sort of traditional Calumny, that the Devotees have rais'd against him. But such I desire to peruse the Life of Petronius without prejudice, and what I here shall offer in his Defence against those Censures which unfair Criticks or gross Ignorance have laid upon him.

We have nothing to fear from any Charge on the Defect of his Wit, and the Purity of his Stile, his Fame for that is too well establish'd all Europe over, and his Party every where too numerous to apprehend an Attaque from that side, for I may venture to assert, that Petronius is not much less admir'd now, than he was in ancient Rome ; for our Age, by an admirable circulation of Temper, has very much of that of the time in which our Author liv'd, and of which he has left us so agreeable a Draught.

This general Inclination to Petronius is not confin'd to those learned Men of my Acquaintance, but reaches all such who have ever discover'd any just claim to Knowledge and a good Taste ; because there is a sort of particular Sympathy betwixt those Persons of Quality who love Petronius, and the Knowledge of the Belle Lettres. For he, of all the Ancients, seems only to have known, and to have had a Taste of that true Gallantry, which at this time finishes the Character of Politeness. With such Address he attaques the Defects of the Understanding *and* Wit, *or the* Frailties *of the* Heart, *in that* Painting *which he has left us of the* Manners *of his* Age, *that he every where keeps up his* Force *and* Energy, *according to the different* Characters *of his* Persons *introduc'd.* These *and his other admirable* Qualities *gave him such a* Value *with the* Prince *of* Conde, *a* Man *of* Spirit *and* Wit, *that he maintain'd several* Learned Gentlemen *to read* Petronius *to him.*

But to omit nothing that is necessary to compleat the Defence *of our* Author, *we must enquire further than in his* Life, *into the* Spirit *with which he wrote this* Satyr, *what* Design *he had, and how he has executed that* Design. The Men *of* Wit *among the* Greeks *and* Romans *always assum'd the* Principle *of that Sect of* Philosophy *which was most agreeable to his* Temper *and* Genius. All the Authors that have wrote of* Petronius, *assure us, that he was of the* Sect *of* Epicurus, *which* Opinion *they found on several Passages of his* Satyricon, *which seem agreeable to the* Doctrine *of that* Philosopher. But that is but a* Problematick Opinion, *for from the very same Reason we may conclude, that he was of all and every one of the* Sects; *because we find all their different* Opinions *in his* Works: The only Proof *this gives us, is, that his* Wit *lov'd to indulge it self with a* Liberty *in* Writing.

But suppose that he was an Epicurean, *we ought not to look on him with an* Eye *of that* Injustice, *which the* Vulgar *generally do on* Epicurus *himself, whose* Sentiments *are much more pure than is commonly imagin'd.* The Morals *of that Philosopher draw their Principles from* Right Reason ; *and he was far from the usual imputed Absurdities of passing his Life in a perpetual* Debauch : *On the contrary, he observ'd such a* severity *in his* Pleasures, *in his* Endeavours *to deliver Mankind from the tyranny of the* Passions, *that* Seneca *was oblig'd to say much to the advantage of that Philosopher*, That he had given his Followers not one Precept, but what was conformable to Honesty and Justice.

This Testimony which Seneca (*who was himself a* Stoic *by Profession*) *gave him, was a* Condemnation *of the Sect opposite to* Epicurus, *and sufficiently discover'd their* Vanity. *For the* Principles *of the* Stoics, *which would be admirable in the Mouth of a* Christian, *are entirely* ridiculous *in that of those Philosophers : Nor can that Moral claim any Advantage, which dethrones, as I may say, the* Divinity, *and sets Man in the Seat of* Jupiter ; *those who held, that* Pain *was a* Good, *and* Pleasure *an* Evil, *and who directed our whole* Lives *through* Pain *and* Austerity, *had only* excessive Pride *for their* Virtue, *and for their* supream Good *nothing but a* vain Name, *and* Chimerical Glory : *Instead of which, the* Morals *of* Epicurus *were founded on good* Sense, *which taught the* Pagans, *that the* soveraign Good *was to have a* long Life *with* Indolence *and* Pleasure.

Since it is by no means reasonable to expect a Christian *in the person of* Petronius, *we ought to be satisfy'd if we find him an honest* Pagan ; *a Man*

xiv

of good Sense, *who reason'd and liv'd according to the true* Principles *of* Natural Knowledge, *which leaves neither room for* Hope *or* Transgression. *The manner of his* Death *alone may justifie this* Opinion. *His* Death, *indeed, is the most noble of any of all those, which* Antiquity *so much admires. In it you cannot find either* Fear, *or* Affectation, Despair, *or* Pride. Tacitus, *very near his time, describes him to us dying with the same* Tranquility *in which he liv'd. The* Deaths *of* Socrates, *and that of* Cato *of* Utica, *which are the two most celebrated of those Ages, in no measure approach that of* Petronius. *The great* Philosophical Discourses *which the first made, and the* Treatise *of the* Immortality of the Soul, *which the other more than once had recourse to, only shew us how they were* oblig'd *to put off that* Terror, *which their approaching* Fates advanc'd.

It is remarkable, that Tacitus *does not venture to say, that* Petronius *was a* Voluptuary ; *but only, that he adapted his Conduct to his desire of pleasing the* Emperour ; *and we can much less conclude, that his* Manners *were corrupt, because he drew the* Debocheries *of* Nero *and his Court. If we give our selves leave to reflect, that this manner of Writing was the* Mode *of the* Age *he liv'd in, and that he gave himself the* Air *of a severe* Philosopher, *who with Freedom lays open the* Vices *of his* Times, *and explains e'ry thing by its Name ; as* Cicero, *in his familiar* Epistles, *says of the* Stoics, Placet *Stoicis* suo quamque rem nomine appellare. *And the*

same Custom *in the greatest part of the Authors,
who have wrote in his way, ought to convince*
Posterity, *that they ought to entertain no suspicion of
his* Libertinism. *Thus* Martial *says,* Lasciva est
nobis pagina vita proba, *that* if his Epigrams had
the Air of Debochery, yet his Life was regular.
And Catullus *almost to the same purpose assures us.*

Nam castum decet esse pium Poetam
Ipsum ; Versiculis nihil necesse est.

That it is no manner of necessity that the Poet's
Verses be chaste, provided his Life be so. *And*
Petronius *himself, being apprehensive that his*
Writings *might incur some such Censures in his
Time, prevents their Objection in a manner, that
shou'd inform them, that he Wrote not by a* Spirit *of*
Corruption, *but by the* disgust *of a* Court Philosopher ; *who had been offended by the* Disorders *of
the* Emperour *and his* Favourites, *whom he exposes
to their own View in a most Satyrical manner. And
this is so plain, that in his most lively* Descriptions
of their Debaucheries, *he so qualifies and sweetens
the* Images *by the Terms and Expressions, that at
first* Modesty *cannot be shook by it ; and he employs
none of those* gross Words *which the Authors we
have nam'd are e'ry where full of, and which the*
Latin Tongue *allows a certain liberty of using, tho'
the Modesty of* our Language *will not permit it.*

Tho' Fulgentius *tells us, that he wrote* several
Books, *particularly one call'd* Euscius *or* Eustois, *a
Tract against a certain Advocate, whom he calls*

Cerberus Forensis ; *and a Poem, entituled,* Albucia, *against his* Rivals *in a* Lady *of that* Name, *with whom he was very much in* Love *; but this Satyr against* Nero *is all that the* injury of Times *has left us.* This way of agreeably mixing Prose *and* Verse *was invented by* Varro, *which, as* Aulus Gellius *informs us, he call'd* Menippean, *from* Menippus *the* Cynic Philosopher ; *because* Menippus, *before him had treated of things serious in a burlesque or bantering stile or manner.* This kind was call'd mixt Satyr, *to distinguish it from the* Satyrs *in equal* Verse. *We have seen in the foregoing* Age, *in* France, *a* Menippean Satyr ; *an Author of that time having describ'd the* Corruptions *of the* Court *of* Henry III. *in an Allegoric History, call'd,* The Isles of the Hermaphrodites.

It is therefore plain enough, that this Piece of Petronius *is a Species of* Roman Satyr, *which gives us a Draught of* Rome, *or rather of the Court of* Nero, *of his proper* Person, *and loose and abandon'd* Life. *But* Fortune *permitting not this* admirable Piece *to come down to us entire, we have from time to time made new discoveries of parts of it ; in short, this* valuable Treatise *came to us only by piece-meal ; and we have had from pure* Antiquity *handed down to us only some particular* Fragments, *which were preserv'd by the Studious, selected out of such places as pleas'd them best.* In process of time, about Forty *or* Fifty Years *since, the Story of* Trimalchio's Feast *was made perfect by the* Fragments *found in* Dalmatia ; *at last, at the taking of* Belgrade, *we got the rest, which made the* whole Work *compleat, as it now appears in the* English Tongue.

Is there any thing among all the Latin Authors *near so fine as the* History *of the* Ephesian Matron? *or any thing comparable to the Letters of* Circe *and* Polyenos? *or any thing better turn'd, or more gallant, than the* Conversation *and* Address *of that* Lady, *both in her* Disappointment *and* Joy? *And where can we find a* Confidant *more accomplish'd than* Chrisis? *She may be an* Example *to all her* Profession *even to* our days. *Her first* Conversation *with* Polyenos *is wonderfully ravishing, but the* Simplicity *and* Naviety *is not to be imitated.*

All the Learned agree, That this Roman Satyr *is in its kind the most* valuable Remains of Antiquity. *It is a surprizing thing to find what an extent of* Wit *the* Author *has discover'd; and how he has given us so many different* Characters. *When he is* Declaiming, *you see all the Air and Stile of a* Declamator; *when he* Philosophizes, *he is sententious, and gives us charming* Moral Reflections; *when he plays the* Poet, *we can find no* Verses *to compare with his. There never was a* Rapsody *so pleasantly put together, as whatever he puts into the* Mouths *of his* Speakers: *The* Debochee *e'ry where maintains his Character, and the* Whores *are always of a Piece: The* Freedmen *always speak like* Men *without Education; and the* Slaves *ne'r lift their Thoughts or Expressions above the humble level of their Condition: The* Lovers *speak with equal* Gallantry *and* Tenderness. *In short, he sustains the* Characters of all sorts of People *with so universal a Genius, as* Petronius Arbiter ; *and fills his* Satyr *with a vast variety of* agreeable Images *iudiciously dispos'd.*

After what we have said, it is no wonder to find so many Authors speaking of him with such Applause : We find Tacitus *a true Judge of Merit, giving* Petronius *a great deal.* Pliny, Terentianus Maurus, Plutarch, *St.* Jerome, Macrobius, Sidonius, Apollinaris, Isidore *of* Seville, Petrus Crinitus, Turnebius, Scaliger, Justus Lipsius, Casaubon, *and many other Authors of the foremost Rank, have celebrated the* Praises *of* Petronius Arbiter.

Above thirty Grammarians *of all Nations have made* Comments *upon* this Satyr, *tho' it must be freely own'd, that the greatest part of them have by no means been able to penetrate into the difficult places of him, which they have endeavour'd to explain ; nay, they have render'd several of them more obscure than they found 'em in their Author : They often run their Conjecture so far, that like an* Ignis fatuus, *they but lead you quite out of your way.*

There are another sort of Learned Men, *who have taken a Fancy to prove, that the* Petronius *mention'd by* Tacitus, *was not the* Petronius *who wrote the* Satyr *under our consideration ; and, that it was not wrote on the Court of* Nero : *But certainly these* Men *of* Letters *have suspended their* Penetration *while they have been reading this Author, when they could doubt of a thing so evident as this; for we every where through the whole* Satyr *discover, and plainly see the agreement with the Manners of* Nero, *the Customs of those Times. We here find* Seneca, Lucan, Silia, *and the Emperour's* Freed-men. *This you will more plainly see by the* Key *to the* Names *of the* Persons *of this* Satyr. *But* Tacitus *himself points out this* Satyr, *when he mentions the Book sent* Nero *by* Petronius *just before his Death; for he says, our Author describ'd under the borrow'd Names De-bochees, abandon'd Women, and the* Vices *of that* Prince; *as is hinted in the Life of* Petronius. *As for his calling him* C. Petronius, *it was a mistake of the first or later Transcribers, in putting a* C, *for a* T, *which is plain from a Passage of* Plutarch *to this purpose*——As whenever you reproach Debochees with their Infamy, as *Titus Petronius* did *Nero.* *And by this other of* Pliny——*Titus Petronius*, a Man of Consular Dignity, on the point of Death, by reason of the Hatred which *Nero* bore him. *But we no where find any mention of two* Petronius's *in the time of that* Emperor, *and much less can we make two of the* Name, *who lost their Lives by the Hate of* Nero. *'Tis therefore evident, that the* Petronius *mention'd by* Tacitus *was* Titus, *since it is confirmed by* Plutarch *and* Pliny.

But Petronius, *and the* Poets *we have nam'd, are not the only* People *who have made use of such a* liberty of Stile; *but we may justifie their Practice by the Example of many* grave Authors, *as the* Mode *of the* Age. *Let us cast an Eye to* Suetonius, Dion Cassius, Lampridius, Orosius, Xiphilin, *who all take a pleasure to paint in lively Colours the* Vices *of* Nero, Domitian, Heliogabalus, *all whose Pictures they have left us.*

If I should push this Defence *farther in this particular, it is no difficult matter to prove, that the very* Fathers *of the* Church *sometimes speak the* same Language, *and imploy such* Figures, Images, *and* Expressions, *as seem most proper to inspire a* Horrour *of* Vice.

E Veneno Salus.

THE
LIFE
OF
PETRONIUS ARBITER.

Written by Monsieur *St. Evremont* ;
Made 𝕰𝖓𝖌𝖑𝖎𝖘𝖍 by Mr. *Tho. Brown.*

TItus *Petronius* was a Roman Knight, descended from that Branch of the Family of the *Petronius*'s, which deriv'd their Original from the *Sabines*, and who gave so many great Men to the Service of the *Roman* Republick. We cannot doubt but he was brought up with the same prudent Care that they then employ'd at *Rome*, in the Education of Children of Quality, and that his Genius was continually exercis'd and cultivated in the attainment of polite Learning, even from his very Youth ; for in those things the *Romans* were as strict and severe as the *Greeks*. *Petronius* himself was also naturally and more particularly inclin'd to

the Study of good Literature; and it's apparent
that he excell'd in it, by the Ingenuity and Politeness he has discover'd in his Writings.

When he had compleated himself in the first
Rudiments in Learning, he made his appearance at
the Imperial Court of *Claudius;* but his great
Assiduity there was no impediment to the chief
design of perfecting himself in the Liberal Sciences,
and therefore employ'd his leisure Hours in
making *Declamations*, which was the custom of
those times, in order to exercise and enable their
young Men of the first Quality to speak in
Publick, for which purpose they had Schools to
Declaim in, and by this successful method, furnish'd
themselves with so many famous Oratours, both in
their *Senate* and *Armies;* to the great advantage of
their Republick.

The Court of *Claudius* was then the very Seat
or Mansion of Pleasures; for the Empress
Messalina employ'd all her Cares and Thoughts to
make it so, in accommodating it with all imaginable
Delights and Recreations, which she more easily
accomplish'd, by having a great Ascendant over
the Person and Inclinations of the Emperor; for
he being a weak Prince, comply'd with every
thing, provided they accommodated him with a
plentiful Table, for he was an extreme lover of
good Eating, and of drinking Wine even to
excess; and his Courtiers following the Example
of their Prince, Debauchery was no less familiar
with them.

Petronius becoming a Courtier under a Reign
where the manner of living was agreeable to his
Temper, he also became insensibly Voluptuous;
tho' at the same time it was observ'd, that he
took no delight in the brutal Pleasures of Love,

like *Messalina*, nor in those of the Table and Drunkenness with *Claudius;* only in a gallant and delicate manner took a relish of both, rather to gratifie his Curiosity than his Senses. In this manner he employ'd a part of the Day in Sleeping, and dedicated the whole Night to Pleasure and Business. His House was the Rendezvous of the better sort of the People of *Rome:* He pass'd away his time agreeably with those that visited him, and with others was celebrated for *Intrigues.* *Petronius* also procur'd himself a Reputation by an agreeable Employment, and in a method of acting easily, readily and freely, and his natural way of discoursing. One might then represent him in a continual exercise of Wit in Conversation, in the most charming Pleasures of the Table, publick Sights, Gaming, and in spending his Estate, not like a Prodigal and Debauchee, but like a nice and learned Artist in the Science of Voluptuousness.

When *Petronius* had thus pass'd away his Youth, in a Life of so much softness and Tranquility, he took a Resolution, to convince those that doubted of the extent of his Mind and Qualifications, that he was capable of the first and chiefest Employments in the Government ; for putting an Interval to his Pleasures, he accepted the Office of *Pro-Consul* of *Bithynia;* went into that Province, where he discharg'd all the Duties of his Place with great Applause ; but having put a period to that exercise of his Parts, and returning to *Rome*, *Nero*, who succeeded *Claudius* in the Empire, in recompence of the Services, made him *Consul.* This new Dignity gave him a great and ready Access to the Emperor, who at first honour'd him with his Esteem, and afterwards with his

Friendship, in acknowledgment of the sumptuous Entertainments he sometimes gave that Prince, to refresh him when fatigued with Business.

The time of *Petronius*'s Consulate being come to a Conclusion, after having laboured in quest of Glory, without quitting the Court, he reassum'd his first manner of living, and whether it proceeded from his own Inclination, or a desire to please *Nero*, he soon became one of the Emperor's Confidents, who could find nothing agreeable to his Humour, but what was approv'd by *Petronius*; and being thus possess'd of the Authority of deciding what might be acceptable, gave him the Surname of *Arbiter*, as being Master and Controller in those Affairs.

Nero, in the first part of his Reign, acted like a very wise Prince, and apply'd himself with care to the Government of the State : However *Petronius* remembred, that he was naturally inclin'd to Lust and Sensuality, and therefore like an able Politician, being in possession of his Prince's Mind, he season'd it with honest Delights, and procur'd him all the Charms imaginable, in order to remove the thoughts of seeking after others, which peradventure would have been more disorderly, and to be dreaded by the Republick.

Things continu'd in this posture while the Emperor kept within the bounds of Moderation, and *Petronius* acted chearfully under him, as *Intendant* of his Pleasures, ordering him Shows, Games, Comedies, Musick, Feasts, pleasant Seats in the Country, with delicious Gardens, charming Lakes, and all that might contribute towards the making of a Prince's Life happy and delightful.

But the Emperor some time after complying with his Nature, chang'd his Conduct, not only in respect of Governing the Empire, but also in relation to his own Person. He gave ear to the Counsels of others, rather than those of *Petronius*, insensibly plung'd into Debauchery, abandon'd himself to his Passions, and became as morose and wicked a Prince, as before he had been pleasant and equitable.

Nero was a learned Prince, of which he had given sufficient Proofs from his Youth; for at Fifteen Years of Age he pleaded in the *Senate*, in his own Tongue, on behalf of the *Boulonnois*, and in Greek for the *Rhodians*; but his Knowledge was confus'd and much embarass'd.

He also lov'd Men of Wit, and had Courtiers near him, who following the corruption of the Court, treated *Seneca* like a *Pedant*, and could not suffer that he should Preach to them the Exercise of Vertue and Modesty, because they had imbib'd an Opinion, that he himself did not live like a *Philosopher* in that particular.

Thus continuing frequently to ridicule him, it at length insinuated into the Emperor's Mind, and expos'd him to his Contempt, which being joyn'd with his own Knowledge of the unjust ways by which he had acquir'd the immense Riches he was possess'd of, his Contempt grew into Hatred, and his Hate at last caus'd the Ruin of *Seneca*.

And now indeed *Petronius* saw with sorrow, that the Emperor began to hide himself from him, and sometimes to shun him, and that, following his own corrupt Inclinations, he was grown utterly debauch'd, and forgot what he ow'd to his Imperial Dignity, that he would frequently run wild up and down the Streets, and into wicked Places, outraging all he met, and would also offer Violencies to *Roman* Ladies of the best Quality.

The Favour to which *Petronius* was rais'd had also drawn upon him the Jealousie of those who pretended, as well as he, to the Grace and Favour of the Prince, and, among others, that of *Tigillinus*, Captain of the Guards, who was a dangerous Rival. This Man, of obscure Birth and Corrupt Manners, had in a short time acquir'd a great power over the Emperor's Genius, and as he perfectly knew his blind side, began seriously to contrive the Ruin of his Competitor, and by such means, as 'twas thought would also have destroy'd the Empire.

The choice and delicious Pleasures invented by *Petronius* grated the gross Debauches of *Tigillinus*, and foreseeing that the Credit *Petronius* had with the Emperor would always be an Obstacle to his Designs, he therefore endeavour'd to possess himself of the Heart of the Prince ; and finding himself prevail by degrees, he soon engag'd him in the foulest *Brutalities*.

It's true, 'twas no difficult thing to succeed in this attempt, for finding a Nature wholly dispos'd, he quickly, and with little trouble, seduc'd him to embrace such Pleasures, as were neither approv'd nor advis'd by *Petronius*, which were entirely dropt in order to remove his Rival ; for *Nero* had already committed *Parricide* by murdering his Mother, and no sooner hearken'd to the Persuasions of *Tigellinus*, but he signaliz'd his Power, by putting *Sylla* and *Rubellius Plautus* to death, who were both Persons dreaded by them for their celebrated Vertues, and being highly esteemed and in favour with the People. Afterwards, Fury and Brutality render'd themselves Mistresses of his Heart to such an excess, that all manner of Crimes were perpetrated by him.

When the Emperor had confirm'd himself in these Disorders, our ancient Favourite, by the Artifices of the new one, found himself almost without Employment near the Prince, and *Nero* himself could not endure so nice a Witness of his *Infamias*, nor give him so free an entrance into his Pleasures as he formerly enjoy'd.

Tigillinus serving himself of these Dispositions, omitted nothing that might satisfie the Desires of his Prince, by the magnificent Feasts he provided ; and as his Rival (according to *Tacitus*) much surpass'd him in the Science of Pleasures, one might conclude, without fear of being deceiv'd, that those which *Petronius* order'd were of another nature, and had nothing of those disorders in them that were seen in one of the Feasts which that Historian relates as an Example of all the rest, which he describes in this manner : They provided a stately Feast on the Lake of *Agrippa* ; in a Vessel cover'd with Plates of Gold and Ivory; the Rowers were plac'd in their Ranks, which they took according to their Age and Experience in Debauchery. They had sent to the very ends of the Earth for the rarest eatables. The Lake was edg'd with Porches, in which were great numbers of Chambers, fill'd on one side with Women of Quality, who prostituted themselves to the first comers, and the other with naked Courtizans in a thousand lascivious postures ; at Night appear'd in all parts surprizing Illuminations, the Woods and Palaces round about ecchoed with Consorts of Musical Instruments and Songs adapted to the Feast. To conclude this grand Debauch in a famous Action, *Nero* was married a little after, to one of the most corrupted Wretches of this Troop, named *Pythagora*, and that publickly,

with all the accustom'd Ceremonies. They put
upon the Emperor's Head the Espoused's Vail,
sent him two *Auspices*, assign'd him the Marriage-
Portion, adorn'd the Nuptial Bed, lighted Flam-
beaux, and to conclude the Marriage, permitted
that to be seen to the open view of all the
Company, which the Shades of Night hide from
the Eyes in the most lawful Pleasures.

Petronius being extremely disgusted at the
Horrours he saw, insensibly withdrew himself
from Court, and being of a mild and unenter-
prizing Nature, suffer'd things to run in the
train they had form'd, without attempting to re-
establish them in the Condition he had left them.
I am of Opinion, it was about this time that he
took his Pen in Hand to compose this *Satyr*,
which so exactly represents the Nature and
Character of *Nero*, and under the Names of
Debauchees and *Lewd Women*, decry'd all the
Vices of this Prince and his Courtiers.

While *Petronius* liv'd in a retired Tranquility,
Tigillinus labour'd with all his power to destroy
him, and take away his Rival from all possibility
of re-ent'ring into favour ; and knowing that the
Prince's Nature was inclining to *Cruelty*, he insinuated, that *Petronius* was too familiar with
Scevinus, not to be dipt in *Piso's* Conspiracy ; and
for that end having suborn'd one of *Petronius*'s
Slaves to swear against his Master, to deprive him
of all means of justifying himself, they put the
greatest part of his Domestics in Prison.

Nero was well enough pleas'd to find an opportunity of losing a Man who was become a dead
Weight upon his Affairs ; for the Vicious cannot
endure the presence of such Persons, whose sight
reproaches them with their abominable Practices ;

therefore favourably receiv'd the Accusation against *Petronius*, and order'd him to be apprehended at *Cumæ*, when the Emperor made a Voyage thither, where he was one of the Company : But as it required some time to deliberate, whether they ought to put a Man of his consideration to Death, without clearer Proofs of his being guilty of the Crimes he stood charg'd with ; he was so extreamly disgusted, and also weary of living under the Domination of such a *detestable* Prince, that seeing himself so long a time made the Sport of his Caprices, he resolv'd to *dye*. However, that he might not give himself a precipitate Death, he open'd his Veins, and afterwards clos'd them again, that he might have time to enjoy the Conversation of his Friends, who came to see him in his last Moments ; whom he requested to entertain him, not with Discourses of the *Immortality of the Soul*, and the celebrated Axioms that the Pride of Philosophers had invented, to acquire Glory and a vain opinion of their Constancy, but with the recital of some curious Pieces of Poetry.

And to convince the Spectators that he did not *Dye*, but only cease to *Live*, he continu'd his ordinary Functions ; took a particular account of the Demeanour of Domesticks ; recompenc'd some of his Slaves, and chastis'd others ; set himself as formerly at his Table, and also slept very quietly, insomuch, that he rather seem'd a Man in perfect Health than one that was dying ; so that his Death, tho' *Violent*, appear'd to his Friends as if it had been *Natural*.

Now, as *Petronius* abhorr'd the People of *Nero*'s and *Tigillinus*'s Character ; so he would never condescend to the baseness of imitating those Animals, who dying in these wretched Times by the order of this Prince, made him their Heir, and stuff'd their Testaments with *Elogies* on the Tyrant and his Favourite.

But on the contrary, being possess'd of a *Goblet* of precious Stones, which cost him above 2000 Pistoles, and out of which he commonly drank, he broke it to pieces, that *Nero* might not have it after his death ; and after this, thought fit to present him this *Satyr*, writ against him, and having seal'd it up, tore off the Seal again, for fear (after his Death) they might employ it as an Instrument to destroy those in whose Hands it might be found.

This made *Nero* extremely chagrine, to see his infamous Actions made known to *Petronius ;* and having levell'd his *Suspicion* upon all those who he thought might discover his Secrets, at last fix'd it upon the Wife of a *Senator*, named *Silia*, with whom he had been *too familiar ;* but because she was also a great Friend of *Petronius*'s, he imagin'd that, by a particular grief, she had hazarded a discovery of what had been more her Interest to conceal ; upon which she was exil'd.

It was in the Year of the Foundation of *Rome* 819, (under the Consulate of *Caius Suetonius Paulinus*, and of *Lucius Pontius Telesinus*) that City lost so great a Person.

A

K E Y,

BY A

Person of Honour.

ENcolpius, a Word which takes its Original from the *Greek*, and signifies *I insinuate*. So *Petronius* nam'd this Person ; because he related, from the beginning to the end, all the Adventures of this *Roman*, who frequently in his Morals insinuated the Horrour of Vice.

Ascyltos, in Greek, signifies *Indefatigable*, a Name well adapted to this young Man, who was handsome, vigorous, and endow'd with the choicest Talents of Nature.

Gito, in the same Language, signifies *Neighbour*, a Term of Friendship, as if he had said, *my Inseparable*; for *Gito* did not abandon *Encolpius*, till he was forc'd by *Ascyltos*.

These three Persons serve only to embellish the History, their Conduct is the Portraicture of the disorderly Life of young People. They were Associates in all sorts of Friponeries and Debaucheries, and wore the habit of Philosophers to cover their designs.

xxxii

Agamemnon, a Professor of Eloquence, whose Character is that of a true *Pedant*, and under his Name, *Petronius*, who had in view all the Orators of his time, particularly designs *Seneca*, who was *Nero's Præceptor*, and a *Stoic* Philosopher ; the same whom this Prince describ'd under the Name of *Trimalchio*, and whom he calls his *Master*, in the Feast he made for his Friends. The Author gives him the Name of a great King ; peradventure in imitation of *Varro*, who has also describ'd a *Declamator* under the name of *Agamemnon* ; because *Homer*, the chief of the *Greeks*, harangues like an Orator. We see also that *Martial* has pointed another under the Name of King *Attalus*, and calls these publick *Haranguers*, proud Kings and Triflers ; for really, in ancient Times, they often enough gave this Title to *Rhetoricians* by way of derision, to mock them out of the vain pomp of their affected Eloquence and swelling windy Style. So in some places we find *Seneca* preaching *Frugality* and *Poverty* in the midst of Riches and a plentiful Table, which was nothing less than appearing what he was not, as *Suillus* made apparent, when he accus'd him for taking Money to plead the Causes of his own Parties, in opposition to the *Cincian* Law. *Tacitus* also reproach'd him ; *That he had always a great Animosity against the Friends of* Claudius. *That his Studies being to promote insignificant Trifles, and to cajole young Scholars in their Ignorance, he envy'd all those that were endow'd with a Masculine uncorrupted Eloquence, and employ'd it in defence of their fellow-Citizens. That he was made Treasurer of* Germanicus, *That he introduc'd Adultery into the Prince's Palace. That it was easie to judge which was most culpable, he that receiv'd a voluntary*

Recompence for his honest Industry; or he that labour'd to support unjust Causes at the Bar in Courts of Judicature, and corrupt Ladies of the first Quality. That it ought to be known, by what kind of Wisdom or Precepts of Philosophy, in only four Years time, he possess'd the Favour and Graces of Nero, *and acquir'd three Millions of Riches.* That he search'd all Rome *for such as had no Children, to make them fall into the Snares he had laid, to oblige them to make their* Testaments *in his Favour.* That by exorbitant Usury, *he exhausted the Wealth of* Italy *and the Provinces,* &c. I have, you see, been very particular, and have related these Passages almost entire, because the Author frequently insists upon them in many places of this Satyr, where occasionally he falls upon *Seneca;* which you will find at large in the Work it self.

Lycurgus, a *Roman* Knight, Friend of *Ascyltos,* whose House in the Country was pillag'd in a pleasant Adventure.

Quartilla, Priestess of *Priapus.*

Psyche, Waiting-woman to *Quartilla.* This word in *Greek* signifies *the Soul,* and was a Name of tenderness given to a Courtizan.

Pannychis, a little Girl, very pretty. The Name is *Greek,* and signifies *Night,* proper enough for Whores; because anciently the greatest Debaucheries were practis'd in the Night, and so it continues among the nicest sort of this Tribe to this day, and particularly at *Rome.*

The History of these three Adventurers comprehends Truths that are unknown to us. Their business is to give Diversion, to shew the Address, Effronteries, and Debaucheries of lewd Women.

Trimalchio is compounded of two *Greek* words and signifies in Latin, *ter mollis,* to express a Man consummated in all kinds of Debauchery. 'Tis, the Name of a Rich *Freeman*, who made a sumptuous Banquet ; a vain Person, learn'd, but confus'd having his Wit cross-wise, and his manners entirely corrupted. The Author purposely made this *Hero* ridiculous, and extremely loaded his Picture, that he might the more resemble *Nero*. *Bourdelot* assures us, that anciently this Emperor was represented on *Medals* in these words, *C. Nero. August. Imp.* and on the reverse, *Trimalchio*, which according to the *Commentator*, shews how much they are deceiv'd, who pretended that *Petronius* describ'd *Seneca* under that Name. *Nero* is also represented under the Person of a *Franchise* or Freed-man, and that for two reasons. 1. Because he had a perfect conformity with the Vices of that sort of People. 2. To reproach him with the too great Familarity he held with them : Which caus'd *Tacitus* to say, That *Franchis'd* Persons were never in so much Credit as under the Reign of *Nero*.

Fortunata, Wife to *Trimalchio*. This Woman was of obscure Birth, and also had been a Slave ; so that his marrying her was a reproach to himself.

Seleucus, *Phileros*, *Ganymedes*, *Echion*, *Niceros*, *Plocrime*, were a Troop of *Freed-men*, invited to a Feast by *Trimalchio*, which was never known in *Rome* before that time.

Norbamus, under this Name must be understood *Tigillinus*, Captain of *Nero*'s Guards, and his Favourite.

Hermeros, a very impudent Freed-man of *Trimalchio*'s.

Habinnas, an inferiour Magistrate, who, accompanied by his wife, went to *Trimalchio* at the latter end of the Repast, with attendance, and in the Majesty of *Prætor*, as one who design'd to build a

Mausoleum, of which he had laid the Plan according to his Genius : Which is a piquant piece of Raillery, design'd by the Author to scoff at *Nero*'s intentions, to erect an Eternal Monument to his own Memory.

Scintilla, Wife of *Habinnas*, under which appellation you have a Character of those superficial Women, that have no solidity in them.

Eumolpus, besides his being a Poet, and in a forlorn Equipage, was a great Deboshee, and had suffered many Disgraces under this Name ; the Author represents the management of *Nero* in making Verses, in which he was so strongly conceited of his own Abilities, that he put to death all that succeeded in that Art, better than himself. Another End was, to give himself the liberty of representing *Nero* under different Characters, all ridiculous, and under different Names, the principal whereof were *Trimalchio*, *Eumolpus*, and *Polyænus*.

Corax, Servant to *Eumolpus*.

Lycas, Captain of the Ship, a very debauch'd Person, who provok'd the Anger of the Gods.

Doris, Wife of *Lycas* and Mistress of *Encolpius*.

Tryphæna, a perfectly fine Courtizan, belov'd of *Lycas*, and to whom there happen'd pleasant Adventures with *Encolpius* and *Gito*.

Esius, a Passenger in the Ship commanded by *Lycas*, who caus'd all the troubles that befel them.

Polyænos, a Name taken by *Encolpius*, disguised like a Slave in *Crotona* under which Name *Petronius* describes an Adventure that happen'd to *Nero* with a *Roman* Lady. The character of *Polyænos* is extremely fine, and might have done *Nero* honour, if the Author had not first represented him under the vile Person of a Slave, which part this Emperour often acted, in running about the Streets in the Night, and frequenting infamous Places, which shew'd his Impuissance, and doubtless, was a great mortification to him, to find his Weaknesses in this kind so openly discover'd. Further we have reason to believe, that *Petronius* also shew'd how easily he could embellish his Work, and do himself Honour by his excellent Wit, which shines in all these incomparable Descriptions.

Circe, a Lady of *Crotona*, amorous of *Polyænus*, by whom it may be reasonably conjectur'd, that the Author would be understood of *Silia*, a *Roman* Lady, who was married to a *Senator*, and banish'd, as you heard already in the Life of *Petronius*, under suspicion of revealing *Nero's* Secrets, out of grief for what happen'd to the Author : For if this Prince drown'd in Debauchery, and who, without shame, made himself a Spectacle of contempt in the midst of *Rome*, could be concern'd to see his Pleasures turn'd to Ridicule in this Satyr ; there is great appearance, that the Picture of his Weakness in this Instance touch'd him most sensibly ; and by consequence, that the Adventure had rather relation to *Silia*, than any other.

Chrysis, Waiting-woman to *Circe*, and her Confident. This Name is *Greek*, and signifies *Dorea*, or *Fine* ; an Epithet given to *Venus*, and was voluntarily taken by the ancient Courtizans.

Proselenos, a Sorcerer, that *Chrysis* led to *Polyænos*.

Enothea, a Priestess of *Priapus*.

Philumena, another Lady of *Crotonia*, who sometimes serv'd her self of her Beauty to get Visiters, and upon the Reputation of *Eumolpus's* being rich presented him with her Son and Daughter, who were both very young and very handsome, that they might profit by his good Instructions. Under this Name *Eumolpus*, *Petronius* describes *Nero's Novitates Stupri*, as *Tacitus* says, new-invented ways of Whoring and Filthiness.

The Places where these Adventures pass'd, are *Naples* and *Crotona*, under whose Names the Author chose to draw the natural Portraiture of *Rome*.

THE SATYRICON.

The Works of Petronius Arbiter

I FORMERLY promis'd you an Account of my Adventures, and am now resolv'd to be as good as my Word, being opportunely met ; not only to improve our Learning, but to make merry with pleasant Tales, and a free Conversation.

Fabricius Vejento has already, with a world of Wit, expos'd the Juggle of Religion, and withal discover'd with what Impudence and Ignorance *Priests* pretend to be inspir'd : But are not our wrangling Pleaders possess'd with the same Frenzy, who harangue their Audience ? These Wounds I receiv'd in defence of your Liberty ; this Eye was lost in your Service ; give me a Hand to lead me to my Children, for my wounded Hams are too feeble to support me.

Yet even this might pass for tolerable, did it put young beginners in the least way to well-speaking : Whereas now, what with the irregular swelling of Matter, and the empty rattling of

Words, they only gain this, That when they come to appear in publick, they think themselves in another World. And therefore I look upon the young fry of Collegiates as likely to make the most promising Blockheads, because they neither hear nor see any thing that is in use amongst Men : But a company of Pirates with Chains on the shoar ; Tyrants issuing Proclamations to make Children kill their Fathers ; the Answers of Oracles in a Plague-time ; that three or more Virgins be sacrific'd to appease the angry Gods ; dainty fine Words without any Substance, like a Dish prettily garnish'd without any Meat in it, and every thing so done, as if 'twere all Spice and Garnish.

Such as are thus bred can no more judge aright, than those that live in a Kitchin not stink of the Grease : Give me, with your favour, leave to say, 'twas you first lost the good Grace of Speaking ; for with light idle gingles of Words, to make sport, you have brought Oratory to this, That the substance thereof is become invalid and effeminate.

Our Youth were not confin'd to this way of declaiming when *Sophocles* and *Euripides* influenc'd the Age : Nor yet had any Garret-Professor debauch'd their Studies, when *Pindar* and the nine *Lyrick* Poets durst not attempt the inimitable Numbers of *Homer :* And that I may not derive my Authority from Poets only, 'tis certain neither *Plato* nor *Demosthenes* ever put in practice these

affected Declamations. Their chaste Orations were
neither turgid, painted, or adulterate, but had all
the Ornaments and Charms of a Natural Beauty.

This windy and irregular way of babling came
lately out of *Asia* into *Athens;* and having, like
some ill Planet, blasted the aspiring Genius of their
Youth, at once corrupted and put a period to all
true Eloquence.

After this, Who came up to the height of
Thucydides? Who reach'd the Fame of *Hyperides?*
Nay, there was hardly a clean Verse, but all were
of the same strain, and died with their Author.
Painting also had the same fate, after the boldness
of the *Egyptians* ventur'd to bring so great an Art
into Miniature.

At this and the like rate I was upon a time
declaiming, when one *Agamemnon* made up to us,
and looking sharply on a Person whom the Mob
with such diligence gave attention to, he would
not suffer me to declaim longer in the Portico,
than he had sweated in the school ; "But, young
" Man, said he, because your Discourse is beyond
" the common apprehension, and, which is not
" often seen, that you are a lover of Understand-
" ing, I won't deceive you : The Masters of these
" Schools are not to blame, who think it necessary
" to be mad with mad Men : For unless they teach
" what their Scholars approve, they might, as *Cicero*
" says, keep School to themselves : like flattering
" Parasites, who when they come to great Mens
" Tables, study nothing more than what they

3

" think may be most agreeable to the Company,
" (being sensible they shall never effect their
" Designs, unless they first charm the Ear) so a
" Master of Eloquence, Fisherman-like, unless he
" first baits his Hook with what he knows the
" Fish will bite at, may wait long enough on the
" Rock without hopes of catching any thing.

" Where lies the Fault then? Parents ought
" to be sharply reprehended, who are unwilling
" their Children should observe a strict Method in
" their Studies ; but in this, as in all things else,
" they are so fond of making a Noise in the
" World, and in such haste to arrive at their
" Wishes, that they hurry Youth into the Publick
" e're they have well digested what they have
" read, and put Children, before they are past
" their Sucking-bottle, into the Lists of Eloquence;
" than which, by their own Confession, nothing is
" harder to attain : Whereas if they would suffer
" them to come up by degrees, that their Studies
" might be temper'd with grave Lectures ; their
" Affections fashion'd by the Dictates of Wisdom ;
" that they might work themselves into a Mastery
" of Words ; and for a long time hear, what
" they're inclin'd to imitate, nothing that pleas'd
" Children wou'd be admir'd by them. But now
" Boys trifle in the Schools, young Men are
" laugh'd at in Publick, and, which is worse than
" both, what ill Habits are foolishly assum'd in
" Youth, we refuse to acknowledge in Age.

" And that I may not be thought to have

" condemn'd *Lucilius's* manner of Writing, I will
" also my self give you my Thoughts in Verse.

By Liberal Arts would you acquire Renown,
And rise to Power by Honours of the Gown?
Strict in your Life, of Conversation chaste,
Far from the Court with just precaution haste,
The Haughty Great *but very rare attend,*
Nor drink too deeply *to oblige a Friend.*
Let no soft Vows your blooming Youth engage,
And flye the luscious Accents *of the Stage,*
Whether the Bard of fair Briseis *Sings,*
Of stern Pelides *and the Fate of Kings,*
Or wounded Gods, *the immortal Verse inspire*
Atrides Wrongs, *or burnt* Scamander's *Ire :*
Let Homer's *Muse your early Studies guide,*
And largely drink of that enchanting Tide.
Next let Philosophy employ your Thought,
And Maxims learn the Wise Athenian* *taught,*
From thence———
A fresh Career, with rapid Courses run,
And equal him† oppos'd great* Philip's *Son.*

While I was wholly taken up with *Agamemnon,*
I did not observe how *Ascyltos* had given me the
slip, and being still intent upon his Discourse, a
great crowd of Scholars fill'd the Portico, to hear,
(as it appear'd afterwards) an extemporary Decla-
mation, of I know not whom, that was descanting
on what *Agamemnon* had said ; while therefore they

* *Socrates.*   † *Demosthenes.*

5

ridicul'd his Advice, and condemn'd the method of the whole, I took an opportunity of getting from them, and ran in quest of *Ascyltos:* But the hurry I was in, with my ignorance where our Inn stood, so distracted me, that what way soever I went, I return'd the same, till tir'd in the pursuit, and all in a sweat, I met an old Herb-woman: *I beseech you Mother*, says I, *do you know whereabouts I dwell?* Pleas'd with the humour of the question, *Why should I not?* answer'd she; and rising up, went on before me: I thought her no less than a Witch: But having led me into a bye Lane, she threw off her Pyebal'd Patch'd Mantle, *and here*, says she, *you can't want a Lodging.*

As I was denying I knew the House, I observ'd a company of *Beaux* reading the Bills o'er the Boxes, on which was inscrib'd the Name of the respective Whore and her Price; and others of the same Function naked, scuttling it here and there, as if they would not, yet would be seen: When too late I found my self in a Bawdy-house, cursing the Hag that had trapan'd me thither, I cover'd my Face, and was just making off through the midst of them, when in the very Entry *Ascyltos* met me, but as tired as my self, and in a manner dead; you'd have sworn the same old Woman decoy'd him there. I could not forbear laughing, we saluted each other, and I ask'd him what business he had in so scandalous a place? he wip'd his Face, *And if you knew*, reply'd he, *what has happen'd to me——* As what, says I.

He faintly reply'd ; *When I had rov'd the whole City without finding our Inn, the Master of this House came up to me, and obligingly proffer'd to be my Guide ; so through many a cross Lane and blind turning, having brought me to this House, he drew upon me, and press'd to a closer Ingagement. In this Affliction the Whore of the Cell also demanded a Reward for the use of her Apartment ; and that loose Fellow laid such violent Hands on me, that had I not been too strong for him, I had got the worst of it.*

While *Ascyltos* was telling his Tale, in come the same Fellow, with a Woman, none of the least agreeable, and looking upon *Ascyltos*, entreated him to walk in and fear nothing, for if he would not be Passive he might be Active : The Woman on the other hand press'd me to go in with her. We follow'd therefore, and being led among those little Apartments, we saw many of both Sexes imploy'd in the Boxes, * so that we concluded all of them had drank a Love Potion.*

We were no sooner discover'd, but they wou'd have attack'd us with the like Impudence, and in a trice one of their number with his Coat tuck'd under his Girdle, laid hold on *Ascyltos*, and having thrown him cross a Couch, would have charg'd him in the rear : I presently ran to help the under-most, * and uniting our forces, we made Nothing of the troublesome Fool.* *Ascyltos* went off, and flying, left me expos'd to their Violence ; but thanks to my Strength and Courage, I got off without Injury.

I had almost traverst the City round, * when in the dusk of the Evening I saw *Gito* at the Bench of our Inn * ; I placed my self by him, and enquir'd what *Ascyltos* had got us for Dinner? the Boy sitting down, began to wipe away the Tears that stood in his Eyes ; I was much concern'd at it, and ask'd him the occasion ; he was slow in his answer, and seem'd unwilling to inform me ; but mixing Threats with my Entreaties ; *'Twas that Brother or Comrogue of yours*, said he, *that coming ere while into our Lodging, wou'd have violated my Virtue : When I cry'd out, he drew his sword, and if thou art a* Lucreece, said he, *thou hast met a* Tarquin.

I heard him, and pointing at *Ascyltos*, what say'st thou, thou Catamite, whose very Breath is infectious?

Ascyltos at first pretended to be mightily sur-priz'd, but presently putting my Hand aside, in a higher Voice, cry'd out, *Must you be prating, thou Lascivious Cut-throat,* * who was condemn'd for murdering thine Host,* * and sav'd only by the breaking of the Rope? You make a noise, you Night-Pad, whose top Mistriss was but a Bawd. On what account did you and I keep Company formerly? Upon the same, I suppose, the Boy is admitted the honour of your Conversation.*

And who but you, *interrupted I*, gave me that slip in the Portico? *Why, what a wise Man of* Gotham, continu'd he, *must I have been, when I was dying for hunger, to hear Sentences, forsooth, as much to the purpose as the ratling of broken Glasses, or the expounding of Dreams?* by Hercules, *thou wert by much the greater Rogue of the two, who to get a meals Meat, did not blush to commend an insipid Poet.* When at last, turning from Scolding to Laughing, we began to be in a better humour, and to talk of our Affairs with a little more sedateness.

But a sense of the late Injury still sticking in my Stomach, *Ascyltos, said I,* I find we shall never agree together, therefore let's divide the common Stock, and each of us set up for himself: You are a piece of a Scholar, and I'll be no hinderance to your Projects, but think of some other way; for otherwise we shall run into a thousand Mischiefs, and become scandalous all over the Town.

Ascyltos was not against the Project; *And since we have promised,* said he, *as Scholars, to sup together, let's husband the Night too; and to morrow I'll get me a new Lodging, and some Comrade or other.*

'Tis Nonsense, *said I,* to defer what we desire: I had for a considerable time Intentions to part with *Ascyltos,* looking upon him as a Person who too narrowly observ'd my Actions; but a stronger Motive to it was, that I might renew my old friendship with *Gito.*

Ascyltos taking the Affront, impatiently, without answering, flew away in a fury; I was too well acquainted with the weakness of his Mind, and the violence of his Love, not to fear the effects of

so sudden a breach, and therefore made after him,
both to observe his Designs and to prevent them ;
but losing sight of him, I was a long time in
pursuit of him to no purpose.

When I had search'd the whole Town, I
return'd to my Cellar, where, the Ceremony of
Kisses being over, I got my Boy to a closer
Embrace, and enjoying my wishes thought my self
happy even to Envy : Nor had I done when
Ascyltos stole to the Door, and forcing the Bolt,
found us diverting our selves ; upon which,
clapping his Hands, he fell a laughing, and
turning me about, *What*, said he, *most reverend
Gentleman, what were you doing, my brother in
Iniquity ?* Nor was he content with Words only,
but untying the Thong that bound his Wallet, he
belabour'd me heartily, and mingling Reproaches
with his Blows, *As you like this, desire a second
parting.*

‘Being thus surprized, I took little notice of the
‘ Injury, but politickly turn'd it off with a laugh ;
‘ for otherwise I must have come to an Engage-
‘ ment with my Rival : Whereas sweetning him
‘ with a counterfeit Mirth, I brought him also to
‘ laugh for company : *And you*, Eucolpius, began
‘ he, *are so wrapt in Pleasures, you little consider
‘ how short our Money grows, and what we have left
‘ will turn to no account : There's nothing to be got in
‘ Town this Summer-time, we shall have better luck
‘ in the Country ; let's visit our Friends.*

‘Necessity made me approve his Advice, as well

' as conceal the smart of the Lash; so loading *Gito*
' with our Baggage, we left the City, and went to
' the House of one *Lycurgus*, a *Roman* Knight;
' who, because *Ascyltos* had formerly been his
' Comrade, entertain'd us handsomely; and the
' Company we met with in the place, made our
' Entertainment the more agreeable: For, first
' there was *Tryphæna*, a very beautiful Woman,
' who came with one *Lycas*, the owner of a Ship,
' and Master of a small Seat that lay contiguous to
' the Sea.

' The Delight we receiv'd in this place was more
' than could be exprest, tho' *Lycurgus*'s Table was
' thrifty enough, you must know we were all pro-
' miscuously imploy'd in Affairs of Love: The
' fair *Tryphæna* pleas'd me, and readily inclin'd to
' my wishes; but I had scarce given her the
' Courtesie of the House when *Lycas* storming to
' be thus nickt in his Amours, accus'd me at first
' of underhand-dealing; but soon from a Rival
' addressing himself as a Lover, he pleasantly told
' me, I must repair his Damages; and ply'd me
' hotly: But *Tryphæna* having my Heart, I could
' not lend him an Ear. The refusal made him the
' sharper; he follow'd me wherever I went, and
' getting into my Chamber at Night, when Entreaty
' did no good, he fell to downright Violence; but
' I rais'd such an out-cry, that I wak'd the whole
' House, and by the help of *Lycurgus*, got rid of
' him for that time.

' At length perceiving *Lycurgus*'s House was

'not for his purpose, he would have persuaded me
'to his own ; but I rejecting the proffer, he made
'use of *Tryphæna*'s power over me ; and she the
'rather persuaded me to yield to him, because she
'was in hopes of living more at liberty there.   I
'I follow'd therefore whither my Love conducted
'me ; but *Lycurgus* having renew'd his old·Con-
'cern with *Ascyltos*, would not suffer him to absent
'himself : At last we agreed, that he shou'd stay
'with *Lycurgus*, and we go with *Lycas* : Moreover
'it was concluded, that every one of us, as oppor-
'tunity offer'd, should pilfer what he could for the
'benefit of the common Stock.

'*Lycas* was overjoy'd at my Consent, and so
'hastned our departure, that, taking leave of our
'Friends, we arriv'd at his House the same Day.

'But in our Passage he so order'd the matter
'that he sat next me, and *Tryphæna* next to
'*Gito*, which he purposely contriv'd, to shew the
'notorious Lightness of that Woman ; nor was he
'mistaken in her, for she presently grew amorous
'of the Boy : I was quickly jealous, and *Lycas* so
'exactly remark'd it to me, that he soon confirm'd
'my suspicion of her.   On this I began to be
'more condescending to him, which made him all
'Joy, as being assur'd the Unworthiness of my
'new Mistress wou'd beget my Contempt of her,
'and resenting her slight, I should be more easily
'induc'd to receive him favourably.

'So stood Affairs while we were at *Lycas*'s :
'*Tryphæna* was desperately in love with *Gito* ;

' *Gito* again as wholly devoted to her; I car'd
' little for the sight of either of them; and *Lycas*
' studying to please me, found me every day some
' new Diversion: In all which also his Wife
' *Doris*, a fine Woman, strove to exceed him, and
' that with so much gaiety, that she presently
' expell'd *Tryphæna* from my Heart: I gave her
' the Wink, and she return'd her Consent by as
' wanton a Twincle; so that this dumb Rhetorick
' going before the Tongue, secretly convey'd to
' each other our mutual Inclinations.

' I knew *Lycas* was jealous, which kept me
' Tongue-ty'd so long, and the love he bore his
' Wife made him discover to her his inclination to
' me: But the first opportunity we had of talking
' together, she related to me what she had learn'd
' from him; and I frankly confess'd it, but withal
' told her how absolutely averse I had ever been
' to't: Well then, quoth the discreet Woman, we
' must try our Wits, according to his own
' Opinion, the Permission was one's, and the
' Possession another's.

' By this time *Gito* had been worn off his Legs,
' and was gathering new strength, when *Tryphæna*
' return'd to me, but disappointed of her expecta-
' tion, her Love chang'd to a downright Fury;
' and, all on fire with following me to no purpose,
' she got into my Intrigue both with *Lycas* and his
' Wife: She made little reckoning of his Wanton-
' ness with me, as well knowing it wou'd hinder
' no Grist from coming to her Mill: But for

' *Doris*, she never left till she had found out her
' private Amours with me, and discover'd them to
' *Lycas;* whose Jealousie being superior to his
' Love, ran all to Revenge; but *Doris*, advertis'd
' by *Tryphæna*'s Woman, to divert the Storm,
' forbore any clandestine Meetings.

' As soon as I perceiv'd it, having curs'd the
' Treachery of *Tryphæna*, and the Ingratitude of
' *Lycas*, I began to think of retiring, and Fortune
' favour'd me: For a Ship consecrated to the
' Goddess *Isis*, laden with rich Spoils, had the day
' before run upon the Rocks.

' *Gito* and I laid our Heads together, and he was
' as willing as my self to be gone ; for *Tryphæna*
' having exhausted his strength, began now not to
' be so fond of him. Early the next Morning
' therefore we march'd towards the Sea, where with
' the less difficulty we got on board the Vessel,
' because we were no strangers to *Lycas*'s Servants,
' who at that time took care of her : They still
' honouring us with their Company, it was not a
' time to filch any thing ; but leaving *Gito* with
' them, I took an opportunity of getting into the
' Stern, where the Image of *Isis* stood, and strip'd
' her of a rich Mantle, and Silver Trimming ; and
' also having turn'd other good Booty out of the
' Master's Cabin, I stole down by a Rope, unseen
' of any but *Gito;* who also gave them the slip and
' sneakt after me.

' As soon as I saw him I shew'd him the Pur-
' chase, and both of us resolv'd to make what

'haste we could to *Ascyltos*, but *Lycurgus*'s House
'was not to be reach'd the same day : When we
'came to *Ascyltos* we shew'd him the Prize, and
'told him in short the manner of getting it, and
'how we had been the meer make-game of Love :
'He advis'd us to prepossess *Lycurgus* with our
'Case, and make him our Friend ere the others
'could see him ; and withal boldly to assert, That
the ill usage of *Lycas* was the only cause why we
stole away so hastily ; which when *Lycurgus* came
to understand, he would at all times protect us
from our Enemies.

Our flight was unknown till *Tryphæna* and
Doris were got out of Bed ; for we daily attended
their Levy, and waited on them while they were
dressing ; but, when contray to our usual custom
we were found missing, *Lycas* sent after us, and
especially to the Seaside, for he had heard we made
that way, but not a word of the Pillage, for the
Ship lay somewhat to Sea-ward, and the Master
had not yet return'd on board.

But at last it being positively known we were
run away, and *Lycas* becoming uneasie at our
absence, fell in a desperate passion with his Wife,
whom he suppos'd to be the occasion of our
departure : I pass over what Words and Blows he
gave her, knowing not the particulars : I'll only
say, *Tryphæna*, the Mother of Mischief, had put
Lycas in the head, 'twas probable we had taken
Sanctuary at *Lycurgus*'s, where she persuaded him
to go in quest of the Fugitives, and promis'd to

bear him Company, that she might load us with just Reproaches.

The next day they accordingly set forward, and came to his House ; but we were out of the way : For *Lycurgus* was gone to a Festival in honour of *Hercules*, held at a neighbouring Village, and had taken us with him, of which when our Adversaries were inform'd, they made what hast they could after us, and met us in the Portico of the Temple. The sight of them very much disordered us : *Lycas* eagerly complained of our flight to *Lycurgus*, but was received with such a contracted Brow, and so haughty an Air, that I took Courage upon't, and opening my Throat charg'd him with his lascivious Attempts upon me, as well at *Lycurgus*'s as in his own House ; and *Tryphæna* endeavouring to stop my Mouth, had her share of the Infamy ; for I set out her Harlotry to the Mob, who gather'd about us to hear the Scolding : And, as a Proof of what I said, I shew'd them poor limber-Ham'd *Gito*, and my self also, whom vicious Practices had even brought to our Graves.

The Shout of the Mob put our Enemies so out of Countenance, that they went off heavily, but contriving a Revenge ; and therefore observing how we had put upon *Lycurgus*, they went back to expect him at his House, and set him right again. The Solemnity ending later than was expected, we could not reach *Lycurgus*'s that Night, and therefore he brought us to a half-way House, but left us asleep next Morning, and went home to dispatch some business, where he found *Lycas* and *Tryphæna* waiting for him, who so order'd the matter with him, that they prevail'd with him to deliver us up. *Lycurgus*, naturally barbarous and faithless, began to contrive which way to betray us, and sent *Lycas* to get some Help, whilst he secur'd us in the Village.

Thither he came, and at his first entry treated us in the same manner as *Lycas* had done : After which, wringing his Hands together, he upbraided us with the Lye we had made of *Lycas*, and taking *Ascyltos* from us, lock'd us up in our Chamber, where we lay, without so much as permitting him to speak in our defence ; but carrying him to his House, he set a Guard upon us, till he himself should return.

On the Road *Ascyltos* did what he could to mollifie *Lycurgus* ; but neither Entreaties mingled with Love, nor Tears, could do any good upon him : It came into our Comrade's Head to set us at Liberty by other Methods ; and being all on fire at *Lycurgus*'s Restiness, refus'd to lodge with him that Night, and by that means the more easily put in execution what he had been thinking on.

The Family was in their dead Sleep when *Ascyltos* took our Baggage upon his Shoulders, and getting through a Breach in the Wall, which he had formerly taken notice of, came to the Village by break of Day, and meeting no one to stop him, boldly enter'd it, and came up to our Chamber ;

which the Guard that was upon us had taken care
to make fast ; but the Bar being of Wood, he
easily wrench'd it with an Iron Crow, and waken'd
us ; for we soundly snor'd, in spight of all our ill
Fortune.

Our Guard had so over-watch'd themselves,
that they were fall'n into a deep Sleep, which was
the Reason we only wak'd at the breaking of the
Door. To be short, *Ascyltos* came in, and briefly
told us what he had done for our sake : On this
we got up ; and as we were rigging our selves, it
came into my Head to kill the Guard, and rifle
the Village ; I told *Ascyltos* my Mind : He liked
the rifling well enough, but disapprov'd the other
Proposal, and gave us our desired Liberty without
Blood, for being acquainted with every corner of
the House, he pick'd the Lock of an Inner-room
where the Moveables lay, and bringing us into it,
we stole what was of most value, and got off while
it was yet early in the Morning ; avoiding the
common Road, and not resting till we thought our
selves out of danger.

Then *Ascyltos* having gotten heart again, began
to amplifie the Delight he took in having pillag'd
Lycurgus ; of whose miserableness he complain'd
with just reason ; for he had neither paid him for
his Nights service, nor kept a Table that had
either Meat or Drink on't, being such a miserable Scoundrel, that, notwithstanding his infinite
Wealth, he deny'd himself the common Necessaries
of Life.

A'ternate Streams curst Tantalus surround,
Whose flatt'ring Surge with blushing Fruits abound.
The wanton Banquet with malicious haste,
Flies from the Wretch that perishes to taste:
Such is the Miser's Fate, who 'midst his Store,
(Fearing to use) is miserably poor.

Ascyltos design'd for *Naples* the same day, had I
not acquainted him how imprudent it was to take
up there, where, according to all probability, we
were in likelihood to be sought after : And therefore, said I, let's keep out of the way for the
present, and, since we have enough to defend us
from want, stroul it about till the Heat be over.
The Advice was approv'd, and we set forward for
a pleasant Country Town, where we were sure to
meet some of our Acquaintance that were taking
the benefit of the Season : But we were scarce got
half way, when a showre of Rain discharging it
self upon us like Buckets, forc'd us into the next
Village ; where entring a House of Entertainment, we saw a great many others that had also
struck in thither to avoid the Storm. The throng
kept us from being taken notice of, and gave us
the opportunity of prying here and there, what we
might filch in a crowd ; when *Ascyltos*, unheeded
of any body, took a Purse from the Ground, in
which he found several pieces of Gold ; we leap'd
for Joy at so fortunate a beginning ; but fearing
lest some or other might seek after it, we slunk
out at a Back-door, where we saw a Groom sadling

his Horses; but, as having forgot somewhat, he ran into the House, leaving behind him an Embroider'd Mantle fastned to one of the Saddles: In his absence I cut the Straps, and under the covert of some Out-houses, we made off with it to a neighbouring Forest.

Being more out of danger among the Thickets, we were contriving where we should hide the Gold, that we might not be either charg'd with the Felony, or robb'd of it our selves: At last we concluded to sew it in the Lining of an old patcht Coat, which I threw over my Shoulders, and entrusted the Care of the Mantle to *Ascyltos*, with an intent to get to the City by Cross-ways: But as we were going out, we heard some-body on our left hand speak to this purpose: They shall not escape us; they came into the Wood; let's separate our selves and beat about, that we may the better discover and take them. This put us into such a fright, that *Ascyltos* and *Gito* fled thro' Briars and Brambles towards the City; but I turn'd back again in such a hurry, that without perceiving it, the precious Coat dropt from my Shoulders; At last being quite tir'd, and not able to go any further, I laid me down under the shelter of a Tree, where I first mist the Coat: Then Grief restor'd my strength, and up I got again, to try if I could recover the Treasure; I wander'd backwards and forwards to no manner of purpose; till spent and wasted with toil and sorrow, I got into a Thicket, where having tarried four Hours, and half dead with the horrour of the place, I sought the way out; but going forward, a Country Man came in sight of me: Then had I occasion for all my stock of Confidence; nor did it fail me: I went up roundly to him, and making my moan how I had lost my self in the Wood, desir'd him to tell me the way to the City: He pitying my Figure (for I was as pale as Death, and all bemir'd) ask'd me, if I had seen any one in the Wood? I answer'd, not a Soul—on which he courteously brought me into the High-way, where he met two of his Friends, who told him, they had travers'd the Wood thro' and thro', but had lit upon nothing but a Coat, which they shew'd him.

It may easily be believed I had not the Courage to challenge it, tho' I knew well enough what the value of it was: This afflicted me more than all the rest; however, bewailing my Treasure, the Country-man not heeding me, and Feebleness growing upon me, I slacken'd my pace, and jogg'd on slower than ordinary.

It was longer e're I reach'd the City than I thought of; but coming to the Inn, I found *Ascyltos* half dead, stretcht upon a Straw Pallat, and fell on another my self, not able to utter a word: He missing the Coat, was in a great disorder, and hastily demanded of me, what was become of it: I, on the other hand, scarce able to draw my Breath, resolv'd him by languishing Eyes, what my Tongue would not give me leave to speak:

At length recovering by little and little, I plainly told him the ill Fortune I had met with : But he thought I jested, and tho' the Tears in my Eyes might have been as full Evidence to him as an Oath, he yet questioned the truth of what I said, and would not believe but I had a mind to cheat him. During this, *Gito* stood as troubled as my self, and the Boys sadness increas'd mine : But the fresh pursuit that was made after us, distracted me most. I opened the whole matter to *Ascyltos*, who seem'd little concern'd at it, as having luckily got off for the present, and withal assur'd himself, that we were past danger, in that we were neither known, nor seen by any : However, it was thought fit to pretend a Sickness, that we might have the better Pretence to keep where we were : But our Monies falling shorter than we thought of, and Necessity enforcing us, we found it high time to sell some of our Pillage.

It was almost dark, when going into the Brokers Market, we saw abundance of things to be bought and sold; of no extraordinary Value, 'tis true, yet such as might be safely disposed of at that time by the Persons who stole them. We also had the Mantle with us, and taking the opportunity of a blind Corner, fell a shaking the skirt of it, to see if so glittering a Shew would bring us a Purchaser : Nor had we been long there, e're a certain Country-man, whom I thought I had seen before, came up to us, with a Woman after him, who beginning to inspect the Mantle more narrowly, as on the other side did *Ascyltos* our Country Chapman's Shoulders, they presently startled him, and struck him dumb : Nor could I my self behold 'em without being concern'd at it, for he seemed to me to be the same Fellow that had found the Coat in the Wood, as in truth he was : But *Ascyltos* doubting whether he might trust his Eyes or not, and that he might not do any thing rashly, first came nearer to him as a Buyer, and taking the Coat from his Shoulders, began to cheapen, and turn it more carefully. O the wonderful vagaries of Fortune! for the Country-man had not examined a Seam of it, but carelessly look'd on it as a Purchase for a Beggar.

Ascyltos seeing the Coat unript, and the Person of the Seller contemptible, took me aside from the Crowd : And don't you see, Brother, said he, the Treasure I made such moan about is return'd? That's the Coat with the Gold in't, all safe and untoucht : What therefore shall we do, or what course shall we take to get our own again?

I was now comforted, not so much that I had seen the Booty, but had clear'd my self of the Suspicion that lay upon me, and was by no means for going about the Bush, but downright bringing an Action against him, That if the Fellow would not give up the Coat to the right Owner, we might recover it by Law.

Law bears the Name, but Money has the Power;
The Cause is bad whene'er the Client's Poor:

Those strict-life'd Men that seem above our World
Are oft too modest to resist our Gold.
So Justice, like other Wares, are sold;
And the grave Judge that nods upon the Laws,
Wak'd by a Bribe, smiles, and approves the Cause.

Ascyltos on the other side afraid of the Law, Who, said he, knows us in this place, or will give any Credit to what we say? I am clear for buying it, tho' we know it, to be our own, and rather recover the Treasure with a little Money, than embroil our selves in an uncertain Suit ; but we had not above a couple of Groats ready Money, and that we design'd should buy us somewhat to eat. Lest therefore the Coat should be gone in the mean time, we agreed, rather than fail, to sell the Mantle at a lower price, that the Advantage we got by the one, might make amends for what we lost by the other.

As soon therefore as we had spread open the Mantle, the Woman that stood muffled by the Country-man, having pryingly taken notice of some tokens about it, forcibly laid both Hands on't, and setting up her Throat, cry'd out, Thieves, Thieves !

We on the other part were very much surpriz'd at the Accident, yet lest we should be wanting to our selves in this Extremity, we got hold of the tatter'd Coat, and as spitefully roar'd out, *They have robb'd us of it.* But our case was in no wise like theirs, and the Rabble that came in upon the

Out-cry, ridicul'd, according to their manner, the weaker side, in that the others made claim to a rich Mantle, and we to a ragged Coat, scarce worth a good Patch. At this *Ascyltos* could hardly keep his Countenance; but the noise being over, We see, said he, how every one likes his own best, Give us our Coat, and let them take the Mantle.

The Country-man and the Woman lik'd the exchange well enough, but a sort of Pettifoggers, most of whose business was such Night Practice, having a mind to get the Mantle in their own Custody, as importunely required, that both Mantle and Coat should be left in their Hands, and the Cause should be determin'd on the Morrow: For it was not the things alone that seem'd to be in dispute, but quite another matter to be enquir'd into, *to wit*, a strong suspicion of Robbery on both sides.

At last it was agreed to put both into some indifferent hand, till the Right was determin'd; when presently one, I know not who, with a bald Pate, and a fiery Face full of Pimples, a pettifogging kind of a Solicitor, steps from among the Rabble, and laying hold on the Mantle, said, He'd be Security it should be forth-coming the next day: when in truth his Intention was, that having gotten it into Hucksters hands, it might be smuggled amongst him and his Companions, as believing we would never come to own it, for fear of being apprehended for stealing it. For our part we were as willing as he; and an Accident be-

friended both of us : For the Country-man
thinking scorn of it, that we demanded to
have the patcht Coat given us, threw it at
Ascyltos's Head, discharging us of every thing but
the Mantle, requiring that to be secur'd as the
only Cause of the Dispute. Having therefore
recover'd, as we thought, our Treasure, we made
all the haste we could to the Inn, and having shut
the Door upon us, made our selves Merry, as well
with the judgment of the Rabble as of our
Detractors, who with so much circumspection had
restor'd us our Money.

While we were ripping the Coat and taking out
the Gold, we overheard somebody asking mine
Host, what kind of people those were that just
now came in : And being startled at the question,
I went down to see what was the matter, and
understood that a City sergeant, who, according to
the Duty of his Office, took an account of all
Strangers, had seen a couple come into the Inn,
whose Names he had not yet Register'd, and therefore enquired of what Country they were, and
what was their way of living.

But mine Host gave me such a blind Account
of it, that I began to suspect we were not safe
there ; whereupon, for fear of being taken up, we
thought fit to make off for the present, and not to
return back again till it was late in the Night, but
leave the care of our Supper to the management
of *Gito*.

We had resolv'd to keep out of the broad

Streets, and accordingly took our Walk thro' that quarter of the City, where we were likely to meet least Company ; when in a narrow winding Lane, which had no Passage thro', we saw, a little distance before us, two handsome well-drest Ladies, and followed them at a distance to a Chappel, which they entred, and from whence we heard an odd humming kind of a Noise, as it came from the hollow of a Cave : Curiosity also made us go in after them, where we saw a number of Women, as mad as if they had been Sacrificing to *Bacchus*, and each of them an Amulet (the Ensign of *Priapus*) in her Hand.   More than that, we could not get to see, for they was no sooner sensible of our being amongst them, but they set up such a Shout, that the Roof of the Temple shook again, and withal endeavoured to lay Hands on us ; but we scamper'd away, and made all the haste we could to our Inn.

We had scarce eaten the Supper which *Gito* had got ready for us, when a more than ordinary knocking at the Door put us into another Fright ; we look'd as pale as Death, and in fear demanded who was there? Answer was made, Open the Door and you'll see : While we were talking, the Bolt dropt off and fell down of its own accord, and the Door miraculously flew open, on which, a Woman with her Head veil'd came in upon us, the very same who a little before was with the Country-man in the Market : And what, said she, do you think to put a Trick upon me? I am *Quartilla*'s Maid, whose Sacred Recess you so lately disturb'd : She is at the Inn-gate, and desires to speak with you : You need not be uneasie, she neither blames your Inadvertency, or has a mind to resent it, but rather wonders what God brought such civil Gentlemen into her Quarters.

We were silent as yet, and gave her the hearing, but not the least inclin'd to grant any part of her Requests, when in came *Quartilla* her self, attended with a young Girl, and sitting down by me, fell a weeping : Nor here did we put in a word, but stood expecting what would be the event of these Tears which she commanded at her discretion. At last, when the Showre was over, she disdainfully turn'd up her Hood, and wringing her Hands together, What Impudence, said she, is this? or where learnt you these Shams, and that Slight of Hand you have so lately been beholden to? By my Faith, I am sorry for ye; for no one beheld what was unlawful for him to look upon, but went off severely punisht : and sincerely our part of the Town hath so many Deities in it, you'll sooner meet with a God than a Man : Don't believe I come here with any Sentiments of Revenge, I am rather affected with Compassion for your Youth than angry at the Injuries you have done me, which, I believe, were not done with a Design, but unawares you had the Misfortune to perpetrate them, and an inexpiable abomination.

For my part, it troubled me all Night, and threw me into such a shaking, that I was afraid I had gotten a *Tertian* Ague, on which I took a Remedy to have made me Sleep; but the God appeared to me, and commanded me to rise and find you out, as the likeliest way to take off the violence of the Fit. Yet I am not so much in pain for a Cure, but that a greater Anguish strikes me to the Heart, and will undoubtedly make an end of me, for fear, in one of your youthful Frolicks, you should declare what you saw in *Priapus*'s Chappel, and disclose the Mysteries of the Gods amongst the Vulgar. Low as your Knees, I therefore lift my Hands t'ye, that you neither make a Jest of our Night-worship, nor dishonour the Rites of so many Years, which not every one, even among our selves, is throughly acquainted with.

After this she fell a crying again, and with many a pitiful Lamentation, fell flat on my Bed; when I, at the same time, between Pity and Fear, bid her take Courage and assure her self, that we would neither divulge those Holy Mysteries, nor, if the God had prescrib'd her any other Remedy for her Ague, be wanting freely to assist in the Cure, even with the hazard of what was dearest to us.

At this Promise of mine, becoming more chearful, she fell a kissing me thick and threefold, and changing her Tears into Laughing, she comb'd up some Hair that hung over my Eyes with her Fingers: And I, said she, am Friends with you, and remit the Injury I intended against you; but if you

shou'd refuse me the Medicine I entreat of you
for the Ague, I have those that will be ready by to
Morrow, who shall both vindicate my Reputation,
and revenge the Affront you have put upon me.

Contempt's uncivil, to Command is rude;
Love does no Force upon the Fair intrude.
The best Revenge is, to neglect an Ill,
The Wise forgive, or Kissing kindly Kill.

Then clapping her Hands together, fell into so
violent a fit of Laughter, that she gave us reason
to apprehend she had some designs against us; the
Woman which came in first, and the Girl that
accompanied *Quartilla* were in the same humour.
Their Mirth seemed so odd and unnatural, that we
who saw no reason for so sudden a change, stood
amaz'd, and sometimes lookt upon the Women,
and sometimes upon one another.

During these Transactions, saith *Quartilla*, I
have commanded, That no Flesh alive be permitted
to come into this Inn to day, that I may be at
liberty to receive the Medicine for my Ague without interruption.

Ascyltos was in a little confusion, but I was so
surpriz'd, that I had not power to utter a word:
But the Company put me in heart again, for they
were but three Women, and if they had any
design, must yet be too weak to effect it against
us, who if we had nothing more of Man about us,
had yet that Figure to befriend us: We were all
ready for the Engagement, and I had so contriv'd

the Order of Battle, that if it must come to a Rencounter I was to make my part good with *Quartilla*, *Ascyltos* with her Woman, and *Gito* with the Girl.

While I was thus contriving the matter, *Quartilla* address'd her self to me to cure her of her Ague, but finding herself disappointed, she flew away in a Passion, and returning in a little while, commanded some Persons in disguise forcibly to convey us into a more magnificent Palace.

Here all our Courage fail'd us, and nothing but certain Death seem'd to appear before our Eyes.

When I began, If, Madam, you design to be more severe with us, be yet so kind as to dispatch us quickly, for the nature of our Offence is not so heinous, that we ought to be rack'd to death for it : Upon which her Woman, whose Name was *Psyche*, spread a Carpet on the Floor, and fell examining the inside of my Breeches, but her Labour was lost, all was quite gone. *Ascyltos* muffled his Head in his Coat, as having had a hint given him how dangerous it was to take notice of what did not concern him : In the mean time *Psyche* took off her Garters, and with one of them bound my Feet, and with the other my Hands.

As I lay thus fetter'd, Madam, said I, this is not the way to make me capable of curing your Ladies Ague : I grant it, answered *Psyche*, but I have a Dose at hand will infallibly do it : and thereupon she brought me a lusty Bowl of *Satyrion* (a Love Potion) and so merrily ran over the wonderful Effects of it, that she induc'd me to drink the greatest part of it off: But because *Ascyltos* had slighted her Addresses, she finding his Face turn'd from her, threw what was left upon his Back.

Ascyltos perceiving the Affair was over, Am not I worthy, said he, to get a Sup? And *Psyche* fearing my Laughter might discover her, clapped her Hands, and told him, Young-man, I made you an offer of it, but your Friend here has just now drank it all up.

Is it so, says *Quartilla*, smiling very agreeably, and has *Eucolpius* gulp'd it all down? At last also even *Gito* laugh'd for Company, at what time the young Wench flung her Arms about his Neck, and meeting no resistance, half smother'd him with Kisses.

We would have cry'd out, but there was no one near to help us; and as I was offering to bid em keep the Peace, *Psyche* fell a pricking me with her Bodkin: On the other side also, the young Wench half stifled *Ascyltos* with a Dish-clout she had rubb'd in the Bowl.

Lastly, came leaping upon us an unruly Fellow, in a rough Mantle stuck with Myrtle, girt about him; and one while almost ground us to Powder, and otherwhile disoblig'd us with his Kisses, till *Quartilla*, holding her Staff of Office in her Hand, discharg'd us of the Service; but not without having first oblig'd us to Swear, that so dreadful a Secret should go no further than our selves. Then

came in a Company of Wrestlers, and rub'd us
over with the Yolk of an Egg beaten to Oil:
When being somewhat refresh'd, we put on our
Night-gowns, and were led into the next Room
which had three rich Beds in it, and the rest of
the Entertainment as splendidly set out. The
word was given, and we sate down; when having
whet our Appetites with an excellent Antipast, we
treated our selves with the choicest Wine; nor
was it long e'er we fell a nodding. Is it so, quoth
Quartilla, can ye sleep when ye know it is the
Vigil to *Priapus?* At what time *Ascyltos* snoaring
soundly, and *Psyche* not forgetting the disappointment she had met with, black'd his Face, and
scor'd his Shoulders with a burnt-Stick's end.

For my own part, being over-harrass'd with the
Mischiefs I had suffer'd, I could not get a wink
of Sleep, nor was the rest of the Family, whether
within doors or without, in a much better condition; some lay up and down at our Feet, others
had run their Heads against a Wall, and others
lay dead asleep across the Threshold: The Lamps
also having drank up all their Oyl, gave a weak
and glimmering Light. At this instant got in
a couple of pilfering Rogues to have stolen our
Wine; but while they fell a scuffling among
some Silver Vessels that stood upon the Table, they
broke the Earthen Jarr that held the Wine, and
overthrew a Table with some Plate upon it, and
at the same time also a Cup falling off the Shelf
on *Psyche's* Bed, broke her Head as she lay fast

asleep ; upon which she cry'd out, and therewith discover'd the Thieves, and wak'd some of the Drunkards : The Thieves on the other hand finding themselves in danger of discovery, threw themselves on one of the Beds and fell a snoring as soundly as the rest. The Usher of the Hall being by this time got awake, put more Oyl into the dying Lamps ; and the Boys having rub'd their Eyes, return'd to their charge, when in came a Woman that play'd on the Harp, and ratling its Strings rouz'd all the rest : On which the Banquet was renew'd, and *Quartilla* gave the Word to go on where we left off (Drinking) : The She-Harper also added not a little to our Midnight Diversion.

At last bolted in a most shameless rascal, void of Grace both in Words and Action, and truly worthy of the House wherein he was ; who having compos'd himself in an affected manner, utter'd these Verses.

O Yet ! to Love's mysterious Feast repair,
The Old, the Young, the Ugly, and the Fair,
T' invade each other with soft melting Lips,
With kind Embraces, and with active Hips.

Having done with his Poetry, he smeared our Lips with loathsome Kisses ; then getting on our Bed, he tugg'd stoutly to have turn'd us out of it, but our Resistance render'd his Endeavours altogether fruitless. Great drops of Paint hung like Gum on his Forehead, and came trickling down the wrinkles of his Cheeks like Rain on a naked wall. Nor could I forbear Tears any longer, but being brought to the last Extremity, I beseech you, Madam (says I) have you commanded us to be smother'd?

When gently clapping her Hands together, A very witty Gentlemen, said she, a Man of excellent Parts! what, don't you know these sort of People are always toying? Upon this, that my Companion might not 'scape better than my self, By your Integrity, Madam, said I, does *Ascyltos* alone keep Holy-day among us?

Is it so, said she, even let him have his share too: And therewith the Rascal chang'd his course, and turning to *Ascyltos*, with Tricks and Humours almost beat him to Powder. *Gito* stood laughing all the while, till he had well-nigh split himself, which *Quartilla* perceiving, with much Curiosity enquired whose Boy he was, and I telling her he was my Comrade, Why then, said she, has he not kist me? And so calling him to her, she fell to kissing him smartly; this young Gentlemen, says the Old Lady, may do well enough for a Whet, and get me an Appetite to Morrow; but having made so full a Meal already, it is not my way to put a Churl upon a Gentleman. With that *Psyche* came tittering to her, and having whisper'd something in her Ear, You are in the right on't, quoth *Quartilla*, 'twas well thought on; and since we have so fine an opportunity, why should not our *Pannychis* partake with us? And

forthwith was brought in a pretty young Girl, that
seem'd not to be above Seven Years of Age, and
was the same that came into our Inn with *Quartilla :*
All approving the design, and desiring the Con-
summation, a Match was struck up between the
Boy and her. For my part I stood amaz'd, and
assur'd them, That neither *Gito*, a modest Lad,
was able to undergoe such a Drudgery, or the Girl
of years to receive it. Is that all, quoth *Quartilla ?*
Is she less than I was when I first enter'd on't ? I
vow, by all that's good, I can't remember that I
ever was a Maid ; for when I was in Hanging-
sleeves, I went to Creep-mouse with little Boys ;
and as I grew in Years, I entertain'd my self with
bigger, till I came to the Age you see ; and truly
I think hence came the Proverb :

She'll bear him a Bull that bore him a Calf.

Fearing therefore my Comrade might sustain
a greater Injury by my delay, I got up to celebrate
the Wedding.

And now *Psyche* put a Flame-colour'd Veil
upon the Girl's Head ; a Satyr led before with a
Flamboe, and a long Train of drunken Women
fell a shouting, and drest up the Bride-chamber ;
Quartilla all a-gog as the rest, took hold of *Gito*,
and dragg'd him in with her : But truly the Boy
made no resistance ; nor seem'd the Girl frighted
at the Name of Matrimony. When therefore they
were lockt up, we stood at the Chamber-Door ;
and *Quartilla* having waggishly slit a Chink in the

Door, as wantonly lookt thro' it; nor content with that, pluckt me to be a Witness of their Diversion, and when we were not peeping, she turn'd her Face to me, and would steal a Kiss.

The Jade's fulsomness had so tir'd me, that I began to devise which way to get off. I told *Ascyltos* my Mind, and he was well pleased with it, for he was as willing to get rid of his Torment, *Psyche:* This might easily have been done, if *Gito* had not been lockt up in the Chamber ; for we were resolv'd to take him with us, and not leave him expos'd unto the mercy of an Ill-house. While we were contriving how to bring about our Design, it so happened that *Pannychis* fell out of bed, and drew Gito after her, without being hurt, but the Girl got a small Knock as she fell, and therewith made such a Cry, that *Quartilla*, all in a Fright, ran headlong in, and gave us the opportunity of getting off, and taking the Boy with us ; when without more ado, we flew to our Inn, and getting to Bed, past the rest of the Night without Fear.

But going out the next Day, whom should we meet with, but two of those Fellows that robb'd us of the Mantle, which *Ascyltos* perceiving, he briskly attack'd one of them, and having disarm'd and desperately wounded him, came in to my Assistance, who was pressing hard upon the other ; but he behav'd himself so well, that he wounded us both, altho' but slightly, and got off himself without so much as a Scratch.

And now came the third Day, on which we were
invited to an Entertainment at *Trimalchio*'s, where
every one might speak his Mind : But having
received some Wounds, we thought it convenient
to withdraw to our Inn as fast as we could, and
our Wounds not being great, we cured them as
we lay in our Bed with Wine and Oyl.

But the Rogue whom *Ascyltos* had hewn down,
lay in the Street, and we were in fear of being
discovered : while therefore we were pensively
considering which way to avoid the impending
Storm, a Servant of *Agamemnon*'s interrupted our
Fears : And don't you know, said he, with whom
you are to Eat to Day? *Trimalchio*, a trim finical
Humourist has a Clock in his Dining-room, contriv'd on purpose to let him know how many
Minutes of his Life he has lost. We therefore
drest our selves carefully, and *Gito* willingly taking
upon him the part of a Servant, as he had hitherto
done, we bad him put our things together, and
follow us to the Bath.

Having in the mean time drest our selves, we
rambled up and down we knew not where, and
being resolv'd to give ourselves all the Diversion
we could, struck into a Tennis-Court, where we
saw an old Bald-pated Fellow in a Carnation-
colour'd Coat, playing at Ball with a company of
Boys ; nor was it so much the Boys, tho' it was
worth our while to observe them, that engaged
our Attention, as the Master of the House himself
in Pumps, who altogether tossed the Ball, and

never struck it after it once came to the Ground, but had a Servant by him with a Bag full of them, and enough for all that play'd.

We observ'd also other new things; for in the Gallery stood two Eunuchs, one of whom held a Silver Bason, the other counted the Balls; not those they kept tossing, but such as fell to the Ground. While we admir'd the Humour, one *Menelaus* came up to us, and told us, This is the Gentleman you must sup withal to Night, and that we had seen the beginning of our Entertainment. As he was yet talking, *Trimalchio*, the vainest Man alive, snapp'd his Fingers, at which sign the Eunuch held the Bason to him as he was playing; then calling for Water, he dipped the tips of his Fingers in it, and dry'd them on the Boys head. 'Twould be too long to lay open the whole Scene: We went into the Hummums, and being presently in a Sweat, we descended into a Cold Bath; and while *Trimalchio* was anointed from Head to Foot with a liquid Perfume, and rubb'd clean again, not with Linnen, but the finest Flannel, his three Surgeons ply'd stoutly some Bottles of rich Muscadine; but brawling over their Cups, *Trimalchio* said it was his turn to drink; then wrapt up in a Scarlet Mantle, he was laid on a Chair, supported by six Servants, with four Lacqueys drest in rich Liveries running before him, and by his side a Sedan, in which was carried his Darling, a Squinting and Blear-ey'd over-grown Boy, more ill-favour'd and ugly than his Master *Trimalchio*; who, as they went on, kept close to his Ear with a Flagellet, as if he had whisper'd him, and made him musick all the way. Wondering, we follow'd, and, with *Agamemnon*, arriv'd at the Gate, on which hung a Tablet with this Inscription :

WHATEVER SERVANT GOES OUT WITHOUT HIS MASTER'S LEAVE, SHALL RECEIVE A HUNDRED STRIPES.

In the Porch stood the Porter in a Green Livery, girt about with a cherry-colour'd Girdle, cleansing of Pease in a Silver Charger ; and overhead hung a Golden Cage with a Magpye in it, which saluted us as we entred : But while I was staring at these Novelties, I had like to have broke my Neck backwards ; for on the Left Hand, not far from the Porter's Lodge, there was a great Dog in a Chain painted on a Wall, and over him written in large Capital Letters, TAKE CARE OF THE DOG. My Companions could not forbear laughing ; but I re-collecting my Spirits, pursued my design of going to the end of the Wall ; it contain'd the draught of a Market-place where Slaves were bought and sold, with Bills tackt upon them shewing their Price : There was also *Trimalchio* with a white Staff in his Hand, and *Minerva* with a Train after her entring *Rome* : A little farther was represented after what manner he had learnt to cast Account, and how he was made Auditor ; all exquisitely painted, with their proper Explanations ; and at the end of the Gallery *Mercury* was discovered lifting him by the Chin, and placing him on a Judgment-seat, *Fortune* stood by him with a *Cornucopia*, and the three fatal Sisters weaving a Golden Thread.

I observed also towards the lower-end of the same place a Troop of Light-horsemen, with their Commander exercising them ; as also a large Armoury, in one of the Angles of which stood a Shrine with Household Gods in Silver, a Marble Statue of *Venus*, and a large Golden Box, in which it was said he kept the first Shavings of his Beard. We enquired of the Servant that had the charge of these things, What Pictures those were in the middle ? *The* Iliads *and the* Odysses, said he, *and on the left hand are two Pieces of Sword-playing.* We could not bestow much time to consider them, for by this time we were come to the Dining-room, in the entry of which sate the Steward inspecting Accounts : But what I most admir'd, were those bundles of rods, with their Axes, that were fastned to the sides of the Door, and stood, as it were on the Brazen Prow of a Ship, on which was written :

CINNAMUS, STEWARD OF CAIUS POM-
PEIUS TRIMALCHIO, A MAN OF
QUALITY.

Under the same Title also hung a Lamp with

two Branches, from the Roof of the Room, and two Tablets on either side of the Door ; of which one, according to the best of my remembrance, had this Inscription :

THE THIRD AND SECOND OF THE KALENDS OF JANUARY, OUR PA-TRON CAIUS EATS ABROAD.

On the other was represented the Course of the Moon, and the Seven Stars ; and what Days were Lucky or Unlucky, each distinguish'd by an Imboss'd Studd from one another.

Full of this Luxury we were now entring the Room, where one of his Boys, set there for that purpose, call'd aloud to us, ADVANCE OR-DERLY. Nor is it to be doubted, but we were somewhat concern'd for fear of breaking the Orders of the place. But while we were proceeding accordingly, a Servant stript of his Livery fell at our Feet, and besought us to save him from a Whipping, alledging his Fault was no great matter, and that he had only lost some Cloaths of the Stewards in the Bath, which were hardly worth Eighteen-pence.

We returned therefore in good Decorum, and finding the Steward in the Compting-House telling some Gold, besought him to remit the Servant's Punishment : When putting on a haughty Face, *It is not*, said he, *the loss of the thing which troubles me, but the Negligence of a careless Rascal. He has lost me the Garments I us'd to Feast in, and which a*

Client of mine presented me with on my birthday; no Man can deny them to be right Purple, tho' not the double Dye; but let them be worth what they will, I grant your Request.

Having receiv'd so great Favour, as we were entring the Dining-room, the Servant for whom we had been Intercessors, met us, and kissing us, with many Thanks for the Kindness we had done, *By and by,* says he, *you shall know, that the Wine which my Lord drinks of himself, is oftentimes in the disposition of his Servants.*

At length we sate down, when some Gypsie-Boys coming about us, poured Snow-water on our Heads, and others par'd the Nails of our Feet, with a mighty dexterity, and that not silently, but humming as it were to themselves. I resolv'd to try if the whole Family was good at Singing; and therefore called for Drink, which one of the Youngsters as readily brought me, with an odd kind of Tune; and in the same humour was every one you asked for any thing.

Then came in a sumptuous Breakfast, for we were all seated but only *Trimalchio,* for whom after a new fashion, the chief place was reserv'd. Besides that, as a part of the Entertainment, there was set by us a large Vessel of Metheglin, with a Pannier, in the one part of which were white Olives, in the other black; two broad pieces of Plate covered the Vessel, on the brims of which were engraven *Trimalchio*'s Name, and how many Ounces of Silver they weigh'd, with little Bridges solder'd together, and on them Dormice, strew'd over with Honey and Pepper : There were also piping-hot Sausages on a Silver Grid-iron, and under that large Damsons, with the Kernels of Pomegranates.

In this Condition we were when *Trimalchio* himself was waddled into the Chorus ; and being close bolster'd with Neckcloths and Pillows to keep off the Air, we could not forbear laughing in spight of our teeth : For his bald Pate peep'd out of a Scarlet Mantle, and over the load of Cloths he lay under, there hung an Embroider'd Towel with Purple Tassels and Fringes dingle dangle about it : He had also, on the little Finger of his left Hand, a large Ring of Gold, and on the extream Joint of the Finger next it, one lesser, which I took for all Gold ; but at last it appeared to be jointed together, with a kind of Stars of Steel : And that we might see these were not all his Gallantry, he stripp'd his right Arm, on which he wore a Golden Bracelet, and an Ivory Circle, bound together with a glittering Locket, and a Medal at the end of it : Then picking his Teeth with a Silver Pin, *I had not, my Friends*, said he, *any Inclination to have come among you so soon, but fearing my absence might make you wait too long, I deny'd my self my own satisfaction ; however, suffer me to make an end of my Game.* There followed him a Boy with an Inlaid Table and Chrystal Dice ; and I took notice of one thing more pleasant than the rest ; for instead of black and white Counters, his were all of Silver and Gold.

In the mean while he was squandring his Heap at Play, and we were yet picking a bit here and there, a Cupboard was brought in with a Basket, in which was a Hen Carved in Wood, her Wings lying round and hollow, as sitting on Brood ; when presently the Consort strook up, and two servants fell a searching the Straw under her, and taking out some Pea-hens Eggs, distributed them round the Company :   At this *Trimalchio* changing Countenance, *I commanded my Friends*, said he, *the Hen to be set with Peahens Eggs, and by* Hercules, *I'm afraid they are half Hatcht ; however we'll try if they are yet fit to be Eaten.*

The thing we receiv'd was a kind of Shell, of at least six Pound weight, made of Paste, and moulded into the Figure of an Egg, which we easily broke ; and, for my own part, I was like to have thrown away my share ; for it seemed to me to have a Chick in it ; till hearing a Guest who us'd to Eat at that Table say, *There was some good Bit or other in the Egg-shell ;* I search'd further into it, and found a delicate fat Wheat-ear in the middle of a well-pepper'd Yolk : On this *Trimalchio* stopped his play for a while, and asking the like for himself, declar'd, *If any of us would have more Metheglin, it was at our Service ;* when of a sudden the Musick gave the Sign, and the first Course was scrambled away by a Company of Singers and Dancers ; but in the Bustle, it happening that a Dish fell on the Floor, a Boy took it up, and *Trimalchio* observing the Action, gave him a Box on the Ear, and commanded him to throw it down again ; and presently the Groom of the Chamber came with a Broom and swept away the Silver Dish, with whatever else had fallen from the Table.

When presently came in two long-hair'd *Æthiopians*, with small Leather Bottles, such as they carry Sand in to strew on the Stage, and gave us Wine to wash our Hands, but no one offer'd us Water. We all admiring the Finicalness of the Entertainment, *Mars*, said he, *is a lover of Justice, and therefore let every one have a Table to himself; for having more Elbow-room, these nasty stinking Boys will be less troublesome to us :* And thereupon large double-ear'd Vessels of Glass close plaister'd over, were brought up, with Labels about their necks, upon which was this Inscription.

OPIMIAN MUSCADINE OF AN HUN-
DRED YEARS OLD.

While we were reading the Titles, *Trimalchio* clapped his Hands, and *Alas, alas*, said he, *that Wine should live longer than Man ! Wine is Life, and we'll try if this has liv'd ever since the Consul-ship of* Lucius Opimius, *'Tis right* Opimian, *and therefore make ready ; that which I gave my Guests yesterday was not so generous as this, tho' they were Persons of better Quality that supp'd with me.*

We drank, and admir'd every thing ; when in

came a Servant with a Silver Puppet, so jointed
and put together, that it turned every way ; and
being more than once thrown upon the Table, cast
it self into several figures ; on which *Trimalchio*
came out with his Poetry :

> *Let's do what we can,*
> *This Life's but a Span,*
>   *Exposed to Trouble and Sorrow ;*
> *Then drink my good Friends,*
> *E're our Merriment ends,*
>   *For we may be dead by to Morrow.*

The Applause we gave him was follow'd with
a Service, but respecting the place not so considerable as might have been expected : However,
the Novelty of the thing drew every Man's Eye
upon it ; it was a large Charger with the twelve
Signs of the Zodiak round it ; upon every one
of which the Master-Cook had laid somewhat or
other suitable to the Sign : Upon *Aries*, a sort
of Pease which resembled a Rams-head ; upon
Taurus a piece of Beef ; upon *Gemini* Rumps and
Kidneys ; upon *Cancer* a Coronet ; upon *Leo* an
African Egg ; upon the *Virgin* a lusty Boy ;
upon *Libra* a pair of Scales, in one of which
was a Tart, in the other a Custard ; upon *Scorpio*
a Pilchard ; upon *Sagittary* a Grey hound ; upon
Capricorn a Lobster ; upon *Aquarius* a Goose ;
upon *Pisces* two Mullets ; and in the middle a
Plat of Herbs, cut like a green Turf, and over
them an Honeycomb. During this, a black Boy

carry'd about Bread in a Silver Oven, and with a hideous Voice, forced a Bawdy Song from a Buffoon that stunk like *Assa Fœtida*.

When *Trimalchio* perceived we lookt awry on such course Fare, *Come, come*, said he, *fall to, this is our manner of Eating*.

Nor had he sooner uttered these Words, than the fourth Consort struck up; at which the Waiters fell a dancing; and took off the upper part of the Charger, under which was a Dish of cramm'd Fowl, and the hinder Paps of a Sow that had Farrowed but a Day before, well powder'd, and in the middle a Hare, larded with Finns of Fish on both sides, that it look'd like a Flying-Horse; and on the sides of the Fish four little Images, that spouted a Relishing Sauce on some Fish that lay near them, brought from the River *Euripus*.

We also seconded the Shout begun by the Family, and fell merrily aboard this; and *Trimalchio* no less pleas'd than our selves, cryed *Cut;* at which the Musick sounding again, the Carver humour'd it, and cut up the Meat with such Antick Postures, you'd have thought him a Car-man fighting to the Musick of a Bagpipe.

Nevertheless *Trimalchio* in a lower Note cryed out again *Cut:* I hearing the word so often repeated, suspecting there might be some Joke in it, was not ashamed to ask him that sate next above me, what it meant? And he that had been often present at the like Expressions, *You see*, said he, *him that Carves about, his Name is* Cutter ; *and as often as he says* Cut ; *he both Calls and Commands.*

The Humour spoiled my Stomach for Eating ; but turning to him that I might learn more, I talkt pleasantly to him at a distance, and at last asked him who that Woman was that so often scutled up and down the Room ?

It is, said he, *Trimalchio*'s Wife, her Name is *Fortunata*, she counts her Money by the Bushel ; but what sort of a Person think you she was a little while since ? Pardon me, Sir, you would not have touched her with a pair of Tongs, but now, no one knows why or wherefore, she's as 'twere got into Heaven ; and is *Trimalchio*'s *all in all:* In short, if she says it is Mid-night at Mid-day, he'll believe her. He's so very Wealthy, he can't tell his Riches, but she has an Eye every where ; and when you least think to meet her, she's at your Elbow : She is a very Scold, and indiscreet, a meer Magpye in Bed ; whom she loves she likes, and whom she does not love she dislikes.

Then for *Trimalchio*, he has more Lands than a Crow can fly over ; Bags upon Bags : There lies more Silver in his Porter's Lodge, than any one Man's Estate is worth. And for his Family, Hey-dey, hey-dey, there is not (by *Hercules*) one tenth of them that know their Master. In brief, there is not one of those Fools about him, but he can change him into a Cabbage-stalk. Nor has he occasion to buy any thing, he finds all things at his own Door ; Wooll, Fish, Pepper, nay, Hens-Milk ; look about you and you'll find it. In a word, time was, his Wool was none of the best, and therefore he bought Rams at *Tarentum* to mend his Breed ; as in like manner he did by his Honey, by bringing his Bees from *Athens*. It is not long since but he sent to the *Indies* for Mushroom-Seed : Nor has he so much as a Mule that did not come of a wild Ass. Do you see all these Quilts ? there is not one of them whose Wadding is not the finest Comb'd Wooll, of Violet or Scarlet Colour, dy'd in Grain. O happy Man ! but have a care how you despise those Freed Men, they are rich Rogues : Look on him that sits at the lower end of the Table, he has now the Lord knows what ; and 'tis not long since he was not worth a Groat, and carried Billets and Faggots upon his Back : So it is said, but I know nothing of it my self, but by hear-say, either he got in with an old Hog-grubber, or had to do with an *Incubus*, and found a Treasure : For my part, I envy no Man, if I get any thing, it is a Bit and a Knock. He lately set up this Proclamation.

C. POMPEIUS DIOGENES HAS SOME LODGINGS TO LET, FOR HE HATH BOUGHT A HOUSE.

But what think you of Him who sits in the place of a Slave ? how well was he once ? I do

not upbraid him : He was worth a Hundred
Thousand Pounds, but has not now a Hair of his
Head which is not Mortgaged ; nor, by *Hercules*,
is it his own Fault : There is not a better
humour'd Man than himself ; but those Rascally
Freed Men have cheated him of all : For know,
*when the Pot no longer Boyls, and a Man's Estate
declines, farewel Friends.* And what Trade do
you think he drove ? He was an Undertaker,
and by the Gains of that Employment eat like
a Prince : He had his Wild Boars served up
covered : All sorts of Pastry, Fish and Wild
Fowl, and Cooks for each sort of Provision :
More Wine was spilt under his Table, than most
Men have in their Cellars ; a meer Phantasm :
And when his Estate was going, and he fear'd his
Creditors might fall upon him, he made an Auction
under this Title :

JULIUS PROCULUS WILL MAKE AN
AUCTION, AND SELL SEVERAL
GOODS HE MAKES NO USE OF.

The Dish was by this time taken away, and the
Guests, grown mellow, began to talk of what was
done abroad, when *Trimalchio* broke in upon us,
and interrupted the Discourse ; leaning on his
Elbow, This Wine, said he, is worth drinking,
and Fish must swim ; but do you think I am
satisfied with that part of your Supper you saw in
the Charger ? *Is* Ulysses *no better known ?* what
then ; *we ought to exercise our Brains as well as*

our Teeth; and shew, that we are not only lovers of Learning, but understand it : Peace be with my old Tutor's Bones, who made me a Man amongst Men : No body can tell me any thing that is New to me ; for, like him, I am Master of the Practicks.

This Heaven that's inhabited by twelve Gods, turns it self into as many Figures ; and now 'tis *Aries :* He that is born under that Sign has much Cattel, a great deal of Wooll, is a Blockhead, a Brazen-face, and will be certainly a Cuckold : There are many Scholars, Advocates, and Horned Beasts, come into the World under this Sign. We applauded our Nativity-caster's pleasantness, and he went on again : The whole Heaven is under *Taurus,* and no wonder it bore Football-players, Herdsmen, and such as can shift for themselves. Under *Gemini* are often foaled Coach-horses, Oxen calv'd, and such are born as can claw both sides. I was born my self under *Cancer,* and therefore stand on many Feet, as having large Possessions both by Sea and Land. For *Cancer* suits one as well as the other, and therefore I put nothing upon him, that I might not press my own Geniture. Under *Leo,* Spend-thrifts and Bullies : under *Virgo* Women, Runagates, and such as wear *Iron Garters :* Under *Libra* Butchers, Apothecaries, and Men of Business : Under *Scorpio,* Poisoners and Cut-throats : Under *Sagittary,* such as are Goggle-ey'd, Herb-women, and Beggars of Bacon : Under

Capricorn, poor helpless Rascals, to whom Nature bequeath'd Horns to defend themselves : Under *Aquarius*, Cooks and Paunch-bellies : Under *Pisces*, Caterers and Orators : *And so the World goes round like a Mill, and is never without its Mischief;* Men continually born perish. But for that Tuft of Herbs in the middle, and the Honey-comb upon it, I do nothing without just reason for it : Our Mother the Earth is in the Middle, made round like an Egg, and has all good things in her self, like a Honey-comb.

Most Learnedly, we all cry'd ; and lifting our Hands, swore, neither *Ptolemy* nor *Copernicus* were to be compared with him ; till at last other Servants came in and spread Coverlets on the Beds, on which were painted Nets, Men in Ambush with Hunting-poles, and whatever appertain'd to Hunting : Nor could we yet tell what to make of it ; when we heard a great Cry without, and a pack of Beagles came and ran round the Table ; after this Frolick was over, a large Dish was set before us, and in it a mighty Boar, with a Cap on his Head, (such as Slaves, at their making Free, do usually wear as tokens of Liberty) on his Tusks hung two Wicker Baskets, the one full of Dates, the other of Almonds ; and about him lay little Pigs made of Sweet-meats, as if they were at Suck : They signified a Sow had Farrowed, and hung there as Presents for the Guests to carry home with them.

To the cutting up this Boar, there came (not he

that had served up the Fowl as before, but) a two-handed Fellow with a swinging long Beard, Buskins on his Legs, and a short Embroidered Coat ; who drawing his Wood-Knife, made a large Hole in the Boar's Side, out of which flew a number of Black-birds, which were caught in a trice as they flutter'd about the Room, by some Fowlers, who stood in readiness for that purpose. On which, *Trimalchio* order'd to every Man his Bird ; and, *See*, said he, *What kind of Acrons this Wild Boar fed on :* When presently the Boys took off the Baskets, and distributed the Dates and Almonds among the Guests.

In the mean time, I, who had private Thoughts of my own, was much concerned, to know why the Boar was brought in with a Cap upon his Head ; and therefore having spun out the Thread of my Discourse, I told my Interpreter what troubled me : To which he answer'd, a very Novice can explain to you what it means, for there's no Riddle in it, but 'tis as clear as the Sun. This Boar stood the last of Yester-night's Supper, and dismiss'd by the Guests, returns now as a Free-man among us. I curst my self for a Block-head, and asked him no more Questions, that he might not think I had never before eaten with Men of Fashion.

Before we had made an end of our Discourse, in came a handsome Boy with a Wreath of Vine-Leaves and Ivy about his Head, calling himself now and then *Bromius*, another time *Lycæus*, and presently he said his Name was *Enhyus*, (several denominations of *Bacchus*) he carried about with him a Salver of Grapes, and with a clear Voice, repeated some of his Master's Poetry, at which *Trimalchio* turning to him, *Dionysius*, said he, *be thou Liber*, (i.e.) *Free*, (another Name of *Bacchus*) whereupon the Boy took the Cap from off the Boar's Head, and putting it on his own, *Trimalchio* added, *You will not deny me, but I have a Father, Liber*. We all praised the Conceit, and soundly kissed the Boy as he went round us.

This Scene being over, *Trimalchio* rose up and went to the Close-stool : we also being left at liberty without a Tyrant, fell to some Table-talk.

When presently one calling for a Bumper, The Day, said he, is nothing, 'tis Night before a Cat can lick her Ear, and concluded it best to go streight from Bed to Board. We have had a great deal of Frost, the *Bagnio* has scarce heated me ; but a merry Bottle is Meat, Drink and Cloaths : For my part, I have wound up my Bottom, the Wine is got into my Pericranium ; I am down-right *Dunstable*——

Then *Selucus* took up the Cudgels, And I, said he, do not bath every Day, for he where I use to bathe is a Fuller : Cold Water has Teeth in it, and my Head grows every Day more washy than other ; but when I have got my Dose in my Guts, I bid defiance to the Weather ; But, faith, I was at a Funeral, *Crysanthus* has breathed his last : Well, rest his Soul, he was an honest Fellow, 'tis not long since we were drinking together, and methinks I talk with him now. Alas, alas! we are but Bubbles, meer Mites, yet they have somewhat in them; but we are meer emptiness. You'll say he would not be rul'd; yet not a drop of Water or crumb of Bread went down his Throat for five Days: Well, but he is departed, some say he dyed of the Doctor, but I am of opinion his time was come; for an honest Physician is a great Comfort. However he was decently carried out of his House with a rich Pall over the Coffin, and mightily lamented : He made some of his Servants free ; but his Wife seem'd little troubled. You'll say again, he was not kind to her ; but Women are a sort of Kites that will eat more than a Man can give them, and old Love is soon cold.

At this *Phileros* grew troublesome, and cry'd out, Let us remember the Living : He enjoy'd himself whilst he liv'd, and as he liv'd well so he dy'd well ; and what has he now that any Man moans the want of ? He came from nothing, and to his dying-day would have taken a Farthing from a Dunghil with his Teeth ; therefore, as he grew up, he grew like a Honey comb. He dy'd worth the Lord knows what, all ready Money. But to the matter ; I have eaten a Dog's Tongue, and dare speak truth : He had a foul Mouth, was all Babble, a very Make-bate, not a Man : His Brother was a brave Fellow, a Friend to his Friends, of an open Hand, and kept a full Table :

He did not order his Affairs so well at first as he might have done, but the first Vintage made him up again, for he sold what Wine he would ; and what kept up his Chin was the expectation of a Reversion ; the Credit of which brought him more than was left him, but his Brother taking a Pett at him, devised the Estate to I know not what Bastard : He flies far that flies his Relations. Besides, this Brother of his had Whisperers about him, that were back friends to the other : *But he shall never do right that is quick of belief, especially in matters of Business ;* and yet, 'tis true, he'll be counted wise while he lives, to whom the thing, whatever it be, is given ; not that he ought to have had it. He was, without doubt, one of *Fortune's* Sons ; Lead in his Hand would turn to Gold, and without trouble too, where there are not Rubbs in the way. And how many Years think you he liv'd ? Seventy-odd ; but he was as hard as Horn, bore his Age well, and as black as a Crow.

I knew him some Years ago an Oil-man, and to his last a good Womans Man ; but withal such a Miser, that, by *Hercules,* I think he left not a Dog in his House. He was also a great Whore-master, and a *Jack* of all Trades ; nor do I condemn him for't, for this was the only Secret he kept to himself and carry'd with him.

Thus *Phileros,* and *Ganmiedes* as followeth : Ye talk of what concerns neither Heaven nor Earth, when in the mean time no Man regards

the scarcity of Provisions : I could not, by
Hercules, get a piece of Bread to Day ; and how
do you think this came to pass ? Why the
drought continues : For my part, I have not
fill'd my Belly this Twelvemonth : A plague on
these Clerks of the Market, the Baker and they
juggle together, Claw me and I'll claw thee, which
makes the poorer sort starve, whilst Rich Persons
make Holiday all the Year. Oh that we had
those Lyons I now find here, when I came first
out of *Asia*, that had been to live : The inner part
of *Sicily* had the like of them, but they so handled
the Goblins, even *Jupiter* bore them no Good-will.
I remember *Sasinius*, when he was a Boy, he liv'd
by the Old Exchange ; you'd have taken him for
a Pepper-corn rather than a Man ; where-ever he
went the Earth parch'd under him ; yet he was
a sincere honest Fellow at bottom ; one might
depend on him; a Friend to his Friend, and one
you might boldly trust in the Dark. But how
behav'd he himself on the Bench? He carry'd
all things before him? made no starch'd Speeches,
but was downright, and acted himself what he
persuaded others to : But at the Barr he sounded
like a Kettle-drum, and never feign'd himself
Sick for the matter. I fancy he was like a
Frenchman in his Temper ; for he was so wonderful civil, so ready to salute us by our Names,
we imagin'd him one of us. In his time Bread
was as cheap as Water, a Half-peny Loaf would
have given a Man a Breakfast ; but now a Sheeps-

head will fetch a Shilling :   Alas, alas ! the times,
are every Day worse and worse, like a Cow's Tail,
we grow downward : And why all this ? We have
a Clerk of the Market not worth a Rush, and values
more the getting of a Penny than the Lives of all
Mankind : 'Tis this makes him laugh in his
Sleeve ; for he gets as much Money in a Day as
would purchase an Estate : I know very well how
he got the Fortune he is Master of ; but if we
were Men, he would not enjoy himself as he does ;
but now the People are grown to this pass, that
they are Lyons at home, and Foxes abroad : For
my part, I have eaten up my Cloaths already, and
if Corn holds at the rate it does, I shall be forc'd
to sell my House and all : For what will become
of us, if neither Gods nor Men have Mercy on us ?
Let me never be happy I don't believe all this
proceeds from Heaven ; for no body believes there
is a God ; no one keeps a Fast, or values *Jupiter*
of a Hair, but all stop their Ears to good Advice,
and only trouble their Heads about what they are
worth. Time was when our Matrons went in
Procession with bare Feet, and their Hair dis-
hevel'd, then with sincere Minds they pray'd to
Heaven for Rain, and forthwith it rained by
Pitchers-full ; then, or never, were good times,
every body was in a good Humour : Now we
have no more Reverence for the Gods, than for so
many Mice ; they are bound Hand and Foot, and
by reason of our Irreligion and Prophaneness, our
Fields and Meadows languish and are barren.

59

More civilly, I beseech you, said *Echion*, the Constable of the Hundred, the worse Luck now, the better another time, said the Clown, when he lost his brindled Hog : What falls not out to Day may happen to Morrow ; and so Life passes away. By *Hercules*, a Country is said not to be the better for having many People in it, tho' ours at present labours under that difficulty, but it is no fault of hers : We must not be nice, Heaven is equally distant every where ; were you in another place, you'd say Hogs walked here ready dress'd : And now I think on't, we shall have an excellent Show these Holydays, a Fencing-prize exhibited to the People ; not of Slaves bought for that purpose, but it will consist of Freemen. Our Patron *Titus* has a large Soul, but is a very Devil in his Drink, and cares not a straw which side gets the better : I think I should know him, for I belong to him ; he's of a right Breed both by Father and Mother, no Mungril. They are well provided with Weapons, and will fight it out to the last : The Stage will look like a Butcher's Shambles, and he has wherewithal to do it ; his Father left him a vast Sum, what tho' he makes Ducks and Drakes of a thousand Pound, his Estate will never feel it, and he always carries the Reputation of it. He has his Waggon Horses, a Woman-Carter, and *Glyco*'s Steward, who was caught kissing his Mistress ; what a bustle's here between Cuckolds and Cuckold-makers ! But this *Glyco* a damnable Rich Huncks, condemn'd his Steward to fight

with Beasts ; and what was that but to expose and make a Beast of himself ? Where
lay the Servant's Crime who perhaps was oblig'd
to do what he did ? She rather deserv'd to
be brain'd, than the Bull that tossed her ; but
he that cannot come at the Breech, thrashes at
the Pack-saddle : yet how could *Glyco* expect
Hermogine's Daughter should make a good End ?
she'd have skin'd a Flint ; *like begets its like :*
Glyco might do what he would with his own ; but
it will be a Brand on him as long as he lives ; nor
can any thing but Hell blot it out ; however every
Man's Faults are to himself. I perceive now what
Entertainment *Mammea* is like to give us ; he'll be
at Two-pence Charges for me and my Company ;
which if he does he will put *Narbanus* clean
out of Favour ; for you must know, he'll live at
the full height ; yet, in truth, what good has he
done us? He gave us a Company of pittiful
Sword-players, but so old and decrepit, that had
you breath'd on them, they'd have fallen flat on
their Faces : I have seen many better at a Funeral
Pile ; he would not be at the charge of Lamps
for them ; you'd have taken 'em for a parcel of
Dunghil Cocks fighting in the Dark : one was a
downright Fool, and gouty into the bargain ;
another Crump-footed, and a third half dead,
and Ham-strung : There was one of them a
Thracian, that made a Figure, and kept up to
the Rule of Fighting ; but, upon the whole
matter, all of them were parted, and nothing

came of this great block-headed Rabble, but a down-right running away : And yet, said he, I made you a Show, and I clap amongst the rest for Company ; but cast up the account, I gave more than I receiv'd ; one good turn requires another, You *Agamemnon* seem to tell me, what would that troublesome Fellow be at ; because you can speak and not do, you are not of our Form, and therefore ridicule what poor Men say ; tho', set aside your Book-learning, we know you are a meer Blockhead. Where lies the matter then ? let me perswade you to take a Walk into the Country, and see our Cottage, you'll find there somewhat to eat ; a Chicken, a few Eggs, or the like : The bad Weather had like to have broke us all, yet we'll find enough to fill our Bellies. Your Scholar, my Boy *Cicero*, is mightily improved, and if he lives, you'll have a Pupil after your own Heart ; he is pretty forward already, and whatever spare-time he has, he spends it at his Book : He's a witty Lad, well-featur'd, takes a thing without much Study, tho' yet he is but sickly : I kill'd three of his Linnets the other day, and told him the Weasels had eaten them ; yet he found other things to play with, and has a pretty knack at Painting : He has a perfect Aversion to *Greek* but seems better inclin'd to *Latin* ; tho' the Master he now has humours him in the other ; nor can he be kept to one thing, but is still craving more, and will not take pains with any. There is also another of this sort, not much troubled with Learning, but very diligent, and teaches more than he knows himself : He comes to our House on Holidays, and whatever you give him he's contented ; I therefore bought the Boy some Ruled Books, because I would have him get a smattering in Accounts and the Law ; it will be his own another day : He has Learning enough already, but if he loses what he has got— I design him for a Trade, a *Barber*, a *Parson*, or a *Lawyer*, which nothing but the Devil can take from him : How oft have I told him, Thou art, Sirrah, my first begotten, and believe thy Father, whatever thou learnest 'tis all thy own : See, there's Sir *Clodpate* the Lawyer, if he had not been a Scholar he might have starved, or have hang'd himself ; but now do but look upon his Purple Robes, I'll warrant he thinks himself as good as my Lord Chief-Justice.   Letters are a Treasure, and a Trade never dies.

To this, or the like purpose, we were bandying it about, when *Trimalchio* return'd, and having wip'd the Ointment from his Face, and wash'd his Hands, Pardon me, my Friends, said he, I have been Costive for several Days, and my Physicians were to seek about the matter, when a Suppository of Pomegranate Wine, with Turpentine and Vinegar reliev'd me ; and now I hope my Belly may be asham'd if it keep no better Order ; for sometimes I have such a rumbling in my Guts, you'd think an Ox bellow'd ; and therefore if any of you has a mind to ease himself, he need not blush for the matter ; there's not one of us born without some defect or other, and I think no torment greater than wanting the benefit of going to Stool, which is the only thing even *Jupiter* himself can't prevent : What do you grin, *Fortunata*, you that break me so often of my Sleep by Night ? I never deny'd any Man to do that in my Room might pleasure himself; and Physicians will not allow us to keep any thing in our Bodies longer than needs must ; therefore if you have any further occasion, every thing is ready in the next Room : Water, Chamber-pots, Close-stools, or whatever else may be needful ; believe me, being hard bound, affects the Head, and disturbs the whole body; I have known many a Man lost by it, when they have been so modest to themselves as not to tell what they ailed.

We thank'd him for his Frankness, and the Liberty he gave us, and to suppress our Laughter, set the Glass about again ; nor did we yet know that in the midst of such Dainties we were, as they say, to clamber another Hill ; for upon the flourish of Musick the Cloth being taken away, there were brought in three fat Hogs with Collars and Bells about their Necks ; and he that had the charge of them told us, the one was two Years old, the other three, and the third full grown. I took it at first to be a Company of Tumblers, and that the Hogs, as the manner is, were to have shewn us some Tricks, till *Trimalchio*, breaking in upon my Expectation, Which of them, said he, will you have for Supper ? for Cocks, Pheasants, and the like, are but Country Fare, but my Cooks have Coppers will boil a Calf whole. And therewith commanding a Cook to be call'd for, he prevented our Choice by ordering him to kill the largest, and with a loud Voice ask'd him, Of what Rank of Servants in that House he was ? to which he answering, Of the fortieth : Were you bought, said the other, or born in my House? Neither, said the Cook, but left you by *Pansa*'s Testament. See then, said *Trimalchio*, that you dress it as it should be, or I'll send you to the Galleys. On which the Cook being sensible of his Power, went into the Kitchin to mind his Business.

But *Trimalchio* turning to us with a pleasanter look, ask'd us if the Wine pleased us, if not, said he, I'll have it chang'd ; and if it does, let me see it by your drinking : I thank the Gods I do not buy it, but have every thing that may get an Appetite growing on my own Grounds hard by the City, which no Man that I know of has but my self ; and yet it has been taken for *Burgundy* and *Champaigne*. I have a Project to joyn *Sicily* to my Lands on the Continent, that when I have a mind to go into *Africa*, I may Sail by my own Coasts. But prithee, *Agamemnon*, tell me what *moot-point* was it you argued to day ; for tho' I plead no Causes my self, yet I have had a share of Letters in my time ; and that you may not think me out of Love with them now, I have three Libraries, the one *Greek*, the other two *Latin* ; therefore, as you love me, tell me, what was the state of the Question : The Poor and the Rich are Enemies, said *Agamemnon :* And what is Poor, answer'd *Trimalchio ?* Spoke like a Gentleman, reply'd *Agamemnon.* But making nothing of the matter, If it be so, said *Trimalchio,* where lies the Dispute ? and if it be not so, 'tis nothing.

While we all humm'd this and the like stuff, I beseech you, said he, my dear *Agamemnon,* do you remember the Twelve Labours of *Hercules,* or the Story of *Ulysses,* how a *Cyclops* put his Thumb out of Joint with a Mawkin ? I've read such things in *Homer* when I was a Boy ; nay, saw my self the *Sybil* of *Cuma* hanging in a Glass Bottle : And when the Boy ask'd her, *Sybil, what would you have ?* She answer'd, *I would die.*

He had not yet run to the end of the Rope, when an overgrown Hog was brought to the Table. We all wonder'd at the Expedition which had been us'd, thinking a Capon could not have been dress'd in that time : and what increas'd our Surprize was, this Hog seem'd larger than the Boar which was just now brought before us : When *Trimalchio* looking more intent upon him, What, what, said he, are not his Guts taken out ? No, by *Hercules,* they are not : Bring hither, bring hither this Rogue of a Cook. And when the Fellow stood hanging his Head before us, excusing himself, that he was so much in haste he forgot it. How, forgot it, cry'd out *Trimalchio !* Do you think he has given it no Seasoning, is it neither pepper'd or salted ? Strip him : When in a

trice it was done, and the Cook was placed
betwixt two Executioners : We all of us began
to interceed for him, as a Fault which might now
and then happen, and therefore begged his pardon ;
but if ever he did the like again, there was no
body would speak for him ; tho', for my part, I
think he deserv'd what he got : And so turning
to *Agamemnon*'s Ear, This fellow, said I, must be
reckoned a careless Rascal ; could any one forget
to Bowel a Hog ?   I would not, by *Hercules*, have
forgiven him, if he had serv'd me so in the
dressing of a Mackeril.   But *Trimalchio*, it seems,
had somewhat else in his Head ; for bursting into
a Laughter, You, said he, that have so short
a Memory, let's see if you can do your Office.
On which the Cook, having put on his Coat again,
took up a Knife, and pretending to tremble,
ripp'd up the Hog's Belly, from whence immediately tumbled out a heap of Hogs-puddings
and Sausages.

After this, as it had been done of it self, the
Family gave a Shout, and cry'd out, *Health and
Prosperity to* Caius !   The Cook also was pre-
sented with Wine, a Silver Coronet, and a
Drinking-bowl, on a broad *Corinthian* Plate :
which *Agamemnon* more narrowly viewing ; I am,
said *Trimalchio*, the only person that has the true
Corinthian vessels.

I expected that according to his usual Insolence,
he would have told us they had been brought from
Corinth ; but he pursued his Discourse with more

discretion : And perhaps, said he, you'll ask me why I am the only Person that have them. And why the Copper-smith from whom I buy them, is called *Corinthus?* and what is *Corinthian* but what is made by *Corinthus?* And to shew you I am a Man of Letters, I'll tell you from whence the Word *Corinthian* takes its Original. When *Troy* was taken by *Hannibal* a cunning mischievous sort of a Fellow, he gathered all the Gold, Silver and Brazen Statues together he could find, and caused Fire to be set to the Pile. The Statues melting, intermixt their different Metals together, of which the Goldsmiths made Candlesticks, Sconces, and Salvers ; so that *Corinthian* Vessels are a Miscellany of Gold, Silver and Brass ; but neither this or that Metal in particular, pardon me what I say ; I like Glass Cups better, others are not of my Opinion : If Glass was not so brittle, I would rather have it than Gold ; but now 'tis of a very inconsiderable value.

There was an Artist who made Glass Vessels so tough and hard, that they were no more to be broken than Gold and Silver ones : It so happen'd, that the same Person having made a very fine Glass Mug, fit for no Man, as he thought, less than *Cæsar* himself, he went with his Present to the Emperour, and had admittance ; both the Gift and the Hand of the Workman was commended, and the design of the Giver accepted. This Artist, that he might turn the admiration of the Beholders into astonishment, and work himself the more into the Emperor's favour, beg'd the Glass out of *Cæsar's* Hand ; and having received it, threw it with such a force against a paved Floor, that the most solid and firmest Metal could not but have received some hurt thereby. *Cæsar* also was equally amaz'd and troubled at the Action ; but the other took up the Mug from the Ground, not broken but only a little buldg'd, as if the Substance of Metal had put on the likeness of Glass ; and therewith taking a Hammer out of his Pocket, he hammer'd it as if it had been a Brass Kettle, and beat out the Bruise : and now the Fellow thought himself in Heaven, in having, as he fancied, gotten the Acquaintance of *Cæsar*, and the Admiration of all Mankind ; But it fell out quite contrary to his expectation : *Cæsar* asking him if any one knew how to make this malleable Glass but himself, and he answering in the Negative, the Emperor commanded his Head to be struck off ; For, said he, if this Art were once known, Gold and Silver will be of no more esteem than Dirt.

As for Silver, I affect it ; I have several Waterpots more or less, whereon is the Story how *Cassandra* kill'd her Sons, and the dead Boys are so well Emboss'd, you'd think them real. I have also a drinking Cup left me by an Advocate of mine, where *Dædalus* puts *Niobe* into the *Trojan Horse*, as also that other of *Hermerotes*, that they may stand as an Evidence there is truth in Cups, and all this Plate is Massy ; nor will I part with what I understand of them at any rate.

69

While he was thus talking, a Boy let fall a Cup out of his Hand ; on which, *Trimalchio* looking over his Shoulder at him, bad him be gone, and kill himself immediately ; for, said he, thou art careless and mind'st not what thou art about. The Boy hung his Lip, and besought him ; but he said, To what end dost thou intreat me, as if I required some difficult matter? I only bid thee obtain this of thy self, that thou be not careless again : But at last he forgave him upon our Entreaty. Hereupon the Boy run round the Table and cry'd, *Water without doors, and Wine within.* We all took the Jest, but more especially *Agamemnon*, who knew on what account he had been invited thither.

Trimalchio in the mean time hearing himself commended, drank more heartily and was merrier than before ; and being within an Ace of quite out, Will none of you, said he, desire my *Fortunata* to Dance? Believe me, there's no one leads up a Country Dance with a better Grace? And with that flourishing with his Hand, he began to act the part of a Scaramouch, the Family all the while singing, *Youth it self, most exactly Youth it self;* and he had gotten into the middle of the Room, but that *Fortunata* whisper'd him, and I believe told him, such Whimsies did not become his Gravity : Nor was there any thing more unsteady than his Humour ; for one while he inclin'd to the Advice of *Fortunata*, and another while to his natural Inclination : But what disturb'd the

Pleasure we took to see her Dance, was his Notary's coming in ; who, as they had been the Acts of a *Common-Council*, read aloud.

The Seventh of the Kalends of *August*, born in *Trimalchio's* Mannour near *Cumanum*, thirty Boys and forty Girls : There were also brought from the Threshing-floor into the Granary, Five hundred thousand Bushels of Wheat. The same day broke out a Fire in a Pleasure-Garden that was *Pompey's* which first began in one of the Bayliff's Houses.

How's this, said *Trimalchio !* when were those Gardens bought for me ? The Year before, answered his Notary ; and therefore not yet brought to Account.

At this *Trimalchio* fell into a Passion ; And whatever Lands, said he, shall be purchased for me hereafter, if I hear nothing of it in six Months, let them never, I order you, be charg'd or brought to any Account of mine. Then also were read the Orders of the Clerks of the Market, and the Wills of his Foresters, Rangers, and Park-keepers, by which they disinherited their Relations, and with ample praise of him, declared *Trimalchio* their Heir. Next that, were recited the Names of his Bayliffs ; and how one of them that made his Circuits in the Country, turn'd off his Wife for having taken her in Bed with a Barber. We were inform'd also, that the Door-keeper of his Baths was turn'd out of Office ; that one of his Auditors was found defective in his Accounts, and that the dispute between the Grooms of his Chamber was ended.

At last came in the Dancers on the Rope ; and a Punch-belly'd Blockhead holding out a Ladder, commanded his Boy to hop upon every Round of it singing, and to dance a Jigg on the top, and then to tumble through burning Hoops of Iron with a Glass in his Mouth. *Trimalchio* was the only person that lik'd this Diversion, but withal, he said, he did not admire it ; for there were only two Sights he was desirous to see, and those were Flyers on the High-rope, and Cock-fighting ; and that all other Creatures and Shows were Trifles : For, said he, I bought once a set of *Stroulers*, and chose rather to make them *Merry-Andrews* than *Comedians ;* and commanded my Bag-piper to Sing in Latin to them.

While he was chattering at this rate, a Boy chanc'd to stumble upon him, on which the Family gave a Shriek ; the same also did the Guests ; not for such a Beast, whose Neck they could willingly have seen broken, but for fear the Supper should have an unlucky end, and they be forc'd to lament the death of the Boy.

Whatever it were, *Trimalchio* gave a deep Groan, and leaning upon his Arm as if it had been hurt, the Physicians ran thick about him, and *Fortunata* amongst the foremost with her Hair about her Ears, and a Bottle of Wine in her Hand, still howling, miserable unfortunate Woman she was ! Undone, she was undone.

The Boy on the other hand, ran under our Feet, and beseech'd us to procure him his Pardon : But I was much concern'd, lest our Interposition might make but a scurvey end of the matter ; for the Cook that had forgotten to disbowel the Hog was still in my Thoughts. I began therefore to look about the Room, for fear somewhat or other might drop through the Ceiling ; while the Servant that had bound up his Arm in white instead of scarlet colour'd Flannel, was soundly beaten : Nor was I wrong in my Conjecture, for in lieu of another Course, came in an Order of *Trimalchio*'s, by which he gave the Boy his Freedom, that it might not be said, so Honourable a Person had been hurt by his Slave. We all commended the Action, and from thence fell into a Chat of the instability of all Humane Affairs. You're in the right, said *Trimalchio*; nor ought this Accident to pass without Recording ; and so calling for the Journal, he commanded it to be Enter'd ; and presently, without much thinking, tumbled out these Verses.

What's least expected falls into our Dish,
And Fortune's more indulgent than our Wish :
Therefore, Boy, fill the generous Wine about.

This Epigram gave us an occasion to talk of the Poets, and *Marsus* the *Thracian* was thought most deserving the Bays, till *Trimalchio* (turning to one in the Company) I beseech you, said he, tell me the difference between *Cicer* the

Orator, and *Publius* the Poet? for my part, I think one was the more Eloquent, the other the honester Man; for what could be said better than this?

> *Now sinking* Rome *grows weak with Luxury*,
> *To please her Appetite cram'd Peacocks die*,
> *Whose gaudy Plumes a modish Dish supply.*
> *For her the* Guinnea *Hen and Capon's drest:*
> *The Stork it self for* Rome's *luxurious Taste*,
> *Must in a Cauldron build its humble Nest*,
> *To please each Sense to foreign Worlds we haste*,
> *Perfume our Wines, and by our Smell we Taste.*
> *Now* Ceylon *Spice;* Anchovies *Spain bestows:*
> *For us the Orange and the Limon grows.*
> *To fetch Cavier we found* Geneva's *Lake*,
> *And our own Shoars luxuriously forsake.*
> *The* Grecians *Oyl, the* Germans *Hams afford:*
> Calabria *Wine, to cheer the wanton Lord.*
> *High-relish'd Sauce, unknown in happier times*,
> *We fetch from* Spain *and Sunburnt* Indian *Climes.*
> *Bambooes and Mangoes loaded Nature waste*,
> *Decay our Strength, yet urge the wearied Taste.*

But now we are talking, which, in the Opinion of the Learned, are the most difficult professions to understand? I think a Physician and a Banker: A Physician, because he knows a Man's very Heart, and when the Fits of an Ague will return; tho' by the way, I hate them mortally; for by their good will I should be always taking one Slip-sop or other: And a Banker, because he'll find out a piece of Brass, tho' 'tis plated with Silver.

There are also brute Beasts which are laborious ; to Oxen we are beholden for the Bread we eat ; and to Sheep, for the Wooll that makes us so fine. But, O horrid ! we both eat the Mutton, and make us warm with the Fleece. I take the Bees for Divine Creatures ; they give us Honey, tho' 'tis said they stole it from *Jupiter*, and that's the reason why they Sting : For where-ever you meet any thing that's sweet, you'll ever find a Sting at the end of it.

He went so far as to exclude *Philosophers* from Business, while the Memoirs of the Family were carrying round the Table, and a Boy, set for that purpose, read aloud the Names of the Presents appointed for the Guests to carry home with them. *Wicked Silver, what can it not do !* Then a Gammon of Bacon was set on the Table, and above that several sharp Sauces, a Night-cap for himself, Pudding-pies, and I know not what kind of Birds : There was also brought in a Rundlet of Wine, boiled off to a third part, and kept under Ground to preserve its strength : There were also several other things I can give no account of ; besides Apples, Scallions, Peaches, a Whip, a Knife, and some Presents had been sent him ; as Sparrows, a Flye-flap, Raisons, *Athenian* Honey, Night-gowns, Judges Robes, dry'd Paste, Table-books, with a Pipe and a Foot-stool : After which came in a Hare and a Sole-Fish : And there was also a

Lamprey, a Water-rat with a Frog at his Tail, and a bundle of Beets.

We laugh'd at these Whims ; there were five hundred more of them which I have now forgot : But when *Ascyltos*, who could not keep his Temper, shak'd his sides and laught at every thing so heartily, that he was ready to cry, a Free-man of *Trimalchio*'s that sate next above me, grew hot upon't : And what, said he, thou Sheep, what do you laugh at ? does not this Magnificence of my Master please you ? you're richer than he, forsooth, and eat better every Day ; by the God of this place, had I sate near enough you, I would have hit you a Box on the Ear before now : A hopeful Scoundrel, that mocks others ; some rascally Night-walker, *not worth the very Urine he makes ;* and should I throw a Chamber-pot on his Head, he knows not where to dry himself. I am not, by *Hercules*, quickly angry, *yet Worms are bred even in tender Flesh.* He laughs, and what Jest does he laugh at ? what Wooll did his Father give for the Bantling ? Is he a *Roman* Knight ? I am the Son of a King. How came I then, say you, to serve another ? In this I humour'd my own Fancy, and had rather be a Citizen of *Rome* than a tributary King, and now hope to behave myself so, as to be no Man's Jest. I walk like other Men, undisguiz'd, and can show my Head among the best, for I owe no Man a Groat : I never had an Action brought against me in my life, nor can any Man, abroad or at home, say to me, Pay me what thou owest. I

have purchased a pretty Farm in the Country,
and have everything suitable to it : I have twenty
Persons in Family, besides Dogs : I ransom'd my
Bond-woman, lest another should wipe his Hands
on her Smock ; and between our selves, she cost
me more than I'll tell you at present. I was made
a Captain of Horse without buying my Com-
mission, and hope to die in such a manner, that
I shall have no occasion to blush in my Grave :
But you that are so inquisitive concerning others,
never consider your self : Can you see a Mote in
another Man's Eye, and not perceive a Beam in
your own ? Your Master then is ancienter than
your self, an't please him ; but yet thou, whose
Milk is not yet out of thy Nose, that canst not
say Boh to a Goose, must you be making Obser-
vations ? Are you the wealthier Man ? If you
are so, Dine twice, and Sup twice in a Day ; for
my part, I value my Credit more than Treasures :
Upon the whole matter, where's the Man that ever
dunn'd me twice ? Thou Pipkin of a Man, more
limber, but nothing better than a Strop of wet
Leather, I have served forty Years in this House,
and came into it at Man's Estate ; this Palace was
not then built, yet I made it my business to please
my Master, a Person of Honour, the parings of
whose nails are more worth than thy whole Body.
I met several Rubs in my way, but, by the help
of my good Angel, I broke through them all :
This is truth ; it is as easie to make a Hunting-
horn of a Sows Tail, as to get into this Family.

What makes you in the Dumps now, like a Goat
at a heap of Stones ?

On this *Gito*, who stood behind him, burst out
a laughing ; which the other taking notice of, fell
upon the Boy ; and, Do you, said he, laugh too,
you curl-pated chattering Magpye ? Are these
Holy-days ? why how now, Sirrah, is it the Month
of *December ?* Are you come to Age yet, I pray ?
What would this Skeleton dropt from a Gibbit,
this Crows-meat, be at ? I'll find some way for
Jupiter to plague thee, and him that taught thee
no better manners, or never let me eat a good
Meal's-meat again : I could——Sirrah, but for
the Companies sake I spare thee, tho' either we
are mightily in the wrong of it, or they are Sots
themselves that carry no better a Hand over thee ;
for without doubt the proverb is true, *Like Master
like Man.* I am hot by Nature, and can scarce contain my self ; give me but a Mess of Pease Pottage,
and I care not Two-pence for my Mother. Very
well, I shall meet thee abroad, thou Mouse, thou
very Mushroom : May I never thrive more, but I'll
drive that Master of thine into a branch of Rue ;
nor shalt thou, by *Hercules*, get out of my Clutches,
tho' thou couldst call *Jupiter* to thy assistance : I
shall off with those Locks, and catch thee when
that sorry Master of thine shall be out of the way ;
thou wilt certainly fall into my Hands, and either
I know not my self, or I'll make thee leave this
Buffoonry : Tho' thy Beard were of Gold, I'll
have thee bruised in a Mortar, and him that first

taught thee : I never studied *Geometry*, *Criticism*, *and meer Words without Sense*, but I understand the fitting of Stones for Buildings, can run you over a hundred things, as to Metal, Weight, Coin, and that to a tittle ; if you have a mind, you and I will try it : I'll lay thee a Wager, thou Wizard, and tho' I know not a word of *Rhetorick*, thou'lt presently find thou hast lost : If you beat the Bush, I'll catch the Hare : Resolve me, I say, which of us runs, yet never stirs out of his place ? Which of us grows bigger, and yet is less ? Do you scamper ? can't you tell what to make of it, that you look so like a Mouse in a Trap ? Therefore hold thy Tongue, or don't provoke a better Man than thy self, who thinks thee but a Scoundril of Nature, perchance thou fanciest me taken with those yellow Locks, which thou hast already vowed to some Whore or other. O lucky Opportunity ! come, let's walk to the *Exchange*, and see which of us can borrow Money : You'll be satisfied then, I am a Man of Reputation ; a pretty thing, is it not to be drunk ? So may I grow Rich whilst I live, and die well ; but the People will brain me if I sit not on your Skirts as close as the Coat to your Back : He's a precious Tool too, whoever he were, that taught thee ; a piece of green Cheese, no Master I am sure. I have learn'd as well as another Man, and my Master said it would be my own another Day. Save your Worship ! get home as fast as you can, but look well about you, and have a care how you speak irreverently of your Betters, or vie Estates with them ; he that does it, his Purse shall pay for it :   For my self, I thank God, you see me in the Condition and Circumstances I am.

Ascyltos was making answer to his Railing, when *Trimalchio*, pleased with the good Grace with which his Freed-man deliver'd himself, Go to, said he, no more of this wild Talk, let us rather be Merry ; and you, *Hermeros*, bear with the Young-man, his Blood is all in a Ferment ; be thou the sober Man ; he that is overcome in this Quarrel, gains the Victory : Even you your self, when you were such another Capon, could cry nothing but *Coco, Coco*, and had no Heart at all. Let us therefore, which is the better of the two, be heartily Merry, and expect some Admirers of *Homer*, that will be here presently.

Nor were the words scarce out of his Mouth, when in came a Company of Players, and made a rustling with their Spears and Targets. *Trimalchio* lean'd on his Pillow, the *Homerists* ratled out Greek Verses as arrogantly as they were us'd to do, and he read a Latin Book with a loud Voice ; whereupon Silence being made, Know ye, said he, what Fable they are upon ?

Diomedes and *Ganymede* were two Brothers, and *Helen* was their Sister ; *Agamemnon* stole her away, and shamm'd *Diana* with a Hind in her stead, as *Homer* Sings in this place ; and also how the *Trojans* and the *Tarentines* fell into Civil Wars ; but at last he got the better of it, and Married his Daughter *Iphigenia* to *Achilles*; on which *Ajax* run mad. And there's an end of the Tale.

On this the *Homerists* set up a Shout, and a young boiled Heifer with an Helmet on her Head, was brought to the Table; *Ajax* followed, and with a drawn Sword, as if he were distracted, fell upon the Beef, cutting it now in one place, then in another, still acting as if he was Lunatick; till having cut the Heifer into Joints, he took them upon the point of his Sword, and distributed them to the Company. Nor had we much time to admire the Conceit; for of a sudden the Roof gave a crack, and the whole Room shook: For my part, I got on my Feet, but all in a confusion, for fear some Tumbler might drop on my Head; the same Fear also possest the rest of the Guests, who stood staring and expecting what new thing would come from the Clouds: when straight the main Beams of the Ceiling open'd, and a vast Circle was let down, all round which hung Golden Garlands and Alabaster Pots of sweet Ointments.

While we were required to take up these Presents, I chanced to cast an Eye upon the Table, where lay a fresh Service of Cheese-cakes and Tarts, and in the midst of them a bak'd Image of the God which presides over Orchards, stuck round with all sorts of Apples and Grapes, as they commonly draw that Figure.

We greedily reached our Hands towards it, when of a sudden, a new Diversion gave us fresh Mirth; for all the Cheese-cakes, Apples and Tarts, upon the least touch, threw out a delicious liquid Perfume, which fell upon us.

We judging the Mess to be Sacred, that was so religiously and magnificently garnish'd, stood up and began a Health to the *August Founder*, the *Father of his Country* : After which Reverence, falling to catch that catch could, we filled our Napkins ; and I plundered more furiously than the rest, who thought nothing too good to bestow upon *Gito*.

As these things were doing, in came three Boys in white, their Coats tuck'd about them, two of whom set on the Table three Houshold Gods, with Broaches about their Necks, and the other bearing round a Goblet of Wine, cry'd aloud, be the Gods Favourable ! The Name of this, said he, is *Cobler*, that other's *Good-luck*, and the third's *Spend-all* : The Image of *Trimalchio* was also carry'd round the Hall, and every one having kiss'd it, we thought it shame not to follow the Example of the rest of the Company.

After this, when all of us had wish'd him Health and Happiness, *Trimalchio* turning to *Niceros*, You were wont, said he, to be a good Companion, but what's the matter we get not a word from you now ? Let me entreat you, if you wish me well, do not break an old Custom.

Niceros pleased with the frankness of his Friend : Let me never thrive, said he, if I am not ready to caper out of my Skin to see you in so good a Humour, therefore whatever Stories I tell shall be

pleasant, tho' I am afraid those grave Fops may
laugh ; but let them look to't, I'll proceed nevertheless ; for what am I the worse for any one's
laughing ? I had rather they should laugh at my
Jest than at my Person.

When he had thus spoke——he began this
Tale——

I was once upon a time a Servant, and I dwelt
in a narrow Lane, in the same House where
Gavilla now lives ; there, by the good pleasure of
the Gods I fell in Love with the Wife of
Tarentius ; he kept an Eating-House. Ye all
knew *Melissa Tarentina,* a pretty little smart Lass,
and very Beautiful ; but, by *Hercules,* I fell in
Love with her more for her good Humour than
any other Reason, If I ask'd her a Favour, she
never deny'd me ; and for what Money I got, I
made her my Cash-keeper ; nor did she ever fail
me when I had occasion for it. It so happen'd,
that a She-companion of hers had dy'd in the
Country, and she was gone thither ; how to see
her I could not tell ; *but a Friend is seen at a dead
lift ;* it also fell out that my Master was gone to
Capua to dispatch some Business : I laid hold of
the opportunity, and perswaded mine Host to take
a Walk in the Evening four or five Miles out of
Town, you must know he was a bold Fellow, and
durst have fac'd the Devil : The Moon shone as
bright as Day, and about Cock-crowing we fell in
with a Burying-place, and certain Monuments of
the Dead : my Man loiter'd behind me a Star-

gazing, and I sat down expecting him, and fell to
Singing, and numbring them ; when looking round
me, what should I see but mine Host strip'd stark
naked, and his Cloaths lying by the High-way-side.
The Sight surpriz'd me very much, and I stood
stock still as if I had been dead ; but he piss'd round
his Cloaths, and of a sudden was turn'd to a Wolf :
Don't think I Jest ; I would not tell a Lye for
Ten thousand Pounds.   But as I was saying, after
he was turn'd to a Wolf, he set up a howl, and
fled to the Woods.   At first I knew not where I
was, till going to take up his Cloaths, I found
them also turn'd to Stone.   Some Men would
have dy'd for fear, but I drew my Sword, and
killing all the Ghosts that came in my way, lighted
at last on the place where my Mistriss was : I
enter'd the outward Door ; my Eyes were sunk in
my Head, the Sweat ran off me by more streams
than one, and I was just breathing my last, without thought of recovery, when my *Melissa* coming
to me, began to wonder why I walk'd so late ;
and if, said she, you had been here a little sooner,
you might have done us a kindness ; for a Wolf
came into the Farm, and has made a dreadful
havock of the Cattle ; but tho' he got off, he has
no reason to laugh, for a Servant of ours ran him
through the Neck with a Pitch-fork.   As soon as
I heard her, I could not hold open my Eyes any
longer, and ran home by Day-light, like a Vintner
whose House had been robb'd : but coming by the
place where the Cloaths were turn'd to Stone, I

saw nothing but a puddle of Blood ; and when I
got home, found mine Host lying in Bed like an
Ox in a Stall, and a Chirurgeon dressing his Neck.
I understood afterwards he was a Fellow that
could change his Skin ; but from that Day forward
could never Eat a bit of Bread with him, no,
if you'd have kill'd me.   Let them that don't
believe me, examine the truth of it ; and if I
tell you a Lye, may my good Angels forsake me.

The Company were all in a maze, when, Saving
what you have said, quoth *Trimalchio*, if there be
Faith in Man, my Hair stands on end, because I
know *Niceros* is no Trifler ; he has good grounds
for what he says, and is not given to idle talking :
Nay, I'll tell ye as horrible a thing my self ; but
see there, what's that behind the Hangings ?

When I was yet a long-hair'd Boy, for even
then I liv'd a pleasant Life, I had a Minion, and
he dy'd : He was, by *Hercules*, a Pearl, a Paragon,
nay, Perfection it self : But when his poor Mother
lamented him, and we also were doing the same,
some *Witches* got round the House on a sudden,
you'd have taken them for a Pack of Hounds
hunting a Hare.   We had then in the House a
Cappadocian, a tall Fellow, stout and hardy, that
would not have stept an Inch out of his way for
Jupiter himself.   He boldly drew his Sword, and
wrapping his Coat about his left Arm, leap'd out
of the House, and, as it might be here, (no harm
to the thing I touch) ran a Woman clean through.
We heard a pittiful Groan, but, not to lye, saw

no body at all. Our Champion came in and threw himself on a Bed, but all black and blue, as if he had been thrashed with a Flail ; for it seems some ill hand had touch'd him. We shut the Door, and went on with our Mourning ; but the Mother taking her Son in her Arms, and stroaking him, found nothing but a Bolster of Straw ; it had neither Heart, Entrails, nor any thing, for *the Faries*, belike, *had stollen him out of his Cradle, and left a Wad of Straw instead of him.* Give me Credit, I beseech ye, *Women are craftier than we are, play their Tricks by Night, and turn every thing Topsy-turvy.* After this, that tall swinging Fellow of ours never came to himself again, but in a few Days Died raving mad.

We all wonder'd, as not doubting what he said, and kissing the Table in reverence to him, desir'd the Privilege of the Night, and that our Places might be kept till we return'd.

And now we thought the Lamps look'd double, and the whole Room seem'd quite another thing ; when *Trimalchio* again, I speak to you *Plorimus*, won't you come in for a share ? Will he entertain us with nothing ? you us'd to be a pleasant Companion, could sing a Song and tell a Tale with the best ; but alas ! alas ! the times are chang'd. My Horses, said the other, ran away with my Coach, I have been troubled with the Gout ever since. When I was a young Fellow, I sung so long, I had well nigh brought my self into a Consumption. What do you tell me of Songs, Tales, or Barber's

Shops? Who ever came near me but one, only *Apelles;* and thereupon setting his Hand to his Mouth, whistled out somewhat, I know not what, which afterwards he swore was *Greek.* As he was mimicking the Trumpets, *Trimalchio* looking on his Minion, called him *Cræsus:* Yet the Boy was blear-ey'd, and employ'd himself in swathing a little black Bitch with nasty Teeth, and overgrown with Fat, in green Swaddling-clouts, the Boy set her half a Loaf upon the Table, which she refusing to eat, he cram'd her with it: On which *Trimalchio* commanded the Guardian of his House and Family, *Scylax,* to be brought; when presently was brought in a beautiful Mastiff in a Chain, who having a Hint given him by a scrape of the Porter's Foot, lay down before the Table; whereupon throwing him a Manchet, There's no one, said he, in this House of mine, loves me better than this Dog. The Boy highly resenting it, that *Scylax* should be so commended, threw the Bitch on the Floor, and challeng'd the Dog to have a Rubbers with him. On this *Scylax* after the manner of Dogs, set up such a hideous Barking, that it fill'd the Room; and snapping at him, almost tore off a Locket of Jewels which *Cræsus* wore on his Breast; nor did the Scuffle end here, for a great Candlestick being thrown down upon the Table, broke several Crystal Glasses, and threw the scalding Oyl upon the Guests.

Trimalchio, not to seem concern'd at the loss, kissed the Boy and commanded him to get on his

Back ; nor was it long e're he was a Cock-horse, and slapping his Master's Shoulders, and laughing cry'd out, *Fool, fool, and how many of them have we here ?*

Trimalchio thus kept under for a while, commanded a Bumper to be fill'd and given round to the Waiters, with this further Order, That whoever refused it should have it poured down his Collar. Thus one while we were grave, and another while merry.

After this came Junkets and Forc't-meats upon the Table, the very remembrance of which, if I may be believ'd, will not yet down with me ; for there were several cram'd Hens given about under the notion of Thrushes, and Goose Eggs with Caps upon them ; which *Trimalchio*, not without Ostentation, press'd us to Eat ; adding withal, that their Bones were taken out.

Nor were the words scarce out of his Mouth, when a Beadle rapp'd at the Door, and one in white, with a company of Roisters following him, came in upon us : For my part I was not a little surpriz'd ; and, by his Lordliness, taking him for the Mayor of a Town, and our selves within his Liberties, was getting upon my Feet. *Agamemnon* laught to see me so concern'd, and bade me sit still ; for, said he, this *Habinias* is a Captain of Horse, a good Mason, and has a special way with him in making Monuments.

Recover'd again with his Words, I kept my Seat, and wholly fix'd my Eye on *Habinias* : He came in Drunk, lolling on his Wife's Shoulders, with some Garlands round about him, his Face all trickling down with Ointment, he seated himself at the head of the Table, and incontinently call'd for Wine and hot Water.

Trimalchio was pleased with the Humour, and calling for a bigger Glass, asked him what Entertainment he had from whence he came?

Every thing, said the other, but your Company, for my Inclination was here; tho' by *Hercules*, all was very well. *Scissa* kept a Nine-days Feast for his Servant *Miscellus*, whom he enfranchiz'd after he was dead: It is said he had a round Sum in the Chequer, for they reckon he died worth 50000 Crowns; yet this was all done in good order, tho' every one of us was oblig'd to pour half his Wine on the Grave.

But, said *Trimalchio*, what had ye to Eat? I'll tell ye, quoth *Habinas*, as near as I can, but sometimes I forget my own Name: However, for the first Dish we had a goodly Porker, with a Garland about him, and Puddings, Goose-gibblets Lamb-stones, Sweet-breads, and Gizzards; then there were also Beets, and Houshold-bread of his own baking, for himself, which I had rather have than White; it makes a Man strong, and I never complain of what I like. The next was a cold Tart, with excellent warm Honey, right *Spanish*, running upon it. I eat little of the Tart, but more of the Honey; I tasted also the red Pulse, and Lupines, by the advice of *Calvas*, and several

Apples, of which I carry'd away two in my Handkerchief; for if I bring home nothing to my little she-Slave, I shall have Snubs enough ; this Dame of mine puts me often in mind of her. We had also on a Side-table the Haunch of a Bear, which *Scintilla* tasting e're she was aware, had like to have vomited her Heart up : I on the other hand, eat a pound of it or better, for methought it tasted like Boars-flesh ; and, said I, if a Bear eats a Man, why may not a Man much more eat a Bear ? To be short, we had Cream Cheese, Wine boil'd off to a third part, fry'd Snails and Chitterlings, Livers, Eggs, Turneps, Mustard, and a Bowl that held a Gallon. Don't disturb me, *Palamedes* ; there were also handed about a Basket of Sugar-cakes, of which we wantonly took some, and sent away the Gammon of Bacon. But tell me, *Caius*, I beseech you, what's the matter that *Fortunata* sits not among us ? How came you to know her, quoth *Trimalchio?* till she has gotten her Plate together, and distributed what we leave among the Servants, not a Sup of any thing goes down her Throat.

But unless she sits down, replied *Habinas*, I'll be gone ; and was getting up, but that the word being four times given about for her, she came at last in a greenish Gown, and a Cherry colour'd pair of Bodice, beneath which might be seen her Petticoat and Embroider'd Garters ; then wiping her Hands on her Neckcloth, she plac'd her self on the Bed whereon *Scintilla*, the Wife of *Habinas*,

was seated ; and having given her a Kiss, told
her, it was in Compliment to her that she was
there. At length it came to this, that she took
off her weighty Bracelets, and shewed them to
Scintilla ; which she admiring, she also unbuckled
her Garters and a Net-work Purse, which she said
was of the finest Gold.

Trimalchio observ'd it, and commanding all to
be laid before him, See, said he, this Woman's
Finery, and what Fools our Wives make us ; they
should weigh six Pound and a half ; yet I've
another made by the famous Jew which weighs
ten : And that he might not be thought to be a
Lyar, he call'd for his Gold Scales, and commanded
them to be weigh'd : Nor had *Scintilla* more wit
than t'other, for pulling a Golden Box out of her
Bosom, which she called *Good-luck*, she took out
of it two large Pearl Pendants, giving them in like
manner to *Fortunata* to view : See, quoth she,
what 'tis to have a kind Husband, I am sure no
Woman has a better. What, said *Habinas*, hast
thou put the Sham on me ? thou toldst me thou
couldst be contented with Glass Beads ; and for
this trick, if I had a Daughter, I'd cut her Ears
off, tho' there were no more Women in the World.
This it is to Piss warm and drink cold.

Mean time the Women being toucht with the
Expression, fell a twittering, and being got mellow,
fell to Kissing one another, one commended the
Mistriss of the House, t'other the Master : when
during this chit chat, *Habinas* stealing behind

Fortunata, gave her such a toss on the Bed, that her Heels flew as high as her Head, on which she gave a squeak or two, and finding her Thighs bare, blushing, hid her Head in *Scintilla's* Bosom.

This Entertainment held a while, till *Trimalchio* calling for another Course to entertain his new Guests, the Servants took away the Tables that were before us, and having brought others, strew'd the Room with Pindust, mixt with Vermillion and Saffron ; and what I never saw before, the Dust of a Looking-glass ground to Powder.

When immediately, says *Trimalchio*, I could have been contented with the Dishes we have had already ; but since we have got other Tables, we must also have another Service ; and if there be any thing worth our having, bring it.

On which a spruce Boy that served us with warm Water, began to imitate a Nightingale ; till *Trimalchio* giving the Word, a Servant which waited on *Habinas*, set up another Humour, and, as I believe, commanded by his Master, bellow'd out ;

Mean time Æneas had forsook the Shore.

Nor was I ever acquainted with a harsher sound ; for besides his mean, barbarous, and Peasant-like way of expressing himself, he so stuft it with scraps of Verses, that even *Virgil* then first disrelish'd me ; till at last he was so tir'd, that he could hold no longer : D'ye think, said *Habinas*, this Boy has learn'd nothing? I bred him with Stroalers that follow the Fairs : Nor has he his Fellow, whether he mimicks a Muliteer or a Buffoon. This Never-be-good has abundance of Wit ; he's a Taylor, a Cook, a Baker, a Jack of all Trades, and but for two Faults, were exact to a Hair : He's crack-brain'd, and snores in his Sleep : For that Cast of his Eye I value it not, he looks like *Venus*, and therefore his Tongue is ever running ; and were that Eye out, he were worth the Money I gave for him.

On which *Scintilla* interrupting him, told him he was a naughty Man, for not telling all his good qualities : He's a Pimp too, said she, if not worse, but I'll take care he receive his Reward for that.

Trimalchio laugh'd, and said, He knew he was a *Cappadocian*, that made as much of himself as he could, and, by *Hercules*, I commend him for't ; when will you find such another ? but, *Scintilla*, you must not be Jealous : Believe me, and I know you too ; may I enjoy the Health you wish me, I play'd at Leap-frog so long with our Boy, that my Master grew jealous, and sent me to dig in the Country ; but little said is soon amended.

Hereupon this Rascally Servant, as if he had been praised all this while, produc'd an earthen Candlestick, and for half an hour, or better, imitated the Hautboys, *Habinas* singing the Base to him, and blabbering his under Lip with his Finger ; that done, he went into the middle of the

Room, and clattering some Canes together, one while he imitated the Bagpipes, and danced a Jigg to his own Musick; and another while with a ragged Frock and a Whip, Aped the Humours of a Carrier, till *Habinas* calling him, first kiss'd him, and then drank to him, which the other pledg'd; and wishing him better and better, I give you, said he, a pair of Buskins.

Nor had there ever been an end of this Trumpery, had not the last Service of Black-birds, baked in good Pye-crust, with Raisins and Chesnuts, been brought up, and after them Peaches, so stuck with Prickles, that they look'd like Hedge-hogs: Yet this might have been born with, if the next Dish had not been such, that we should have rather chose to have starv'd than to have touch'd it: For when it was set upon the Table, and, as we thought, look'd like a good fat Goose, with Fish and all kind of Fowl round it, Whatever you see here, said *Trimalchio*, is all made of the same substance.

Like a cunning Loon, I strait apprehended what it might be; and turning to *Agamemnon*, I marvel, said I, whether they be all mash'd together, or made of Loam; for, in a Saturnal at *Rome*, myself saw the like imaginary Supper.

Nor had I scarce said it, when—quoth *Trimalchio*, So may I grow in Estate, not in Bigness, as my Cook made all this you see out of a single Hog; there is not an excellenter Fellow in the World than himself; he shall, if you please, make you a

Poll of Ling of a double Tripe ; a Plover of fat Bacon ; a Turtle of a Spring of Pork ; and a Hen of a Collar of Brawn ; and therefore a Fancy took me to give him a Name suitable to his Parts ; you must know I call him *Dædalus:* And because he understands his Business, I had Chopping-Knives of the best Steel brought him from *Rome;* and with that, calling for them, he turn'd them over, and admiring them, offer'd us the liberty of trying their Edge on his Cheek.

Immediately on this came in two Servants quarrelling about their Collars, at which each of them had a large Earthen Pot hanging ; and when *Trimalchio* determined the matter between them, neither of them stood to his Sentence, but fell to Club-law, and broke each others Pots.

This drunken Presumption put us out of order ; yet casting an Eye on the Combatants, we saw Oysters and Scollaps falling from the broken Pots, and another Boy receiv'd them in a Charger, which he carried round to the Guests.

Nor was the Cook's Ingenuity short of the rest, for he brought us a Dish of broil'd Snails, on a Silver Gridiron, and with a shrill unpleasant Voice, sang as he went. I am asham'd to relate what followed, which was never heard of till then : Some Boys came in with a Bason of liquid Perfumes, and first binding our Legs, Ancles, and Feet with Garlands, anointed them with it, and put what remained amongst the Wine Vessels and the Lamps.

And now *Fortunata* began to Dance, and
Scintilla's Hands went faster than her Tongue;
when, says Trimalchio, Sit down *Philargyrus*, I
give you leave, and you, *Carrio*, because you're an
honest Fellow; and you, *Minophilus*, bid your
Comrade do the like; what shall I say more?
The Family so crowded upon us, that we were
almost thrust off our Seats; and who should be
seated above me, but the Cook who had made a
Goose of a Hog, all stinking of Pickle and
Kitchen-stuff; not yet content that he sate
amongst us, he fell immediately to personate
Thespis the Tragedian, and dare his Master to a
Wager, which of them two should win the Prize
next Wrestling.

Trimalchio abash'd at the Challenge; My
Friends, said he, even Servants are Men; and
however oppress'd by Ill Luck, sucked the same
Milk our selves did; and for mine, it shall not
be long e're I make them Free without prejudice to my self: To be short, I enfranchise all
of them by my last Will and Testament.

I give *Philargyrus* a Country-Farm, and his She-
Comrade; to *Curio*, an Island, with a twentieth
part of my Moveables, a Bed and its Furniture;
for I make *Fortunata* my Heiress, whom I recom-
mend to all my Friends, and publish what I
design to have done, to the end my Family may
love me as much now as they will when I am
dead.

All thanked their Master for his kindness;

and he, as having forgotten Trifles, called for a
Copy of his Will, which he read from one end to
the other, the Family all the while sighing and
sobbing ; afterwards turning to *Habinas*, Tell me,
my best of Friends, said he, do you go on with
my Monument as I directed you? I earnestly
entreat you, that at the Feet of my Statue you
carve me my little Bitch, as also Garlands and
Ointments, and all the Battles I have been in, that
by your Kindness I may live when I am dead :
Be sure too that it have an hundred Feet as it
fronts to the High-way, and as it looks towards
the Fields, two hundred : I will also, that there
be all sorts of Fruit and Vines round my Ashes,
and that in great abundance : For it is a gross
mistake to furnish Houses for the Living, and
take no care of those we are to abide in for
ever : And therefore, in the first place, I will
have it Engraven,

LET NO HEIR OF MINE PRETEND
TO THIS MONUMENT.

And that I may receive no Injury after I am
dead, I'll have a Codicil annext to my Will,
whereby I'll appoint one of my Freed-Men the
Keeper of this Monument, that the People make
not an House-of-Office of it. Make me also, I
beseech you, on this my Monument, Ships under
full Sail, and my self in my Robes sitting on the
Bench, with five Gold Rings on my Fingers, and
scattering Moneys among the common People ; for

you know I have ordered you a Funeral-Feast, and Two-pence a piece in Money. You shall also, if you think fit, carve me some of these Beds we now sit on, and all the People making their Court to me. On my right Hand place my *Fortunata*'s Statue, with a Dove in one Hand, and with the other leading a little Dog in her Hand: As also my *Cicero*, and some large Wine Vessels close Cork'd, that the Wine don't run out; and yet carve one of them as broken, and a Boy weeping over it; as also a Sun-dial in the middle, that whoever comes to see what's a Clock may read my Name whether he will or no. And lastly, have a special consideration whether you think this Epitaph sufficient enough.

HERE RESTS CAIUS POMPEIUS TRIM-
ALCHIO, PATRON OF THE LEARNED.
A TROOP OF HORSE WAS DECREED
HIM, WITHOUT SUING FOR, AND
MIGHT HAVE BEEN A SENATOR,
WOULD HE HAVE ACCEPTED IT.
A PIOUS MAN, HONEST, VALIANT,
AND TRUE TO HIS FRIEND. HE
RAISED HIMSELF FROM LITTLE OR
NOTHING, BUT LEFT BEHIND HIM
A PRODIGIOUS ESTATE, YET NEVER
HEARD A PHILOSOPHER. FARE-
WEL TO YOU ALSO.

This said, *Trimalchio* wept plentifully, *Fortunata* wept, *Habinas* wept, and the whole Family set up a Cry, as if it had been his very Funeral, nay, I also whin'd for Company : When, says *Trimalchio*, Since you know we must die, why don't we live while we may ? so may I live my self to see you happy ; as, if we plunge ourselves in the Bath we shall not repent it : At my Peril be it, I'll lead the way, for this Room is grown as hot as an Oven. Say you so, quoth *Habinas*, nor am I afraid to make two days of one ; and therewith got up barefoot and follow'd *Trimalchio*.

I on the other hand turning to *Ascyltos*, asked him what he thought of it, for if I but see the Bath, I shall swoon away.

Let's drop behind then, said he, and whilst they are getting in, we'll slip off in the Croud.

The Contrivance pleas'd us ; and so *Gitto* leading the way through the *Portico*, we came to the outer-most Gate, where a chained Dog bolted upon us so furiously, that *Ascyltos* fell into the Fish-pond. I who had been frighted at the painted Dog, and now gotten as drunk as *Ascyltos*, while I endeavour'd to get hold of him, fell in my self ; at last the Porter's coming in saved us, for he quieted the Dog, and drew us out ; but *Gitto*, like a sharp Rascal, secured himself, for whatever had been given him at Supper to carry home with him, he threw it the Dog, and that mollified him.

But when shivering with Cold, we desir'd the Porter to let us out : You're mistaken, said he, if you think to go out the same way you came in, for no Guest ever did that yet : They come in at one Gate and go out at another.

In this sad pickle, what should we do ? we found ourselves in a new kind of Labyrinth, and for Bathing, we'd enough of it already : However, Necessity enforcing us, we prayed him to shew us the way to the Bath ; and *Gitto* having hung out our Cloaths a-drying in the Porch, we entered the Bath, which was somewhat narrow, and sunk into the Earth, not unlike a Rain-water Cistern ; in this stood *Trimalchio* stark naked : Nor could we avoid his humours ; for nothing, he said, pleased him better than to Bathe in a Crowd ; and that very place had, in times past, been a Grinding House. Being weary at length, he sate down, and provok'd by the noisiness of the Bath, set up his drunken Throat, and fell a murdering some Songs of *Menecrates*, as they that understood him told us.

Other Guests ran round the Cistern with their Arms across, and made a clamarous noise with their Mouths ; others either try'd to take up a Ring from the Pavement with their Hands bound behind them, or put one Knee to the Ground, to kiss their great Toes backward.

While they thus entertain'd one another, we went into the Hot-house that had been heated for *Trimalchio*, and being now recover'd of our Drunkenness, were brought into another Room, where *Fortunata* had set out a fresh Entertainment.

Above the Lamps I observed some Womens
Gewgaws. The Tables were massy Silver, the
Earthen Ware double gilt, and a Conduit running
with Wine ; when, said *Trimalchio*, This day, my
Friends, a Servant of mine open'd a Barber's Shop ;
he's well to pass, a thrifty Fellow, and a Favourite
of mine : Come, let the Floor have Drink as well
as ourselves ; and for our part, we'll sit to it till
Day-light.

While he was yet speaking, a Cock crow'd, at
which *Trimalchio* grew disorder'd, and commanded
the Wine to be thrown under the Table, and the
Lamps to be sprinkled with it ; then changing a
Ring to his Right Hand, It is not for nothing,
said he, this Trumpeter has given us notice ; for
either the House should be on fire, or one of the
Neighbourhood will kill himself : Far from us
be it, and therefore whoever brings me this ill
Prophet, I'll give him a Reward.

When immediately a Cock was brought in, and
Trimalchio commanding to have him drest, he was
torn in pieces by that exquisite Cook, who a little
before had made us Fish and Fowl of a Hog, and
put in a Stew-pan, and while *Dædalus* was taking
a lusty draught, *Fortunata* ground Pepper.

After which *Trimalchio* taking some of the
Banquet, bid the Waiters go to Supper, and let
others supply their Places.

Whereupon came in another Rank of Servants,
and as the former going cry'd out, Farewel, *Caius*,
those coming in, said, Sit thou merry, *Caius*.

And here our Mirth first began to be disturb'd, for a Beautiful Boy coming in among those new Servants, *Trimalchio* pluck'd the Boy to him, and welcomed him over and over : Whereupon *Fortunata*, to maintain her Right, began to rail at *Trimalchio*, calling him pitiful Fellow, one that could not manage himself, a shame and scandal to all honest Women, and a very Dog. *Trimalchio*, on the other hand, all confounded and vex'd at her Taunts, threw a Goblet at her Head : She fell a roaring as if she had her Eyes beat out, and clapt both her Hands before her Face.

Scintilla also stood amaz'd, and covered *Fortunata*, all trembling as she was, in her Bosom ; the Boy also put a cold Pitcher to her Cheek, on which she lean'd and made a lamentable wailing and blubbering.

But *Trimalchio* did quite contrary ; for, said he, what am I the better for this Graceless Woman ? 'Tis well known I took her out of a Bawdy-House and made her an honest Woman, but now, blown up like a Frog, she bespatters her self ; a very block, no Woman : But this poor Boy, born in a Cottage, never dreams of Palaces. May my good Genius so befriend me, as I'll bring down the Stomach of this seeming Saint, but in her Actions a Whore rampant : As inconsiderable as she makes me, I might have had a Wife with Two hundred and fifty thousand Pistoles, you know I don't Lye ; but she was somewhat in Years, and thereupon my Friend *Jessamin* the Perfumer took me aside, and perswaded me not to let my Family and Name be extinguish'd ; but whilst I am making her Fortune, I have put a Thorn into my own Foot ; but I'll have a care that she dig me not out of my Grave with her Nails : And that you may immediately be sensible, Mistress *Minx*, of what I design to do, I enjoin you, *Habinas*, that you place not her Statue on my Monument, for fear we should fall together by the Ears when I am dead : Nay, that she may know I am able to plague her, she shall not so much as Kiss me when I die. After this, as he persisted to rattle and make a noise, *Habinas* entreated him to give over his Anger ; There's not one of us all, said he, but one time or other does amiss ; we are but Men, not Gods. *Scintilla* weeping, said the same, called him *Caius*, and by his own good Nature, begg'd of him to be pacified.

Trimalchio not able to refrain his Tears any longer, I beg of you, *Habinas*, said he, as you wish to enjoy what you have gotten, if I have done any thing without cause, spit in my Face : I lov'd the Boy, 'tis true, not for his Beauty, but that he's a hopeful thrifty Lad : He has got several Sentences by heart, can read his Book at first sight, saves Money out of his Days Provision, has a little Box of his own to keep it, and two drinking Cups ; and does he not deserve to be in my Favour ? but *Fortunata*, forsooth, will not have it so ; your bandy Legs won't away with it. Be content with your own, thou She-kite, and don't plague me so, thou Harlotry, or otherwise thou'lt find what I am ; thou know'st well enough, if I once set on't, I am immoveable. But we'll remember the Living.

Come, my Friends, let's see how Merry you can be, for in my time I have been no better than your selves, but by my own Industry I am what I am : 'Tis the Heart makes a Man, all the rest is but stuff. I buy cheap and sell dear ; another Man may sell ye other things, but I enjoy my self : And thou Dunghil-raker, art thou yet gruntling, I'll take care hereafter you whimper for something.

But, as I was saying, my Frugality made me the Man I am ; I came out of *Asia* no Taller than this Candlestick, and daily measured my self by it : and that I might get a Beard the sooner, rubb'd my Lips with the Candle-grease ; yet I kept favourite to my Master fourteen Years (nor is it a dishonourable thing to do as one's bid) and the same time satisfy'd my Mistress : You under-stand me, Gentlemen, I'll say no more, for I hate boasting. By this means, as the Gods would have it, the Government of the House was committed to me, and nothing was done but by my Guidance : What need many words ? My Master made me Joint-heir with *Cæsar*, and I got, by his Will, a Senator's Estate ; but no Man thinks he has enough, and I had a mighty desire to turn Merchant. Not to detain you longer, I built five Ships, Freighted them with Wines, which at that time were as precious as Diamonds, and sent them

to *Rome;* you'll think I desired to have it so : All
my Ships founder'd at Sea, 'tis a true Story I tell
you ; *Neptune* swallow'd me in one Day Three
hundred thousand Crowns.   Do you think I broke
upon't ? by *Hercules*, no ; the Loss was but a
Flea-bite : For, as if there had been no such thing,
I built others, larger, better, and more fortunate
than the former ; so that every one esteem'd me
a Man of Courage.   As you know a great Ship
carries a great deal of Force, I loaded them again
with Wine, Beans and Bacon, Unguents, Planes
and other Merchandize :   And here *Fortunata*
shew'd her Affection ; for she sold all that she
had ; nay, strip'd her self to her very Smock, and
put a round Sum of Money in my Pocket ; tho'
yet it was but a Pig of my own Sow.   What the
Gods will is quickly done ; I got an Hundred
thousand Crowns by the Voyage, and forthwith
redeem'd the Lands my Patron had left me, built
me a House, bought Cattle to sell them again, and
whatever I went about gather'd like a Snow-Ball.
But when I grew richer than all the Country
besides, I gave over, and from a Merchant, turn'd
Usurer, and bought Servants.

Thus resolved to give over Trading, a certain
Astrologer that chanc'd to come to this Village
would have perswaded me to the contrary.   He
was a *Grecian*, his Name *Sarapa*, one that held
correspondence with the Gods.   He told me a
deal that I had forgotten, and laid every thing
before me from top to bottom :   He knew all

that I had within me, and told me what I had the Night before to Supper ; and you'd have thought he had liv'd with me all his Life-time.

I desire you'd inform me, *Habinas*, I think you was there, he told me the Intrigue between my Mistress and me ; That I had but Ill luck at Friends ; that no one ever made me a return of my Kindnesses : That I had large Possessions, but nourish'd a Viper in my Bosom : Why should I not tell you all ? I have, by his Account, thirty Years, four Months, and two Days yet to live ; and in a short time shall have another Estate left me.

Thus my Fortune-teller. But if I can join my Lands here to those in *Apulia*, I shall be rich enough : In the mean time, by the Favour of *Mercury*, my Guardian, I have built this House : It was once, you know, a pitiful Cabbin, but now as magnificent as a Temple : It has four Dining-rooms, twenty Bed-chambers, two Marble Porticoes, a Gallery above Stairs, my own Apartment, another for this Viper ; a very good Porter's Lodge, and the House is capable of receiving a thousand Guests : To be short, whenever his Highness comes this way, he had rather lodge here than in his own House, tho' it borders on the Sea : And many other Conveniences it has, which I'll shew you by and by. Believe me, *He that has a Peny in his Purse, is worth a Peny : They that have much shall have more.* And so your Friend, once no better than a Frog, is now a King.

And now *Stichus* bring me the Furniture in which I design to be carried to my Funeral Pile ; bring also the Unguent, and some of that Ointment which I order'd for the cleansing my Bones.

Stichus made haste and brought in a white Coverlet, and Robe of State, and pray'd us to try if they were not fine Wool, and well woven. And see you *Stichus*, said *Trimalchio* smiling, that neither Mice nor Moths come at them ; for, if they do, I'll burn you alive. I will be brought out in Pomp, that all the People may speak well of me.

With that opening a Glass Bottle of Spikenard, he caused us all to be anointed ; and I hope, said he, it will do as much good when I am dead, as it does while I am living : Then commanding the Wine-Vessels to be fill'd again, Now imagine, said he, you are invited to my Funeral Feast. We, by this time nauseated, were ready to vomit ; *Trimalchio* also was got extravagantly drunk, when behold a new Interlude ; he commanded the Cornets to come in, and lying at his full length upon the Bed, with Pillows under him, Suppose me, said he, now dead, say somewhat, I beseech you, in praise of me.

Whereupon the Cornets sounded as at a Funeral ; but one above the rest, a Servant of that Freedman of *Trimalchio*'s who, of all the rest, was the best condition'd, made such a Thundering, that it rais'd the Neighbourhood : On which the Watch, thinking the House had been on fire, broke open the Gate, and making an Uproar after their manner, ran in with Water and Hatchets. When finding so fair an opportunity, we gave *Agamemnon* the slip, and scamper'd off, as if it had been a real Fire.

The End of the First Part.

THE
SECOND PART
OF THE
WORKS
OF
Petronius Arbiter,

In PROSE and VERSE.

Made English by Mr. BURNABY, Mr. THO.
BROWN, Capt. AYLOFF, and Others.

THE

SECOND PART

OF THE

WORKS

OF

Petronius Arbiter,

A Roman Knight.

NOT a Star appear'd to direct us to our Lodging, nor could we meet with any Persons in the Street of whom we might have inquired our Way ; 'twas the very dead of Night : Our little knowledge of the Town, and the Wine we had drank, conspir'd to guide us amiss. When we had wander'd a good while, and hurt our feet with treading upon sharp Stones and Gravel, at length, the diligence of *Gitto* deliver'd us ; for the day before he, apprehending we might be at a loss when we returned from *Trimalchio's,* had providently mark'd every Post and Pillar with Chalk, to that degree, that the darkness of the Night could not render those notices obscure, but their brightness directed us how to find our way. Nor were our Fears over after we were got to our Inn; for my Hostess having taken a plentiful Cup of the Creature, had so entirely lost her Senses, and was fallen into so fast a sleep, that throwing her into the Fire would scarce have wak'd her; and, perhaps, we had been forc'd to have taken up our Lodging in the Street, if a Post belonging to *Trimalchio*, with ten Carriages of his Master's Revenue, had not come to the Door of the Inn at the same time we did; which, without much ado he beat down, and gave us admittance at the Breach.

As soon as ever we had entered our Chamber, I went to Bed, and having made so plentiful a Supper, and burning with Desire, I wholly gave myself up to Pleasure.

Who can the charms of that blest Night declare,
How soft, ye Gods, our warm embraces were!
Our wanton Limbs, like curling Ivy twin'd,
And both our Bodies and our Souls were join'd.
Farewel the World! the Gods would cease to live,
If Joys like these they might in death receive.

But these Dreams of Satisfaction quickly vanish'd, and I immediately found to my cost, that I had no reason to hug my self in my pleasures; *Ascyltos*, naturally prone to Mischief, perceiving me Drunk, and unable to secure my Prize, stole the Boy out of my Bed, and convey'd him to his own, and there revell'd in Joys he had no Title to : *Gitto*, either insensible of the Change put upon him, or cunningly dissembling it, slept unconcern'd at and unmindful of the Vows he had made to the contrary. Rising therefore in the Morning, and finding out the Trick impos'd upon me, by all that's good, I had a strong Inclination to have run them thro' both together, and to have made their Sleep eternal, by sending them into the other World ; but cooler Thoughts taking place, I wak'd my Friend *Gitto* with a good drubbing ; and looking sternly on *Ascyltos*, Since you have play'd the Villain, said I, and broke the common Laws of Friendship, pack up your Matters quickly, and find out another Comrade to abuse.

Ascyltos consented, and after we had made an exact division of our Booty ; Now, says he, let's share the Boy too : I believ'd it a Jest at parting, but he, with a murderous Resolution, drew his Sword ; Nor shall you, added he, think to ingross this Prize, which should, like the rest, be common to us both. I must have my share of him, in case you refuse me, I am resolv'd to take my Dividend no other way but with my Sword. Upon which, I also drew my Sword, and wrapping my Gown about my Arm, stood ready to engage.

The unhappy Boy rush'd between, and, kissing both our Knees, with Tears entreated, that we would not expose our selves in a pittiful Alehouse, nor with our Blood pollute our mutual

Vows and Obligations : But, raising his Voice, says he, If there must be Murder, behold my naked Bosom, hither direct your Fury : 'Tis I deserve Death, who violated the sacred Laws of Friendship.

Upon which we sheath'd our Swords ; and *Ascyltos* first began ; says he, I'll put an end to this difference : Let the Boy himself follow whom he pleases, and enjoy a perfect liberty in the choice of his Friend and Companion.

I that presum'd my long Acquaintance with the Boy had made no slight Impressions on his Nature, was so far from fearing any thing from this Project, that I catch'd at the Proposal ; but I had no sooner given my consent to decide our Contention in the manner *Ascyltos* had offer'd, and to make the Boy the Umpire of our Strife, but *Gitto* jumpt up, and, without the least hesitation, determin'd the Affair in favour of *Ascyltos*.

I, like one Thunder-struck at the sentence, void of Defence, fell flat upon the Bed ; nor had I survived the Loss, if Envy had not put a stop to my Resolution.

Ascyltos proud of the Conquest, goes off with the Prize, leaving me expos'd in a strange place, to the insults of Fortune, whom a little before he had caress'd as a Friend and Partner of his Adventures.

The Gods with Friendship seldom Mortals bless ;
That Sacred Good in Fancy we possess.

Our easy Faith false men with Oaths beguile;
When Fortune frowns the Perjur'd cease to smile.
The good and wretched, Men nor Gods defend;
But poorly fawn, and still the Rich commend.
Thus when the Audience bids the Play begin,
And the last Flourish calls the Actors in;
With tender Words, and with dissembling Art,
This plays a Lover's, that a Father's Part.
The Aged Sire with fond Paternal Care,
Affects his Son as he pursues the Fair.
But when, at length, the unctious Lamps expire
And the Spectators from the Play retire,
Each to his natural Inclination turns,
The Father doats not nor the Lover burns.

I durst not indulge my Grief any longer in that
place, for fear, amongst the rest of my Misfortunes,
one *Menelaus* a School-master, might find me alone
in the Inn; I therefore tyed up my Snapsack, and,
in a Pensive condition betook my self to a retire-
ment near the Sea-side; where, when I had been
mew'd up three Days, reflecting on my despicable
Circumstances, I beat my Breast, as sick as it was,
and, when my deep Sighs wou'd suffer me, often
cry'd out, Why has not the Earth swallow'd me
alive? Why has not the Sea overwhelm'd me?
I have been a Murderer; I have debauch'd the
Wife of *Lycas*; I have fled from Justice; and
even escap'd when I was condemn'd to be hang'd;
but to what purpose? To be an Exile in a strange
Country, to have my name recorded only amongst

Beggars and Vagabonds : And who condemn'd me to this Solitude ?—A Boy ! a Prostitute to all manner of Lust ; who, by his own confession, deserves to die ; who rais'd himself by his Lewdness, and by the same Crime obtain'd his Liberty ; who was Married, as a Girl, by one of his own Sex : And what a Wretch is that other, O ye Gods ! who no sooner arriv'd to be a Man, but perswaded by his Mother, he chang'd himself into a Woman, and assuming the Habit of a Servant-maid, took Service in, and did the drudgery of a Prison ; who having spent his own Paternal Fortune, and chang'd the Scene of his Lust (O horrid Impudence !) like a hot Whore, for one poor Night's Pleasure, sold his Friend. Now the Lovers lie whole Nights lock'd in each others Arms, and who knows but, in the intervals of their Crimes, they may laugh at me, and the solitude I am in : But they shan't go off so, for as I am a Man, free born, and generously bred, I'll make their Blood to expiate the Injury.

Having said thus, I girt my Sword about me ; and lest I should be too weak to maintain the War, I encourag'd my self with a lusty Meal, and making out of doors, like one possest, search'd every place : But whilst, with a wild distracted Countenance, I thought of nothing but Blood and Slaughter, and oft with execrations laid my Hand upon my Sword, a Soldier, or perhaps some Sharper or Foot-pad, observ'd me, and making up to me, said, Brother Soldier, to what Regiment

and Company do you belong? With a great
deal of Impudence, I nam'd him both the Ba-
talion and Company in which I pretended to
serve: My Assurance had near induc'd him to
believe the Lye, when looking down, But Friend,
said he, do the Soldiers of your Company walk in
such Shoes? I began to look guilty, and, by my
trembling, discover'd the Untruth I had told him;
upon which he oblig'd me to lay down my Arms,
and bid me take care of my self. Thus robb'd
both of my Weapons and Revenge, I return'd to
my Lodging, where, by degrees, my Rage abating,
I began in my Mind to thank the Robber.

But finding it difficult to wean my self from the
love of Revenge, I spent half the Night very
pensively; and rising by Daybreak, I rov'd about
every where to ease my self of my Grief, and to
make me forget the thoughts of the Injury I had
receiv'd, till at last going into a publick Gallery,
very wonderful for several sorts of excellent Painting; I saw some pieces by *Zeuxy*'s Hand, that
had not yet yielded to the Injuries of Time: And
not without an awful Reverence consider'd others
done by *Protogenes*, which tho' they were his first
Trials, yet disputed for exactness even with Nature
itself: But on the other side viewing a celebrated
Piece drawn by *Apelles*, I even ador'd the Work of
so great a Master: 'Twas so correctly finish'd,
and so much to the Life, you'd have sworn it a
Picture of the Soul too. One side related the
Story of the Eagle bearing *Jupiter* to Heaven;

the other, that of the fair *Hylas* repelling the Addresses of a lascivious *Naiad :* In another part was *Apollo*, angry with himself for killing his Boy *Hyacinthus*, and to show his love to the deceased, he crown'd his Harp with the Flower that sprung from his Blood.

Tho' I was amongst these Painted Lovers, yet thinking my self alone, I burst out ; And are the Gods themselves not secure from Love ? *Jupiter* in his Heavenly Seraglio not finding one that can please his Appetite, descends to, and sins upon Earth, yet injures no body : The Nymph would have stifled her passion for *Hylas*, had she believ'd the mighty *Hercules*, wou'd have forbid the Banes : *Apollo* changes *Hyacinthus* into a Flower ; and the Artist made every Deity enjoy his Wishes without a Rival ; but I have caress'd, as the dearest Friend, the greatest Villain.

While I was thus talking to my self, there enter'd the Gallery an old Man, with a Face as pale as Age had made his Hair ; he seem'd, I know not how, to bring with him the Ayre of a great Soul ; but viewing his contemptible Dress and Habit, by that very token I immediately concluded him in the number of those Learned Men to whom Rich Men have a mortal Aversion, and to whose Labours Fortune is seldom Favourable. In short, he made up to me, and addressing himself, told me he was a Poet, and, as he hop'd, such a one who could pretend to some Excellencies above the vulgar Rank ; if my Merit, added he,

don't suffer by that Applause that's promiscuously
given to the good and bad.

How therefore, interrupted I, are you so meanly
clad ? On this reason, return'd he, Because
Learning never made any Man Rich.

> *Returning Sails the happy Merchant bless,*
> *And flowing Bowls smiles on his rich Success,*
> *The dusty Plain, and cruel purple Field,*
> *Does to the Brave a wealthy Harvest yield.*
> *The Clergy thrives, and the litigious Bar ;*
> *Dull Heroes fattens with the Spoils of War.*
> *To servile Parasites we Altars raise,*
> *And the kind Wife her vigorous Lover pays :*
> *But starving Wit in Rags takes barren Pain,*
> *And dying seeks the Muses Aid in vain.*

'Tis certain, added he, that a Lover of Virtue,
on the account of his singularity, meets with
Contempt ; for who can approve what differs
from himself ? And those that admire Riches
wou'd fain possess every body, that nothing is
more reasonable than their Opinion ; whence they
ridicule, as well as they can, the Learned few, that
the World may imagine, even these judicious
Persons are as great Slaves to Gold, and equally
desirous of Money as themselves.

'I don't know how Learning and Poverty
'become Relations, said I, and sigh'd. *You justly
lament,* return'd he, *the condition of Scholars.*

'You mistake me, said I, that's not the occasion
'of my Sighs, there's another, and much greater

'Cause : And, as all Men are naturally inclin'd
'to communicate their Grief, I laid open my Case
'to him, beginning with *Ascyltos*'s Treachery, which
'I aggravated ; and, with repeated Sighs, often
'wish'd the Person who had injur'd me had been
'capable of imploring or meriting my Pardon ;
'but he had no such Thoughts, he was a hardned
'Villain, and in Lust more subtil than a Carted
'Bawd.

The Old Man believing me sincere, began to
comfort me ; and the better to effect it, told me
what formerly had happen'd to himself on the like
occasion.

When I was in *Asia*, began he, and concern'd
in the Publick Revenue, I lodg'd at the House of
one *Pergamus*, where the Entertainment did not
tempt me to stay so much, as a very beautiful
young Girl I saw there, Daughter to the Master
of the House : My Contrivance was to act the
Lover unsuspected by her Father ; and to effect
my Wishes I us'd this Method : Whenever in
Mirth we happen'd to discourse of Intrigues, or
private Amours, I dissembled such a strong
aversion to the Ladies, and pretended my modesty
suffer'd so much by the recital of such Gallantries,
that the Mother of the young Virgin look'd upon me
as a Philosopher above the sensual Pleasures of the
World. Upon this, I was desir'd to be Tutor of
the pretty Lady, not only to instruct her in a
method of Study, but also to replenish her Mind
with Principles of Honour and Virtue.

The Charge I had over her Person and Studies, authoriz'd my coming into her Bed-Chamber, at such times as were convenient for her Instructions. It happen'd that an extraordinary Festival was solemniz'd in the Neighbourhood, where both the Father, Mother, and the greatest part of the Family were present; I took the occasion which Fortune presented me with, and went to her Apartment, where I found her upon her Bed, rather pretending to sleep than sleeping; in a very agreeable disorder, the blushing Colour in her Cheeks augmented her Beauty, and tho' her Eyes were shut, I felt their piercing Influence in my Soul, addressing myself therefore to *Venus;* Queen of soft Desires, whisper'd I, Could I have the happiness to kiss the lovely Virgin, and she not know it? to morrow I'll present her with a pair of Turtles. Hearing the Reward, she began to sleep more profoundly than before; whereupon I greedily seiz'd my Wishes: Satisfy'd with this beginning, I stopt there, and early the next Morning perform'd my promise.

The Festival continued, and the following Day permitted me the same, or a greater, liberty than I had taken in the former; when advancing in my Wishes, And if I might discover, said I, the lovely Breasts of my pretty Scholar, I'll have a brace of Peacocks the fairest in all *Asia* at her Service: At this the Maid turn'd about, and gave me the opportunity of touching two snowy Hills, whiter than the *Alps,* or *Apennines;* I bought the

Peacocks, and, like a Man of Honour, perform'd my Word. The third Morning was now arriv'd, and the Family still entertain'd themselves in Diversions sacred to the Gods, I had the like access, and found my Mistress as fast asleep as she was the preceeding Days ; her Conduct inspir'd me with Courage, and, approaching her Ear, Ye Gods, said I, could I now seize that Joy entire, which neither can nor ought to be exprest, to morrow shall make the Charmer Mistriss of a Diamond worth five Hundred Crowns ; upon which she dissembled to sleep on. Wild to enjoy, I prest to her and receiv'd a satisfaction that bounded all my Wishes. You may imagine, that Turtles and Peacocks were easier to be bought than so fine a Diamond ; besides, I thought it Imprudence to alarm the old People, by presenting their Daughter so considerably, who might reasonably conjecture, I should hardly have put my self to so much charge without expectation of a suitable Return. I therefore wav'd my Promise, and return'd to my Mistress's Chamber without the Jewel she expected : I enter'd the Room, and without more Ceremonies, she threw her Arms about my Neck ; And, I beseech you, Sir, where's the Diamond ?

'The difficulty of getting a fine one, return'd 'I, made me defer my Promise, but in a few Days 'I'll be as good as my Word. The Girl well knew the meaning of my delay, and by her Countenance betray'd her Resentment.

This breach of my Word put a stop to our Commerce, but Fortune set us right again ; for not many Days after, another Festival gave me the same Priviledge I had at first : When I found her fast asleep, I began to desire her to be Friends with me, that is, that she would grant me the favours she had for some time kept from me ; she, perfectly angry, return'd no other Answer, than, If you won't be still I'll raise the Family ; but Love forces thro' all difficulties ; tho' she was saying, I'll raise the Family, I rusht upon her, and, meeting with a faint Resistance, seiz'd the Joy I long'd for. She was not displeas'd with my Attempt, but after a long complaint that she was cheated, laugh'd at, and should be abus'd among her Play-fellows, whom she had possest with an Opinion of my being very Rich, since I had pro-mised her so fine a Diamond ; To shew you, added she, that you shan't meet with the same Ingrati-tude from me, if you have inclinations to repeat your Wishes, do it freely : I, laying aside all Quarrels, was easily Friends with her, and having us'd the liberty she gave me, fell fast asleep upon her Bed ; But she that was now in her prime, and fit for Action, not satisfy'd, raising me ask'd, Whether I would have any more ? It was yet no troublesome Province to me ; and when her Weariness confess'd her satisfy'd, I fell asleep again. 'Twas hardly an hour e're she was pushing me with her Elbow, and crying, We lose time : I flew in a great Passion to be so often disturb'd, and turn'd her own Words upon her, Lye still, or I'll raise the Family.

This Discourse amusing my Grief, I began to question the old Gentleman about the Antiquity of some Figures there represented, and the Stories of some others I was not acquainted with ; what might be the reason why the present Age did not arrive to the Excellency of Learning of the Preceeding ones ; why the most excellent Arts were lost, of which Painting had not the least Figure or Mark of its first Beauty and Complexion : Our love of Riches, reply'd he, has been the only root of this, and most other Evils ; for in old time, when Virtue was more admir'd for its own sake, all liberal Arts flourish'd, and the only Emulation among Men, was to make discoveries that might Profit Mankind. 'Twas in those times *Democritus*, not despising an ingenious and inquisitive Poverty, found out the Vertue of most Herbs ; and, lest there might be any Excellence in Stones and Trees, unknown to the Age he liv'd in, spent the rest of his Life in Experiments about them. 'Twas then *Eudoxus* abandon'd the World, to live on the top of a high Mountain, to discover the motions of the Heavens ; and *Crysippus*, the better to qualify his Mind for Invention, went thrice through a Course of Physick.

But to return to Statuary, *Lysippus* with that diligence employ'd himself about one Figure, that, neglecting to earn Bread, he was starv'd for want of meer Necessaries ; and *Myron*, whose brazen

Images of Men and Beasts, you might have mistaken for living ones, dy'd very Poor. But our Age is so wholly devoted to Lewdness, that we are so far from inventing, we even refuse to study those Arts which are already found out to our hands : All the business of our Schools is to fall foul upon the Ancients, and whilst we declaim at their Methods, our Academies are become Seminaries of Vice only : What's our Logick? How little do we know of Astronomy? Where's our Philosophy? What Master of Eloquence could endure to hear it so murder'd as it is in a Pulpit? Who now comes to Church to pray for Wisdom, Health, or Moderation ; we enter the sacred Houses of the Gods with wild unaccountable Desires, and the Petitions we make to Heaven are as foolish and extravagant ; one ardently prays to succeed his Friend both in his Bed and Estate ; another promises a Sacrifice to the Gods, if they'd be pleas'd to take a troublesome Father out of this wicked World : A third, if they'd direct him to a Treasure : A fourth Spark begs the favour of the Immortals, that they would oblige him with an Estate of 500 *l. per Ann.* or so, which a Neighbour of his enjoys, and that the Owner of it may hang or drown himself with all convenient expedition : The very Senate that should shew an exemplary Conduct in Occasions of great Emergencies, have devoted mighty Summs of Gold to Religious Uses : It appears therefore but reasonable for Mortals to

be avaritious of Money, which can charm and
make flexible even the Gods themselves! You
need not wonder why Painting is lost, when Gold
appears more beautiful both above and below,
than any thing *Apelles* or *Phydias* madly fool'd
away their time about : But seeing your Curiosity
is wholly taken up in that Piece, that shews you
a contracted History of the Siege of *Troy*, I'll try
to give you the Story more at large in Verse.

Now twice five Years the Argive *Youth in vain*
Contending, fought on Ilium's *dusty Plain,*
The Wars success, by Jove's *high Will conceal'd,*
No God, or Prophet, to the Greeks *reveal'd.*
Cryses, in vain, on the resounding Shore,
Did Power Marine religiously implore.
Confusion, Sorrow, Care, and Panick Fear,
Did on each Face in gloomy looks appear :
When thus Apollo, *like* Laerte's *Son,*
Shew'd how Troy's *Walls might by Surprize be won.*
Forgetting quite great Hector's *generous Shade,*
And Towers, whose stones immortal builders laid,
Refulgent Beams did round his Temples shine,
And every Accent spoke a Power divine.
Dear to the Gods, proud Ida's *Rising Hill :*
Prodigious Pines, and mighty Cedars fill ;
The stubborn Trees from their lov'd Mountains force
And with the Timber frame a wooden Horse,
As large as those which thro' Heaven's *Regions run,*
And draw the weighty Chariot of the Sun.
Fallacious Doors cut in the wounded side,

And in its Caverns your Batalians hide.
The Greeks obey, and nodding Cedars feel
The glittering Edge of their laborious steel.
With these the Argives build a vast machine,
And plac'd the Fraud near bright Scamander's Green.
With eager haste th' impatient Squadrons march,
And hide themselves in the capacious Arch :
By means ungenerous, aiming to destroy
The gilded Temples of unguarded Troy.
What cruel Fate unhappy Ilium rul'd,
By Grecian Art amuz'd, by Synon fool'd.
The Trojans hop'd, and that Deluder swore
The hostile Fleet had left rich Asia's Shore.
Near Ida's Tomb upon the bloody Plain,
Where Gods were wounded, and Pelides slain ;
Now free from Mars, and Wars ungrateful Broils,
The Phrygians walk'd, recounting late their toils.
All view'd the Horse——
So pleas'd they wept : thus even our cares and fears
When Joy surprizes melt away in Tears.
Enrag'd Laocoon, with Prophetick Fires,
To wound the Horse the wond'ring crowd inspires.
Invoking Heaven he drew his sacred Blade,
Began the War and the first Onset made.
Some Power unseen the dreadful Blow repell'd,
Which might a Pine, or lofty Cedar fell'd.
A second time he try'd his mighty force,
And pierc'd the dire Recesses of the Horse :
Its wounded Sides, and gloomy Caverns groan,
And tremble at the Danger, not their own.
All stood concern'd——

When far at Sea, two fiery Snakes appear,
And o'er the Surge their gilded Bellies rear.
Like lofty Ships on the green Waves they ride,
And with their Breasts the foaming Surge divide.
Their golden Crests with gaudy horror blaze,
Burn sporting Fish, and Gods marine amaze.
Affrighted Neptune *shuns the odd Surprize,*
And to the Beach, and Ouzie Harbour flies.
The Monsters land——
And toward the crowd with humble heads descend
Then rise again, and circularly bend:
Straight round the Horse in glittering Orbs they rol'd,
And Ilium's *Fall in dreadful Hissings told.*
Laocoon's *Sons the horrid Object view'd,*
Fearless of Fate, the unhappy Youths pursu'd.
Safe in their Father's Probity and Truth,
Secur'd by childish Innocence and Youth:
Yet these the Snakes and guilty Gods assail,
And o'er the Boys with impious force prevail:
Their little Hands for Aid, to Heaven they rear;
Each for his Brother feels unusual Fear:
And when the strict Embraces stopt their Breath,
They shew'd fraternal Piety in Death.
Their mournful Father with a Parents care,
Hastes to revenge that Fate he's doom'd to share.
To kill the Sire the Snakes their Forces bend;
Nor does Minerva *her own Priest defend.*
The horrid Omens deep impressions made;
All vote the Horse should be to Troy *convey'd.*
Their Bastions flat the hasty Dardans *beat,*
Aiding the Grecian's *Fraud, and* Synon's *Cheat*

Now Night perswaded Gods and Men to rest;
And Sleep and Wine in cautious Troy *opprest;*
When from the open'd Caverns of the Horse,
Pyrrhus *leaps out, and draws the* Grecian *Force.*
Broke from their Prison and discharg'd from
  dread,
The glittering Troop with wanton motions tread.
The Courser thus, when broke his Reins he feels,
Bounds on the Plain and tries his active Heels.
They draw their Swords, and shake their brazen
  Shields,
Which cast bright horror on the dusky Fields.
Buried in Wine part on the Trojans *light,*
And stretch their sleep to one eternal Night.
Some others make the Phrygian *Altars smoke,*
And against Troy *the* Trojan *Gods invoke.*

When *Eumolpus* had gone thus far in his Po-
etical Harangue, the People that were walking
there, began to fling Stones at him : But he,
conscious of his Merit, cover'd his Head, and ran
away as fast as he could : Fearful lest they should
have taken me for a Poet too, I made after him :
As soon as we had secur'd our selves out of Stone-
shot, I beseech you, Sir, said I, what will you do
with this Disease of yours ? I don't wonder at
the Peoples humour, since I have hardly been
acquainted with you two Hours, and your Entertainment has had more Poetry in it than the
Conversation of a Man. I think I must fill my
Pocket with Stones, that when I perceive you

going into your Fit, I may bleed you in the Head
with one of 'em.

He turn'd to me, and, Dear Child, said he, I
rose to Day without consulting my Fortune ; tho',
'tis confest, I seldom appear even upon the Stage,
but it treats me after the same manner : But that
I may not be at difference with you too, I'll tye
my self up from this humour of Poetry : Well,
well, said I, on that condition I Sup with you ;
upon which, going into the poor Cottage I lodg'd
at, we order'd the Master of the House to get us
a Supper, and in the mean time we went to the
Bagnio, where I saw *Gito* leaning against the Wall,
with Towels and Rubbing-brushes in his hand ;
his dejected Countenance easily convinc'd me he
served on Compulsion. As soon as he saw me,
addressing himself in an humble manner, he told
me, That now he could freely speak to me his
Mind, since I was no longer in such a martial
Posture as obliged him to bely his Affections, and
to hide the true Sentiments of his Soul : Afterwards he entreated me to have Compassion on his
Circumstances, and to deliver him from the Cruelty
of so barbarous a Master. He acknowledg'd himself sorry for the decision he was oblig'd to make
against his own Inclinations ; that I might take
my own satisfaction in punishing him after what
way I pleas'd, for, added he, If I must die, 'twill
be comfort enough to so unhappy a Wretch, to
think that you are pleas'd in't.

I desir'd him not to make a noise with his

Complaints, lest our Design should be discover'd ; and leaving *Eumolpus*, who was versifying in the Bath, we scowered off thro' a dirty Back-entry, as privately as we could, to my Lodgings : Where, shutting the Door, I threw my Arms about his Neck, and, tho' he was all in Tears, half smother'd him with Kisses : Thus we continued in a mutual Silence ; *Gito*'s repeated Sobs so disturb'd him, he could not speak : When after a long time spent in that posture, How unaccountable is it, began I, to love him that once forsook me : And that in this Breast I should feel so great a Wound, yet have no sign of its being there ! What's your pretence for chusing *Ascyltos?* Have I deserv'd such usage ?

You see I make no other Person the Judge, Whose love was greatest, yours or mine ? But I've done my Complaints, and design to forget my Injuries, if I find you sincere.

I could not tell him this without falling into Tears. When, wiping his Face, says he, *Eucolpius*, I appeal to your Memory, whether I left you, or you betray'd me : I must confess, and hope you won't blame me for it, when I saw two at Daggers-drawing, I went over to the strongest.

I could not but admire his Wit, and to convince him of a perfect Reconciliation, seal'd it with repeated Kisses.

'Twas now quite dark, and our Supper was dishing up, when *Eumolpus* knock'd at the Door : I ask'd who was there ? and took an opportunity thro' a Chink, to see whether *Ascyltos* was with him; but finding him alone, I soon open'd the Door: He had hardly seated himself on his Couch, when seeing *Gito* in waiting, On my word, said he, a very *Ganymede* indeed, sure *Eucolpius* you have no reason to complain to Day.

I did not like a beginning which had so much of Curiosity, and was afraid I had entertain'd another *Ascyltos*. *Eumolpus* pursuing his Humour, when the Boy fill'd him a Glass, I had rather, said he, be in possession of thee, than the whole Bagnio; and greedily drinking it off, the Heat I've been in, added he, made this the pleasantest Draught I ever took. For, to deal freely with you, I narrowly 'scap'd a beating when I was in the Bath, for attempting to deliver my Thoughts of it in Verse: And after I was turn'd out of the Bagnio, as I us'd to be out of the Theatre, I search'd every place, crying, as loud as I cou'd, *Eucolpius*, *Eucolpius*: A naked Youth that had lost his Cloaths, as strongly eccho'd back to me, *Gito*, *Gito*: The Boys, believing me mad, hooted at me: But the other was attended with a great concourse of People, that with an awful Admiration prais'd the Youth: For Nature had so largely qualify'd him for a Lover, that his body seem'd less than a part that depended on it: A lustly Rogue! I'll warrant he'll maintain the Field four and twenty Hours: He therefore soon found relief; for a debauch'd Spark, a *Roman* Knight, as was reported, flung his Cloak over him, and took him home, with hopes,

I presume, to engross so great a Prize : But I was
so far from meeting such Civility, that even my
own Cloaths were kept from me, till I brought
one that knew me, to satisfy 'em in my Character :
So much more advantageous is it to be beautiful
in our Persons, than accomplished in our Minds.

Whilst *Eumolpus* was telling his Story, I often
chang'd Countenance, looking pleasantly or
troubled, according as my Rival met with good
Fortune or Displeasure : I suffer'd the old Gentleman to proceed without interruption, lest he should
discover my Concern ; and when he had concluded
his Story, I told him what we had for Supper.

I had hardly given him an account, e're our
Entertainment came in : 'Twas ordinary homely
Fare, but very nourishing : Our half-starv'd
Doctor attack'd it very briskly, but when he had
well fill'd his Belly, he began to tell us, Philosophers
were above the World, and ridicul'd those that
condemn every thing, because 'tis common, and
only admire those things that are difficult to be
had : These vicious Appetites, added he, that despise what they can cheaply come by, never have no
true taste of any thing, but, like sick Men, love
those things that are obnoxious to their Health.

Things got with Pain and Difficulty's rare,
Indulge our Fancies, and oblige the Fair :
We scorn the Wealth our happy Isle brings forth,
But love whatever is of foreign growth :
Not that the Fish the Po, *or* Tyber *breeds,*

Do those excel which chast Sabrina *feeds.*
Not Tyrian *Gods in nobler purple shine,*
Or shew a Dye rich as [Augusta] *thine.*
Nor can the Flocks which breathe th' Iberian *Air,*
With Esham's *Vale, for fleecy Sheep compare.*
But these are cheaply got——
Whilst moving Plains and rough tempest'ous Seas,
Make the dear-bought and far-fetch'd Follies please.
Thus the lewd Spark, blind to domestick Charms,
Flies to a Mistresses polluted Arms :
The Fair enjoy'd, his wanton Passion dies ;
Pleas'd with the coy and fond of her that flies.

Is this, said I, interrupting him, consistent with the Promise you made me not to versify any more to day ? I beseech you, Sir, at least spare us, that never pelted you : For if any of the Inn should find we have a Poet in our Company, the whole neighbourhood would be rais'd, and we should die Martyrs for Company : If nothing else will make you pity us, think of the Gallery and Bath you came from. When I had treated him after this rate, the good natur'd *Gito*, correcting me, said, I did very ill to reflect upon a Man so much elder than my self ; and that having offer'd a Gentleman the Courtesie of my Table, I shou'd not so far forget good Breeding, to affront him when he came : With many the like Expressions, attended with a Blush at their Delivery, that extremely became him.

Happy the Woman, said *Eumolpus*, that's blest

with such a Son ! The Gods encrease your Virtue ;
so much Sense, and so much Beauty we seldom
meet with in any one Person : But lest you should
think your Civility thrown away, you have found
a Lover for it ; I'll make your Praises the Subject
of my Verse ; I'll be both your Instructor and your
Guardian : I'll follow all your Motions : Nor can
Eucolpius think himself injur'd, he loves another.

Eumolpus was oblig'd to the Soldier who had
stole my Sword, otherwise he had felt my Revenge,
which was at first design'd for *Ascyltos: Gito*
reading my Anger in my Countenance, under
pretence of fetching Water, prudently withdrew,
and allay'd my Heat, by removing one Cause of
it : But my Rage reviving, *Eumolpus*, said I, I
had rather you had plagu'd me with your Verses,
and omitted your making Love; 'tis improbable
you and I should agree, you are very Lewd, and
I am very Passionate : Believe therefore I am
Mad, and humour the Frenzy ; that is, be gone
immediately.

At this *Eumolpus* was in great Confusion, and,
without asking the Occasion of my Anger, presently made out of the Room, pulling the Door
after him, he lock'd me in, when I least suspected
it, and stealing the Key out of the Key-hole, run
in pursuit of *Gito*.

The Rage I was in to be so abus'd, put me
upon hanging my self ; and having ty'd an Apron
I found in the Room to the Bedstead, I committed
my Neck to the fatal Noose I had made with its

Strings : When *Eumolpus* and *Gito* came to the Door, and entering, prevented my Design : *Gito's* Grief growing to a Rage, made a great out-cry, and throwing me on the Bed, You're mistaken, said he, *Eucolpius*, if you fancy it possible for you to die before me : I was first in the Design, and had not surviv'd my choice of *Ascyltos*, if I had met with an Instrument of Death : But had not you come to my relief in the Bath, I had resolved to throw myself out of the Window : And that you may know Death is always ready to wait on those that desire it, see I have it in my Power to Die, and am going to end my Life in the same manner you was about to finish yours.

Upon which, having snatched a Razor from *Eumolpus*'s Servant, he cut three or four times at his Throat, and fell down before us ; frightened at the Accident, I cry'd out, and falling upon him e're he had reach'd the Ground, with the same endeavour'd to follow him : but neither had *Gito* any appearance of a Wound, nor did I feel my self hurt : For it happened to be a Dull Razor, made Blunt on purpose to prepare Barbers 'Prentices to handle a sharper ; which was the reason *Eumolpus* did not offer to prevent our mimicking that Death. Nor was his Man in any surprize when the Razor was snatched from him.

While this Scene was acting, the Inn-keeper brought us up the other part of our Supper ; and viewing the ridiculous Posture we were in, I beseech you, Sirs, said he, are ye Drunk, or have you fled from Justice, and are acting it on your selves, or both? And, pray who was going to make a Gallous of my Bed? What's the meaning of these Tricks? I suppose you intend to bilk me of my Reckoning, but you shall smart for it; I'll soon make you sensible who is Master of the House.

What, you Rascal, cries *Eumolpus*, do you threaten? And, without more ado, flung his Fist in his Face: The Innkeeper took up an Earthen Pitcher we so oft had emptied, and throwing it at *Eumolpus*, broke his Forehead, and immediately ran down Stairs: *Eumolpus*, impatient of Revenge, snatching up a great wooden Candlestick, pursued him, and pouring his Blows very thick on the Innkeeper, reveng'd the Injury he had receiv'd with Interest: This put the whole House in an Uproar; the several Companies in the Inn by this time had got Drunk, and reel'd out in confusion, too see what was the matter: During this Skirmish, having got an Opportunity of Revenge I lock'd the Door upon *Eumolpus*; and having us'd him as he us'd me, enjoy'd both Bed and Board without a Rival.

In the mean time the Neighbours, (that came in at the Bustle) and Cooks, with all their Kitching Artillery, set upon *Eumolpus*: One throws at his Head a hot Spit, with a Leg of Mutton upon't; another with a Chopping-knife put himself in Martial posture; but above all the Combatants, a blear-ey'd old Woman was the most remarkable, who tucking up a ragged blue Apron, with one

Shoe off, and another on, lug'd a great Mastiff into the Field of Battle, and set him at *Eumolpus*; who, with his wooden Candlestick, defended himself valiantly against all his Enemies.

We saw all the Passages thro' a Hole that had been made by wrenching the Latch from the Door: How well I wish'd him, you may easily imagine; but *Gito* had compassion, and would have succour'd the distrest *Eumolpus*; upon which, my Anger being still up, I gave the merciful Coxcomb two or three Boxes; he retired to the Bed, and fell a crying; but I lookt eagerly thro' the Door, encouraging the Mob to persist in assaulting *Eumolpus*, and fed myself with the pleasing Spectacle of his Misfortunes: When the Governour of the Island, one *Bargates*, whom the Scuffle had rais'd from Supper, was brought into the Room, supported by the Legs of others, for he was so troubled with the Gout, he cou'd not use his own: And having in his aukward manner, with a great deal of Heat, made a long Harangue against Drunkards and Vagabonds, looking on *Eumolpus*, Ha! what is it you, says he, the Excellent Poet? What——has these Rogues been abusing you all this while? And without more ado, up he goes to *Eumolpus*, and whispering, I have a Maid, says he, that jeers me when I ask her the Question; Prithee, if you have any love for me, Lampoon her into better Manners.

While *Eumolpus* was thus engag'd with *Bargates*, the Cryer of the Town and some other Officers, attended with a great Concourse of People, enter'd the Inn ; and shaking a smoaky Torch, mouths out to this effect, *viz.*

Not long ago ran away from the Bath, a very pretty Boy, with curl'd Hair, by name Gito.

If any Man or Woman, in City or Country, can tell Tale or Tidings of him, they shall have for their Reward one hundred Crowns.

Not far from the Cryer stood *Ascyltos*, very richly habited, who, to encourage any Discoverer shew'd the promis'd Reward in a Silver Charger.

Upon this I order'd *Gito* to steal under the Bed, and thrust his Feet and Hands through the Cords ; that, as *Ulysses* formerly hid himself in a Sheep's-Skin, so extended he might cheat the Searches.

Gito immediately obey'd the motion, and fixing himself as I directed, out-did *Ulysses* in his native Art : But, that I might leave no room for Suspicion, I so dispos'd the Bed-Cloaths, that none could believe any more than my self had lain there.

We had just done when *Ascyltos*, with a Beadle, having searched the other Chambers, came to ours, which gave him greater hopes, because he found the door close barr'd : But the petty Officer he brought along with him, with an Iron Crow, forc'd it open.

Upon *Ascyltos*'s Entry, I threw myself at his Feet, and intreated him, if he had any Memory of our past Friendship, or any respect for one that had shar'd Misfortunes with him, he wou'd, at least, let me once more see *Gito*, who was still dear to me : And to give my counterfeit Entreaties a better colour, I see, says I, *Ascyltos*, you are come with a Design on my Life ; for to what other end could you bring hither those Ministers of Justice ? Therefore satisfy your Rage, behold my naked Bosom, let out that Blood which, under pretence of a Search, you come to seek.

Ascyltos now laying aside his old Grudge to me ; profess'd he came in pursuit of nothing but *Gito*, who had run away from him ; that he did not desire the Death of any Man, much less of one who submitted to his Mercy, and for whom, notwithstanding former Quarrels, he had still a great Kindness.

The Petty Officer put me to more Pain, for taking a Stick out of the Inn-keeper's Hand, he search'd under the Bed with it, and run it into every hole he found in the Wall : *Gito* drew his Body out of the Stick's way, and, breathing as gently as Fear cou'd make him, held his Mouth close to the Cords.

They were hardly gone e're *Eumolpus* bounc'd in upon us, (for the broken Door cou'd stop no body) and, in a great heat, cry'd out, I'll earn the Reward ; I'll run after the Cryer, and let him know how he may get *Gito* into his Hands.

Eumolpus pretending to execute his design, I kiss'd his Knees, and entreated him not to hasten the end of dying Men ; You wou'd be justly

angry, added I, if you shou'd discover to 'em how
you are deceiv'd : The Boy run into the Crowd
undiscover'd, and where he is gone, I my self
don't know.   I beseech you, *Eumolpus*, bring back
the Boy, or even restore him to *Ascyltos*.

Just as I had work'd him to a Belief, *Gito* with
restraining his Breath, sneez'd thrice, so loudly,
that he shook the Bed ; at which *Eumolpus* turning
about, saluted him with, *God bless you, Sir ;* and,
throwing off the Bedding, saw the little *Ulysses*,
who might have rais'd Compassion even in a
bloody *Cyclops:* Then looking upon me, Thou
Villain, says he, how have you banter'd me?
Durst you not tell truth even when you was
catch'd in your Roguery? If some God, that has
the care of Humane Affairs, had not forc'd the
Boy to discover himself, I had wander'd in search
of him to a fine purpose.   But *Gito*, that cou'd
fawn much better than I, took a Cobweb and
apply'd it to the Wound in his Forehead,
exchang'd his Mantle for the other's torn Coat,
and both by his Embraces and Kindness, having
heal'd his Wounds, and mitigated his Passion, he
addrest himself to *Eumolpus:* Our Lives, said he,
most indulgent Father, our Lives are in your
Power ; if you love your *Gito*, convince him that
you do, by preserving him : Oh! that I might
perish by Fire or Water ; I that am the Cause of
all these Dissentions, my Death would put an end
to your Quarrels, and restore you to each others
Friendship.

Eumolpus concern'd at our Grief, and particularly mindful of *Gito*'s Tenderness to him ; surely, says he, you are very indiscreet, who have Souls enrich'd with Virtues, that may make you happy, yet live a continu'd Martyrdom, raising to your selves every Day new occasions of Grief ; I, wherever I am, make my Life as pleasant and free from trouble, as if I expected no more of it : If you'll imitate me, never let Cares disturb your Quiet. *Ascyltos* haunts you here, avoid him by changing Climates, I am taking a Voyage to a foreign Country, and shou'd be glad of your Company : I believe to morrow Night I shall go on board the Vessel : I am very well known there, and you need not doubt of a civil Entertainment.

His advice appear'd to be both wise and profitable ; for at once it deliver'd me from *Ascyltos*, and gave me hopes of living more happily than I had done : Thus oblig'd by *Eumolpus*'s good Nature, I was sorry for the late Injury I had done him, and began to repent of my Jealousie, since it had occasion'd so many Disasters.

At last, with Tears, I beseech'd him to be Friends with me too, for that it was not in a Rival's Power to bound his Rage ; yet, that I wou'd try neither to say, or do any thing that might give just reason of Offence : And hop'd so wise and good a Man as he, would absolutely blot from his remembrance all marks of our former Quarrels : For 'twas with Men as with Countries, on rude and neglected Grounds, Snows continue very long, but where the fruitful Earth was improv'd by Culture, they presently melt off, and glide away, and hardly leave the least Notices behind them : Thus rough and unpolish'd Minds can't discharge their Passions suddenly, but where Souls are enrich'd with Instruction, they but appear, and vanish.

Get your selves ready for a March, and, as you please, either follow or lead me ; and, to confirm the truth of what you say, return'd *Eumolpus*, all my Heat expires in this Kiss.

He had not done speaking, when, hearing the Door move, we turn'd about, and saw a Seaman, with a Beard that made him appear terrible and grim : who saluted *Eumolpus* with a, Why d'ye stay, as if you did not know how soon we must be going.

All immediately prepare for the Journey, *Eumolpus* loads his Servant, who had been all this while asleep ; I and *Gito* pack'd up our Things together, and, thanking our Stars, enter'd the Vessel.

We plac'd ourselves as much out of the way as we could under-Deck ; and it being not yet Day *Eumolpus* fell asleep ; I and *Gito* could not take a wink : When reflecting afresh, that I had taken into my Acquaintance a Rival more powerful than *Ascyltos*, I began to be much troubled ; but wisely allaying my Grief, I thus reason'd with my self : Is it so troublesome to share what we love, when the best of Nature's Works are in common ? The

Sun dispenses his Rays on all. The Moon, with her infinite train of Stars, serves to light even Beasts to their repose. What below can boast an Excellence of Nature above the Waters? Yet they flow in public for the use of all: And Love seems sweeter stol'n, than when it is freely imparted to us: So it is, we esteem nothing unless 'tis envy'd by others; but what have I to fear in a Rival, that Age and Impotence conspire to render disagreeable? Who, when he has an Inclination, his Body jades under him before he can reach the end of his Race.

When I had cheated my self with this Assurance, I muffled my Head in my Coat, and feign'd my self asleep: But on a sudden, as if Fortune had resolved to ruine my Quiet, I heard one above-deck groaning out; And has he scorn'd me? This struck me with a trembling, for it was a Man's Voice, and one I was afraid I was but too well acquainted with, At a greater distance, yet with the same heat, I hear a Woman lamenting, O that some God, said she, would bring my *Gito* to my Arms; tho' he's banish'd thence, how kindly wou'd I receive him!

So unexpected an Accident turn'd us as pale as Death; for my part, I was a long time speechless, as if I had been in a Trance; when trembling with Fear, I pull'd *Eumolpus* by the Coat, who was now asleep; Upon your Honour, Father, said I, who is the Owner of this Vessel, and what Passengers has he on board? He was very angry to be disturb'd : And was it for this Reason, said he, we chose the most private place in the Ship, that none but you your self might disturb us ? Or what will it signify if I tell you, that one *Lycas* a *Tarentine* owns her, and is carrying a Lady called *Tryphæna*, to *Tarentum*.

For a while I stood Trembling like one Thunderstruck, when, opening my Bosom, I cry'd out ; At last, Fortune, thou hast entirely vanquish'd me : For *Gito*, my better half, lean'd on my Breast, and seem'd to be rather dead than living. Our Fear put us into a Sweat, and after our sweating had a little recover'd our Spirits, I fell at the feet of *Eumolpus*, and entreated him to have Compassion of two dying Wretches ; that is, to shew us means of escaping the impending Mischief : Death threatens us, tho' Death, added I, wou'd be more grateful to us, if the happiness of enjoying you, did not make us desire Life.

Eumolpus was glad to serve us, and swore by all that's sacred, he was privy to no design against us ; and that he had very innocently brought us thither, for no other end but our Company, having hir'd the Vessel before he was acquainted with us. But what practices are here against your Lives ? What terrible Pirate commands the Vessel ? Why, 'tis *Lycas*, a very honest Man, that is both Captain and Owner, and also Master of a very plentiful Estate in Land, who having an Inclination to Merchandize, freights his Ship with his own Cargoe : Is this the terrible *Cyclops* ? Is this the dreadful Cut-throat to whom we must pay our Lives for our Passage ? Another Person on board is the beautiful *Tryphæna*, a very emblem of Terror too, who, for her diversion sails about with *Lycas*.

These are the very two, reply'd *Gito*, we strove to avoid : And, in a low Voice, made *Eumolpus*, who trembled at the Story, at once understand the Cause of their Malice and our present Danger.

Eumolpus was so distracted in his Thoughts, he could not advise, but bid each of us give him our Opinion ; I presume, says he, we had even enter'd the *Cyclops* Den, where *Jove*'s Thunder-bolts are forg'd. We must seek a means of Delivery, unless, by sinking the Vessel, we should bury our- selves and the Fears of all future Mischiefs in the Ocean.

No, no, began *Gito*, rather offer the Pilot a Reward to steer the Vessel to some Port ; and affirm, the Sea so disagrees with your Friend, that if he is not so kind, you fear he'll Die : You may colour the Pretence with Tears, and appear much concern'd, that, mov'd with Compassion, the Pilot may grant your Request.

Eumolpus reply'd, This is impossible to be effected, because great Ships with much difficulty are conducted into Harbour ; besides it would seem unlikely, that my Friend should be so dangerously Ill of a sudden ; add to this, that *Lycas* may think himself oblig'd in Civility to visit his sick Passenger : Can you propose to escape by a means that will discover ye? But presuming the Ship could be stopt when under full Sail, and that *Lycas* should omit visiting his Sick on Board, how can we get out but all must see us, with our Heads muffled or bare? If cover'd, we move every one to lend a Hand to sick Persons; if bare, what is it but to cut our own Throats?

A desperate Disease, said I, must have a desperate Cure; I know no better expedient of our Delivery, than to get into the Long-Boat, and, by cutting the Cord, leave the rest to Fortune: Nor do I desire *Eumolpus* to share the danger; for what wou'd it signify to involve an innocent Person in other Mens deserv'd Misfortunes? We shall think our selves happy if Fortune assist our Enterprize.

'Twas well advis'd, said *Eumolpus*, if it cou'd be done; for can you imagine to make the least movement in the Ship, without being taken notice of, when even the distant Courses of the Stars can't escape the Pilot's Diligence? To effect your Design, you must of necessity pass by that part of the Ship which is guarded, near which place the Hasser of the Boat is fastned: Besides, *Eucolpius*, I wonder you did not remember, that in the Boat it self there is constantly a Sailor on Duty, to remove whom from his Post, there is no other way than cutting his Throat, or flinging him over-board: Consider whether either of those attempts you have Courage enough to put in

execution ; for my part, to go with you, I wou'd
refuse no danger where there was the least hopes
of getting off; but, I believe, even in your own
Opinion, you conceive it unreasonable to put so
low a value on Life, and throw it away as a useless
thing. Hear whether you like my Proposal, I'll
put you into two Trunks I have here, and making
holes for you to breathe and eat through, will
place you amongst my other Baggage ; to morrow
Morning I'll alarm the whole Ship, crying out,
My Servants, fearing a greater Punishment, last
Night jumpt into the Sea, that when the Ship
makes to Land, I may carry you off in my
Baggage.

Very well, said I, but will you inclose us so,
that Nature won't be troublesome with her
Evacuations, and can you insure us from Snoring,
if asleep, or Sneezing if awake ; or, because I once
succeeded in a like Deceit, must we meet with a
second time the same success ? But suppose we
cou'd hold out a Day so ty'd up, what shall we do
if we're put to't longer? Will the thoughts of
a quiet Life, or of our adverse Fortune entertain
us ? Our very Cloaths, long bound up, will rot
upon our Backs : Can we, d'ye think, that are
young, and not inur'd to Labour, endure to be
clad like Statues, and wear our Cords as insensibly ?
Since we are yet to seek a way of Escape, for no
Proposal has been made without an Objection, see
what I have thought on : The studious *Eumolpus*,
I presume, never goes without Ink ; is there a

better Expedient than washing our Hands, Face
and Hair with that, to appear like *Æthiopian*
Slaves, when, without putting ourselves upon the
Wreck, we must needs, with pleasure, act a Cheat
that so neatly imposes on our Enemies?

And why wou'd not you have us Circumcis'd
too, interrupted *Gito*, that we may appear like
Jews; and have our Ears boar'd, to perswade
them we came from *Arabia?* And why did not
you advise us to wash our Faces white, that we
might pass for *Frenchmen*, as if our Colour wou'd
make such a mighty alteration? Has a Foreigner
but one mark of distinction? Can you think any
body so ignorant to mistake you for one by that
sign only? Grant our daub'd Faces wou'd keep
their Colour, suppose it wou'd not wash off, nor
our Cloaths stick to the Ink, how can we imitate
their black swoln Lips, the short curl of their
Hair, the Seams on their Foreheads, their circular
way of treading, their splay Feet, or the mode of
their Beards? An artificial Colour rather stains
than alters the Body; but, if you'll be rul'd by a
Mad-man, let's cover our Heads, and jump into
the Sea.

Not God nor Man, cry'd *Eumolpus*, will permit
you to make so lamentable an End; rather pursue
this Advice: My Slave, you might imagine by
the Razor, is a piece of a Barber; let him not
only shave your Heads, but, as a mark of greater
Punishment, your Eye-brows too, and I'll finish
your Disguise with an Inscription on your Fore-

heads, that you may appear as Slaves branded for some extraordinary Villany : Thus the same Letters will at once divert Suspicion, and conceal your Countenances under the Mask of Punishment.

We lik'd the advice, and hasten'd the execution, when stealing to the side of the Vessel, we committed our Heads and Eye-brows to the Barber : *Eumolpus* in the mean time fill'd our Foreheads with great Letters, and very liberally dispens'd the known marks of Fugitives through the other part of our Faces ; one of the Passengers, easing his Stomach o'er the side of the Ship, by the Moon perceiving the reflection of a Barber busy at so unseasonable a time, and, cursing the Omen that he thought presag'd a Shipwreck, ran to his Hammock ; upon which we dissembled the same Fear, but indeed had an equal, though different concern ; and, the noise over, we spent the rest of the Night without resting much.

The next Day *Eumolpus*, when he found *Tryphæna* was stirring, went to visit *Lycas ;* and after he had talk'd with him about the happy Voyage he hop'd from the clearness of the Heavens, *Lycas* turning to *Tryphæna, Methoughts,* said he, *about Midnight the Vision of* Priapus *appear'd to me, and told me, he had lately brought into my Ship* Eucolpius, *whom I sought for. Tryphæna* was startl'd, *And you'd swear we'd slept together,* reply'd she, *for methoughts the Image of* Neptune *having struck his Trident thrice against*

the **Bajæ**, *told me, that in* Lycas's *Ship I shou'd
find my* Gito.

Hence proceeds (said *Eumolpus*, interrupting
'em) that Veneration I pay the Divine *Epicurus*,
who with so much Wit has discover'd such
Illusions.

When in a Dream presented to our view,
Those airy Forms appear so like the true ;
Nor Heaven nor Hell the fancy'd Vision sends,
But every Breast its own Delusion lends :
For when soft Sleep the Body folds in ease,
And from the heavy Mass our Fancy frees,
Whatever 'tis in which we take delight,
And think of most by Day, we dream by Night.
Th' ambitious Brave, who mighty States o'erturn,
Ruin whole Empires, and vast Cities burn,
From fancy'd Darts believes a darken'd Sky,
And sees, in haste, retreating Squadrons fly :
Here conscious Plains a bloody Prospect yield,
And all the purple Horrors of the Field.
There the Kings deceas'd with wondrous Pomp of
  woe,
Late to the Grave in sad Procession go.
He that by Day litigious Knots unty'd,
And charm'd the drowsy Bench to either side,
By Night a Crowd of cringing Clients sees,
Smiles on the Fools and kindly takes their Fees.
The Miser views his glittering heaps of Gold,
And oft the visionary Summs are told ;
Then fancies Thieves disturb his short delight,

He views their masks and wakens with the fright.
To heaven the Merchant does himself address,
Dreaming of Wrecks, religious in Distress.
Huntsmen with Joy th' imagin'd Chase pursue,
Hollow aloud, and see the Stag in view.
The Mistress to her absent Lover Writes,
And, as awake with Flames and Darts indites.
The amorous Wife dreams of her Lover's Charms,
And huggs her Husband with adulterous Arms.
Dogs in full Cry pursue their fearful Game;
And blushing Maids are cautious of their Fame.

But *Lycas* when he had thank'd his Stars for their care of him, That we may not seem, said he, to slight the Divine Admonitions, what hinders our searching the Vessel?

Upon which one *Æsius*, the Passenger that had discover'd us by our Reflection in the Water, cry'd out, These are the Men that were shav'd by Moon-shine to Night. Heaven avert the Omen! I thought the Ceremony of cutting the Nails and Hair was never perform'd but as a solemn Sacrifice to appease a Storm.

Is't so, says *Lycas* in a great heat, did any in the Ship offer to shave themselves, and at Midnight too? Bring them quickly hither, that I may know who they are; they deserve to die a Sacrifice for our common safety.

'Twas I, said *Eumolpus*, commanded it, not wishing Ill to the Ship, but ease to my self; for they are my Slaves, and having long staring

Hairs, I order'd the uncomely sight to be taken away; not only that I might seem to make a Prison of the Ship, but that the mark of their Villany might more plainly appear; and to let you know how richly they deserve the Punishment, among other Rogueries, they robb'd me of a considerable Sum of Money, and spent it in Luxury and Debauches, on a Whore that was at both their Services, whom I catch'd them with last Night. In short, they yet smell of the Wine they profusely gave themselves with my Money.

Lycas, that the Offenders might atone for their Crime, order'd each of 'em forty Stripes. We were immediately brought to the place of Execution, where the enrag'd Seamen fell upon us with Ropes-ends, and try'd to offer our Blood a Sacrifice for their Safety. I bore three Stripes very heroickly. *Gito*, who had not so much passive Valour, at the first Blow set up such an Outcry, that the known sound of his Voice reach'd *Tryphæna*'s Ear; who, in great disorder, attended with her Maids, which were equally surpriz'd, ran to him as we were beating.

Gito's admirable Beauty soften'd their Rage, and seem'd, without speaking, to entreat their Favour; when the Maids unanimously cry'd out, *'Tis* Gito! *'Tis* Gito! *hold your barbarous Hands; help, Madam, 'tis* Gito!

Tryphæna hasten'd to their Outcries, already convinced from whence those complaints proceeded, and with eager haste flew to the Boy.

Upon which *Lycas*, who had now discover'd me as much by my Person as if he had heard my Voice, taking some Parts on content, and looking on others with a more observing Eye ; *Your Servant*, says he, Eucolpius, *'tis no wonder that the Nurse of* Ulysses *discover'd him, after twenty Years absence, by a Scar in his Forehead, when* Lycas *hath found out his Fugitive by a Token nothing so apparent.* Tryphæna having cheated herself into a belief, that those Marks of Slavery we wore were real, wept ; and began, in a low Voice, to enquire what Prison cou'd stop us in our Rambles, or whose cruel Hands cou'd inflict such a Punishment without Reluctancy. *I confess,* added she, *they deserve some Punishment with whom their Masters are so justly angry.*

Lycas was in a great heat at *Tryphæna*'s tenderness. *And thou foolish Woman,* said he, *can you believe those Marks were cut before the Ink was laid on them ? I wish, indeed, they had so branded themselves in reality, that had afforded us the greatest Consolation : Now we are amus'd by the Tricks of the Play-house, and banter'd with a false Inscription.*

Tryphæna, not yet unmindful of our former Amours, was inclin'd to pity us : When *Lycas,* still resenting the Abuse he receiv'd in his viciated Wife, and the Affronts at the Porch of *Hercules*'s Temple, with greater Rage cry'd out, *I thought,* Tryphæna, *you might have been convinc'd, that Heaven has the care of Humane Affairs, since the Gods have not only brought our Enemies into our*

*power, who strove to destroy us, but reveal'd it in
a Vision to us both ; see what you'll get by pardoning
them whom Heaven itself has brought to Punishment ;
for my part, I am not naturally so cruel, but am
afraid the Judgment I shou'd prevent from justly
falling upon others, may light on my own Head.*

This superstitious Harangue turn'd *Tryphæna*
from hindring our Punishment to hasten its
Execution : When she began afresh as highly
to resent the former Affronts that was offer'd
her, as *Lycas* did the Reputation of his Modesty
which he had lost in the Peoples Esteem.

When *Lycas* found *Tryphæna* was as eagerly
inclin'd to Revenge as himself, he order'd our
Punishments to be increas'd ; which when *Eumolpus*
perceiv'd, he endeavour'd to mitigate his Passion
after this manner :

I pity the Wretches, said he, *that lie at your
Mercy* —— Lycas, *they implore your Compassion,
and chusing me as a Man not altogether unknown
to 'em to perform the Office, desire you would be
reconcil'd to them you once held most dear ; Can
you believe 'twas by accident they fell into your
Hands, when all Passengers make it their chief
business to enquire to whose care they are to trust
themselves ? When you are satisfied of their Intentions, can you be so barbarous to continue your
Revenge ? Permit therefore free-born Men to pursue
their Voyage, without being injur'd. Even barbarous
and implacable Masters allay their Cruelty when
their Slaves repent ; and all give Quarter to the*

Enemy that surrenders himself. What can you, or will you desire more? You have at your Feet re-penting Supplicants; they're Gentlemen, and Men of Worth, and, what's more prevailing than both, were once caress'd as your dearest Friends. Had they robb'd you of your Money, or betray'd your Trust, by Hercules, *the Punishment they've in-flicted on themselves might have satisfied your Rage; don't you see the Marks of Slaves on their Faces? Who, tho' free, to atone their Injuries to you, have branded themselves in so slavish a manner.*

To avoid Confusion (interrupted *Lycas*) give me a Reason for all Particulars as I shall ask you, and *First*, If they came with design to surrender themselves, why did they cut off their Hair? for all Disguises are assum'd rather to deceive than satisfy the Injur'd.

Next, If they expected to ingratiate themselves by their Embassador, why have you endeavour'd, in every thing, to conceal them you were to speak for? Whence it plainly appears, 'twas by accident the Offenders were brought to Punishment, and that you have us'd this Artifice to divert our Suspicion.

Sure you thought to create us the Envy of the Spectators, by ringing in our Ears, that they were Gentlemen, and Men of Worth; but have a care their Cause don't suffer by your Assurance; for what ought the Injur'd to do, but Punish, when the Guilty come to receive their Punishment? And if they were my Friends, they deserve to be more severely treated ; for he that wrongs a Stranger is a Rogue, but he that serves a Friend so, is little less guilty than he that Murders his Father.

I am sensible (said *Eumolpus*, answering this dreadful Harangue) that nothing could happen to these unhappy young Men more unfortunate, than the cutting their Hair off at Midnight, which is the only Argument that may perswade you to mistake their voluntary coming here, for accidental ; but I shall as candidly endeavour to undeceive you, as it was innocently acted : Before they imbark'd they design'd to ease their Heads of that, as a troublesome and useless weight, but the unexpected Wind that hasten'd us on board, made 'em defer it ; nor did they suspect it to be of any moment when 'twas done, being equally ignorant of the Ill Omen and Customs of Mariners.

What advantage, reply'd *Lycas*, cou'd they propose to themselves by the loss of their Hair, unless they thought Baldness might sooner raise our Compassion ? Or can you believe I will rest satisfied in your relation ? When addressing himself to me, What Poison, said he, thou Villain has eat your Hair off ? To what God have your sacrilegious Hands offer'd it ?

The fear of Punishment struck me speechless ; nor could I find anything to urge in my Defence against so plain an Accusation. The confusion I was in, my disfigur'd Face, and the baldness both

of my Head and Eyebrows, gave a ridiculous Air
to every thing I said or did ; but when they wip'd
us with a wet Sponge, the Letters melting into
one, spread o'er our Faces such a sooty Cloud,
that it turn'd *Lycas*'s Rage to a perfect loathing.
Eumolpus cou'd not endure to see free-born Men,
against all Law and Justice, so abus'd, and returning their Threats with Blows, not only was our
Advocate, but Champion too. He was seconded
by his Man, and two or three sick Passengers
appear'd our Friends, that serv'd rather to encourage us, than encrease our Force.

Upon which I was so far from begging Pardon,
that, without any respect, I held my Fists at
Triphæna, and plainly told her she should feel
me, if her Lecherous Ladiship, who only in the
Ship deserv'd to be punish'd, was not content to
decline her pretentions to *Gito*.

The Angry *Lycas* was all in a **Rage** at my
Impudence, and very impatient for Revenge when
he found, without being concern'd for my own
Cause, I only stood up for another's.

Nor was *Tryphæna* less disturb'd at my contempt of her ; at what time every one in the
Vessel chose his side, and put himself in a
posture of defence.

On our side, *Eumolpus*'s Slave distributed the
Instruments of his Trade, and reserv'd a Razor
to defend his own Person : On the other, *Tryphæna*
and her Attendance advanc'd arm'd with nothing
but their Nails and Tongues, which last supply'd

the want of Drums in the Army; when the
Pilot crying out, threaten'd he wou'd leave the
Ship to the mercy of the Waves, if they continu'd the bustle, rais'd about the Lust of two
or three Vagabonds.

This did not in the least retard the Fight;
they pressing for Revenge, we for our safety:
In short, many fell half Dead on both sides;
others withdrew, as from great Armies, to be
drest of their Wounds; nor was yet the Rage
of either Party abated.

When *Gito* drawing out that part of him
Tryphæna most admir'd, clapt a bloody Razor
to't, and threatned to cut away the Cause of
all our Misfortune. But *Tryphæna* could not bear
so Ill an Action should be committed, and hastily
flew to prevent it: I often offer'd at my Throat
too, but with as little design to kill my self as
Gito to do what he threatened: He the more
boldly handled his Weapon, because he knew it
to be the same blunt Razor he had us'd before;
which made *Tryphæna* very apprehensive of his
Tragick Intentions.

Upon this both sides drew up their Ranks,
when the Pilot perceiving how comical a War it
was, with much ado he was perswaded to let
Tryphæna dispatch a Herauld to Capitulate:
Articles of Peace, according to the Custom of
Countries, being immediately struck up on both
sides, *Tryphæna* snatch'd an Olive-branch, the
Ensign of Peace, that stuck to the Image of

Prosperity pictur'd in the Ship, and holding it in the midst of us, thus addrest her self.

Good Gods! what Fury does your minds enrage?
When sudden Madness arms you to engage?
Not here her Brother curst Medea *slays;*
Nor Paris *here a guilty Flame obeys,*
And lovely Ruin to his Troy *conveys.*
But slighted Vows these dire Misfortunes send,
And the wrong'd God does for his Fame contend.
The Ocean swells, and the tempestuous Wind,
Is, like our Humours, fierce and unconfin'd.
Without, the Waves a threat'ning War begin,
And Love has rais'd a dreadful Storm within:
Expos'd to Nature's Quarrels and our own,
For former Feuds by gentle Peace atone.
Nor let your wild, ungovern'd Passions be
Rough as the Winds, or angry as the Sea.

When, in a great heat, *Tryphæna* had thus express'd her self, both Armies stood still a while, and reviving the Treaty of Peace, put an end to the War. Our Captain *Eumolpus* prudently us'd the occasion of her repentance, and, having first severely reprimanded *Lycas*, sign'd the Articles: Which were as follow.

Tryphæna, You do, from the bottom of your Heart, promise never to complain of any Injury you have receiv'd from *Gito*; nor to make mention of, or upbraid him with, or study to revenge, directly or indirectly, any Action of his before this Day; and, to prevent your forcing

him to an unwilling compliance, be it further
agreed, that you never Kiss or Hug him without
his Consent, upon the Pain and Forfeiture of five
Pounds : And, that the young Gentleman may
not be bilkt, you are to pay your Money before-
hand.

Item, You *Lycas*, from the Bottom of your
Heart, do promise never to reproach, or insultingly
treat *Eucolpius*, either in Words or Deeds : And
that you will never offer him any Incivility on the
penalty of five Pounds for each time you abuse
him behind his Back.

Conditions thus agreed on, we laid down our
Arms : And, lest any Grudge might still remain,
we wip'd away the memory of all things past by
kissing each other.

All Parties desiring Peace, our Quarrels vanish'd,
and a sumptuous Banquet following, spread an air
of Mirth thro' the whole Company : The Vessel
rung with Songs, which testified our Joy : And
now a sudden Calm hindering the Ship from
making any way, the Crew betook themselves to
several Diversions : An Angler struck a Fish,
which rising, seem'd with haste to meet its ruine :
There another draws the unwilling Prey that he
had betray'd with an inviting Bait : When looking up, we saw Sea-birds sitting on the Sail-yard,
about which, one skill'd in the Art of Fowling,
having plac'd Lime-twigs, made 'em his Booty.
Their downy Feathers flew about in the Air, or
swam upon the Surges of the Sea.

Now *Lycas* began to be Friends with me, and *Tryphæna*, as a Mark of her Love, threw the bottom of the Glass upon *Gito:* By this time *Eumolpus* was got quite drunk, and fell a rallying us that were bald and stigmatiz'd, till having spent his insipid Jests, he return'd to his Poetry; and designing an Elegy on the loss of our Hair, he thus began.

Nature's chief Gift, your lovely Hair, is lost;
Those blooming Locks feel an autumnal Frost:
Your gloomy Brows their banish'd Honours mourn,
Which no kind Spring will gratefully return.
The Charms indulgent Nature gives to day,
Fallacious Gods to morrow take away.
   A thousand Charms did late surround
   Your Heads, with golden Tresses crown'd;
   Charming as Cynthia's *silver Light,*
   Or as the Rosy Morning bright.
   Now all your banisht Beauties seem,
   Dead as Cocytus *sable Stream,*
   From sporting Girls you'll frighted run,
   And, conscious of the Crime you've done,
   You'll Love's soft Battles meanly shun.
   Impending Death you well may fear,
   The awful Tyrant now draws near:
   First with our Beauties he begins,
   And then Life's faded Blossom wins.

He wou'd have condemn'd us to hear more, and I believe worse than the former, if an Attendant of *Tryphæna* had not disturb'd him : Who taking

Gito aside, dress'd him up in her Mistresses Tower ; and to restore him to his perfect Figure, she took a pair of false Eye-brows out of her Ladies Patch-box, and set them on so exactly, Nature might have mistaken 'em for her own Work.

At the sight of the true *Gito*, *Triphæna* wept for Joy, who cou'd not before embrace him with so sincere a satisfaction.

I was glad to see his loss so well repair'd ; yet often hid my Head, as sensibly I appear'd more than commonly deform'd, when even *Lycas* thought me not worth the speaking to : But 'twas not long e're the same Maid came to my relief, and, calling me aside, dress'd me in a Peruke, no less agreeable : For being of a golden Colour, it very much improv'd my Complexion.

But *Eumolpus*, our Advocate, and Reconciler, to entertain the Company, and keep up the Mirth, began to be pleasant on the inconstancy of Women : How forward they were to Love, and how soon they forgot their Sparks ! And that no Woman was so Chast, but her Lust might be rais'd into Fury : Nor wou'd be bring Instances from ancient Tragedies, or Personages notorious to Antiquity, but was ready to entertain us, if we wou'd please to hear, with a Story within the Circle of his own Memory : Upon which, the whole Company giving him attention, he began his Story in this manner.

There was at *Ephesus* a Lady of so celebrated

a Reputation, that the Women of the neighbouring Nations came to pay their Respects to
her, as a Person of extraordinary Vertue : This
Lady at the Death of her Husband, not content
with tearing her Hair, or beating her Breast, those
common expressions of Grief, follow'd him into
the Vault, where the dead Body was plac'd in a
Monument, and, after the *Grecian* Custom, watch'd
the Corps, and whole Nights and Days continu'd
weeping ;   the perswasions of Parents and Relations cou'd neither divert her Grief, or make her
take any thing to preserve Life : The Magistrates
of the Town endeavour'd to perswade her from so
severe a Mortification ; but were oblig'd to retire,
having met with no success in their Attempt : And
thus lamented by all for so singular an Example
of Grief, she liv'd five Days without eating.

All left her but a faithful Maid, whose Tears
flow'd as fast as her afflicted Lady's, and who,
when the Lamp they had by them began to
expire, renew'd the Light : by this time she
became the Talk of the whole Town, and all
degrees of Men confest, she was the only true
Example of Love and Chastity.

In the mean time there happening a Trial of
Criminals, the Condemn'd were order'd to be
Crucify'd near the Vault in which the Lady was
weeping o'er the Corps of her late Husband.
The Soldier that guarded the Bodies lest any might
be taken from the Cross and buried, upon his
Watch observ'd a Light in the Vault, and hearing

the Groans of some afflicted Person, prest with a Curiosity common to Mankind, he desir'd to know who or what it was ; upon which he enter'd the Vault, and seeing a very beautiful Woman, amaz'd at first, he fancy'd 'twas a Spirit, but viewing the dead Body, and considering her Tears and torn Face, he soon guess'd, as the truth was, that the Lady cou'd but ill support the loss of her Husband : He brings his Supper with him into the Vault, and began to perswade the mournful Lady not to continue her unnecessary Grief, nor with vain Complaints consume her Health : That Death was common to all Men ; and many other things he told her, which use to restore afflicted Persons to that calmness they before enjoy'd : But the Lady startled at the Consolation a Stranger offer'd, redoubled her Grief, and tearing her Hair, cast it on the Body that lay before her.

The Soldier however did not withdraw, but with the like Invitations offer'd her somewhat to eat, till her Maid o'ercome, I presume, by the pleasing Scent of the Wine, no longer cou'd resist the Soldiers Courtesie. When refresh'd with the Entertainment, she began to join her Perswasions to win her Lady ; And what Advantage, began she, wou'd you reap in starving your self, in burying your self alive ? What wou'd it signifie to anticipate your Fate ?

D'ye think departed Souls regard our Care?

Will you, Madam, in spite of Fate, revive your

Husband ? Or will you shake off these vain
Complaints, the Marks of your Sex's Weakness,
and enjoy the World while you may ? The very
Body that lies there might advise you to make the
best of your Life.

We obey without reluctance when commanded to
Eat or Live.

The Lady now dry with so long Fasting, suffer'd
her self to be o'ercome ; nor was she less pleas'd
with her Entertainment, than her Maid that
surrender'd.

You know with what Thoughts encouraging Meats
inspire young Persons.

With the same Charms our Soldier had won her
to be in love with Life, he addrest himself to her as
a Lover ; nor did his Person appear less agreeable
to the chaste Lady, than his Conversation ; and the
Maid, to raise her Opinion of him, thus exprest
her self.

And arm'd with pleasing Love, dare you ingage,
E're you consider in whose Tents you are ?

To make short, nor even in this cou'd the Lady
deny him any thing. Thus our victorious Soldier
succeeded in both, she receiv'd his Embraces :
Not only that Night they struck up the Bargain,
but the next, and the next Night after : Having
shut the Door of the Vault, that if any of her

Acquaintance or Strangers had come out of Curiosity to see her, they might have believ'd the most chast of all Women had expir'd on the Body of her Husband. Our Soldier was so taken with his beautiful Mistress, and the privacy of enjoying her, that the little Money he was Master of, he laid out for her Entertainment, and, as soon as 'twas Night, convey'd it into the Vault.

In the mean time the Relations of one of the Malefactors, finding the Body unguarded, took it from the Cross and buried it. The Soldier thus robb'd while he was in the Vault, the next Day, when he perceiv'd one of the Bodies gone, dreading the usual Punishment, he told the Lady what had happen'd ; and added, That with his Sword he would prevent the Judge's Sentence, in case she would be so kind to give him Burial, and make that place at once the fatal Monument of a Lover and a Husband.

The Lady not less Merciful than Chast, protested, That the Gods would never permit her, at one time, to feel the loss of the only Two she held most dear ; I'd rather, added she, hang up the Dead Body of the one, than be the wicked Instrument of the other's Death. Upon which she order'd her Husband's Body to be taken out of the Coffin and fixt to the Cross, in the room of that which was wanting : Our Soldier pursued the directions of the discreet Lady, and the next Day the People wonder'd how the Dead Body was a second time affix'd to the Cross.

The Seamen were pleas'd with the Story. *Tryphæna* not a little asham'd, lovingly inclin'd her Cheek to *Gito*'s, and hid her Blushes; but *Lycas* wore an Air of Displeasure, and knitting his Brows; If the Governour, said he, had been a Just Man, he ought to have restor'd the Husband's Body to his Monument, and hung the Woman on the Cross. I don't doubt it made him reflect on his own Wife, and the whole Scene of our Amours when we robb'd his Vessel. But the Articles he had agreed to, oblig'd him not to complain; and the Mirth that engag'd us, gave him no opportunity to vent his Rage.

Tryphæna entertain'd her self in *Gito*'s Arms, pressing oft his Neck with eager Kisses, and oft disposing his New Ornaments, to make 'em appear more agreeable to his Face.

At this I was not a little out of humour and, impatient of our new League, cou'd neither Eat nor Drink any thing; but with side-looks wish'd a thousond Curses on them both; every Kiss and every Look she gave him wounded me. Nor did I yet know whether I had more reason to repent the loss of my Mistress or my Friend, he having robb'd me of her, and she having deluded him from my Arms: Both were worse than Death to me. And to compleat my Misery, neither *Tryphæna* spoke to me as if I had been her Acquaintance, and once belov'd; nor did *Gito* think me worth conversing with or drinking to: I believe he was tender of the new return of her

Favours, and afraid to give her a second occasion to fall out with him : Grief forc'd a flood of Tears from my Eyes, and I smother'd my Complaints, till I was ready to expire.

When *Lycas* perceiv'd how well, tho' in this trouble, my yellow Ornament became me, he was inflam'd afresh ; and laying aside the haughty Brow of a Master, he put on the Tender Complaisance of a Friend ; but his Endeavours were fruitless. At last, meeting with an entire repulse, his Friendship turn'd to Fury, he endeavour'd to ravish the Favours he cou'd not win by Entreaty ; at what time *Tryphæna* unexpectedly came in, and observing his wantonness, in the greatest confusion he hid his Head, and ran from her.

Upon which *Tryphæna*, possest with a strange Passion, ask'd me, and made me tell her what those Caresses meant ; she was inspir'd with new heat at the relation, and, mindful of our old Amours, offer'd to revive our former Commerce ; but worn off my Legs with those Imployments, I gave her Invitations but an ill return ; yet she, with all the Desires of a Woman, transported by her Passion, threw her Arms about me, and so closely lock'd me in her Embraces, I was forc'd to cry out ; one of her Maids came in at the noise, and believing I would have forc'd from her the Favours I deny'd her Mistress, rusht between us, and loos'd the Bands : *Tryphæna* meeting with such a Repulse, and even raging with desire, took it more grievous at my Hands, and with threats at her going off, flew to *Lycas*, not only to raise his resentments against me, but to join with him in pursuit of revenge.

By the way observe, I had formerly been well receiv'd by this Attendant of *Tryphæna* when I maintain'd a Commerce with her Mistress, upon that Score she resented my converse with *Tryphæna*, and deeply sighing, made me eager to know the occasion ; when she stepping back, thus began ; If you had any sparks of a Gentleman in you, you'd value her no more than a common Prostitute ; if you were a Man, you wou'd not descend to such a Common-sewer ; these Thoughts not a little disturb'd her ; but I was asham'd of nothing more than that *Eumolpus* suspecting the occasion, shou'd, in his next Verses, make our suppos'd Quarrel the Subject of his Drollery, and that my care to avoid it shou'd prove one means of discovering it.

When I was contriving how to prevent his suspicion, *Eumolpus* himself came in, already acquainted with what was done ; for *Tryphæna* had communicated her Grief to *Gito*, and endeavour'd, at his cost, to compensate the Injury I had offer'd her. Upon which *Eumolpus* was on fire, and the more, because this Action was an open breach of the Articles she had sign'd.

When the old Doctor saw me pitying my Misfortune, he desir'd to know the whole Scene from my self ; I freely told him the attempt of *Lycas*, and how the passionate *Tryphæna* had assaulted

me, all which he was already inform'd of ; whereupon he swore a solemn Oath, that he would
vindicate my Cause, and that Heaven was too
just to suffer so many Crimes to go unpunish'd.

While we were thus discoursing, a Storm arose ;
now thick Clouds and raging Waves obscur'd the
brightness of the Day, the Seamen fly to their
Posts as fast as Fear could make 'em, and pulling
down the Sails, leave the Vessel to the mercy of
the Tempest ; for the Wind often veering, made
the Mariners hopeless of any direct Course ; nor
did the Pilot know which way to steer : Sometimes the ungovernable Ship was forc'd on the
Coast of *Sicily*, often, by contrary Blasts, it was
toss'd near the Shores of *Italy* ; and what was
more dangerous than all the rest, on a sudden, the
gathering Clouds spread such horrid Darkness,
that the Pilot could not see over the Fore-castle ;
upon which, all dispair'd of safety, when *Lycas*
threw himself before me, and lifting up his
trembling Hands, I beseech you, *Eucolpius*, began
he, assist the distress'd, that is, restore the sacred
Vest and Timbrel you took from the Image of
the Goddess *Isis* ; pity us according to your usual
Mercy. At what time a Whirlwind snatch'd him
up, and threw him howling amidst the Flood, and
soon a spiteful Wave just shew'd him us, and drew
him back again.

Tryphæna avoided sudden Death by the fidelity
of her Servants, who catch'd her, and plac'd
her, with her best Goods, in the Skiff belonging

to the Vessel ; by which means she got safely to Shore.

I, lock'd in *Gito*'s Arms, not without Tears, cry'd out, And this we have merited of Heaven, that only Death should join us ; but even now, I fear, Fortune will be against it ; for see the Waves threaten to overset the Vessel ; and now the Tempest comes to burst the belov'd Bands that unite us ; therefore if you sincerely love *Eucolpius*, let's embrace while we may, and snatch this last Joy even in spite of our approaching Fate.

When I had thus said, *Gito* threw off his Mantle, and getting under mine, thrust his Head out at top, and that the malicious Waves might not wash us asunder, he inclosed us both in his Girdle ; And 'tis some comfort, said he, to think that by this means the Sea will bear us the longer e're it can divorce us from each others Arms. Or if, in compassion, it should throw us on the same Shore, either the next that passes by wou'd give us a Monument of Stones, which by the common Laws of Humanity, he wou'd cast upon us ; or, at least, the angry Waves that seem to conspire our separation, wou'd unwittingly bury us in one Grave, midst the Sand their Rage wou'd vomit up. I was satisfy'd with my Condition, and, as on my Death-bed, did now contentedly expect the coming Hour.

In the mean time the Tempest, acting the Decrees of Fate, had rent all the Rigging from the Vessel ; no Mast, no Rudder was left, not a Rope or a Plank, but an aukward shapeless Body of a Ship toss'd up and down the Flood.

The Fishermen that inhabited the Sea-side, expecting a Booty, in all haste put out with their Boats ; but when they saw those in the Vessel that cou'd defend their own, they chang'd their design of pillaging to succouring.

After a salute on both sides, unwonted Murmurs, like that of some Beast labouring to get out, proceeded from beneath the Master's Cabin ; upon which, following the sound, we found *Eumolpus* sitting alone, and in his Hand a large Scroll of Paper that he was filling, even to the Margent, with Verses ; we all were amaz'd to see a Man amuse himself with Poetry at a time when he had reason to think each Minute would be his last ; and having drawn him, making a great noise, from his Hole, we endeavour'd to recover him from his Frenzy ; but he was in such a heat to be disturb'd, that, 'Sdeath, said he, let me make an end of this Couplet, it finishes the Poem ; on which I took hold of the Madman, and order'd the still murmuring Poet to be haul'd on Shore.

When, with some trouble, we had got him on Shore, we very pensively enter'd one of the Fishermens Huts, and having supped on part of our Provisions which the Salt-water had spoil'd, we pass'd the Night in a very melancholly condition.

The next Day, as we were proposing how to bestow ourselves, we discover'd a Humane Carcase floating, and gently approaching the Shore : I stood still concern'd, and began, with more diligence, to see if what was presented to our view was real.

When finding it to be a Man's, And who knows, said I, but the Wife of this unhappy Creature, secure at home, expects the return of her Husband; or perhaps a Son, ignorant of the fatal Storm, may wait the wish'd arrival of his Father, who with so many Kisses seal'd his unwilling parting : These are our great Designs ; vain Mortals swell with promising hopes, yet there's the issue of them all ! See the mighty Nothing how it's toss'd !

When I had thus bemoan'd the Wretch, as one unknown, the Sea cast him on Land with his Face, not much disfigur'd, toward Heaven ; upon which I made up to it, and easily knew that the late terrible and implacable *Lycas* was lying at my Feet.

I could not restrain my Tears ; and, beating my Breast, now where's, said I, your Rage ? Where your unruly Passions? Now you're expos'd a Prey to Fish and Beasts ; and the poor Shipwrackt Wretch, with all his boasted Power, has not one Plank of the great Ship he proudly call'd his own. After this, let Mortals flatter themselves with golden Dreams ; let the wary Miser heap up ill-got Wealth for many Years ; 'twas but yesterday this lifeless thing was proud of its Riches, and had fixt the very Day he thought to return. How short, good God, is the poor Wretch of his Design !

But 'tis not the Sea only we have reason to apprehend : The Wars hurry some to Death ; others perish at the Altar, where they were offering up their Devotions ; a third by a Fall hastens his arrival to the Goal of Death ; Eating often kills the Greedy ; and Abstinence the Temperate. If we rightly consider it, in this Sea of Life we may be Shipwrackt every where : But we vainly lament the want of Burial to a Wretch that's drown'd ; as if it concern'd the perishing Carcass, whether Flames, Worms, or Fishes were its Canibals. Whatever way you are consum'd, the end of all's the same. But Fish, they object, will tear their Bodies ; as if Teeth were less gentle than the Flames, a Punishment that we believe is the highest we can inflict on Slaves that have provok'd us ; therefore what madness is't to trouble our Lives with the Cares of our Burial after we are Dead, when the best of us may meet the Fate he vainly strives with so much diligence to avoid ?

After these Reflections, we performed the last Office to the Dead, and, tho' his Enemies, honour'd him with a Funeral Pile ; but while *Eumolpus* was making an Epitaph, his Eyes roam'd here and there to find an Image that might raise his Fancy.

Having freely acquitted ourselves of this piece of Humanity to *Lycas* we pursu'd our design'd Journey, and, all in a Sweat, soon reach'd the head of a neighbouring Hill, from whence we discover'd a Town seated on the top of a High Mountain ;

we did not know it, till a Shepherd inform'd us
'twas *Crotona* ; the most Ancient, and once most
Flourishing City of *Italy :* When we enquir'd of
him what sort of People inhabited this renown'd
place, and what kind of Commerce they chiefly
maintain'd, since they were impoverish'd by so
many Wars ?

Gentlemen, said he, if you have designs of
Trading, you must go another way ; but if you're
of the admir'd sort of Men, that have the thriving
qualifications of Lying and Cheating, you're in
the direct Path to Business ; for in this City no
Learning flourisheth ; Eloquence finds no room
here ; nor can Temperance, Good Manners, or any
Vertue meet with a Reward ; assure your selves of
finding but two sorts of Men, and those are the
Cheated, and those that Cheat. A Father takes
no care of his Children, because the having of
Heirs is such a mark of Infamy, that he who is
known in that Circumstance, dare not appear at
any public Game or Show, is deny'd all publick
Privileges, and only herds among those that all
Men piss upon. But single Men, who have no
tyes of Nature that oblige the disposal of their
Wealth, are caress'd by all, and have the greatest
Honours confer'd on 'em ; they're the only
Valorous, the only Brave, nay, the only Innocent
too. You're going to a City, added he, like a
Field in a Plague-time, where you can observe
nothing but one Man devouring another, as Crows
dead Carcasses.

The prudent *Eumolpus* at a thing so surprizingly new, began to be thoughtful, and confess'd that way to Riches did not displease him. I believ'd it the effect of a Poetick Gaiety, that had not left his Years : When, I wish, continu'd he, I cou'd maintain a greater Figure, as well in Habit as Attendance, 'twould give a better colour to my Pretences : By *Hercules*, I'd throw by the Wallet, and soon advance all our Fortunes.

Promising therefore to supply his Wants, We have with us, said I, the sacred Vest of *Isis*, and all the Booty we made at *Lycurgus*'s Village ; and you have given me such hopes, *Eumolpus*, added I, that were the Goddess her self in my power, I'd pawn her for Money to carry on the Project.

Upon which, said *Eumolpus*, why delay we the bringing our Hands into use ? and if you like the Proposal, let me be Master.

None e're condemn'd a Project that was no charge to him ; therefore to be true to his Interest, we engag'd in an Oath, before we wou'd discover the Cheat, to suffer ten thousand Racks ; and thus, like free-born Gladiators, selling our Liberty, we religiously devoted both Soul and Body to our new Master.

After the solemn Ceremonies of our Oath were ended, like Slaves, at a distance, we salute the Master of our own making : When, beginning to exercise his Authority, he commanded us to report, That our ancient Lord (meaning him) griev'd at the Loss of a Son, who was a great

Orator, and comfort to his Age, was unhappily
forc'd to quit the place of his Abode, lest the
daily Salutes of those that expected Preferments
under him, or Visits of his Companions might be
the continual occasions of his Sorrow ; and the
late Ship-wreck had added to his Grief, having lost
to the value of twenty thousand Crowns ; tho'
he was not so much concern'd at the loss of his
Money, as of his large Retinue ; that, he fear'd,
wou'd make them not proportion their Thoughts
to his Greatness ; and to add, that our Lord had
Mortgages almost on half the Estates in *Africa*,
and mighty Sums at Use on Personal Security ;
and cou'd raise of his own Gladiators, dispers'd
about *Numidia*, a Force able to plunder
Carthage.

After this, that his Actions might agree with his
Condition, 'twas concluded necessary to wear an
Ayre of Discontent ; that he should, with a stately
stiffness, like Quality, often Cough, and Spit about
the Room ; that his Words might come the more
faintly from him ; that in the Eye of the World
he should refuse to eat or drink ; ever talking of
Riches ; and sometimes, to confirm their belief,
shou'd break into these Words : Strange that
such, or such a Mannor shou'd disappoint my
Expectation, that us'd to be blest with so large an
Encrease ! And that nothing might be wanting to
compleat the Humour, as often as he had occasion
to call any of us, he shou'd use one Name for
another ; that it might easily appear how mindful

the Lord was even of those Servants he had left in *Africk*.

Matters thus order'd, having, as all that wou'd thrive, implor'd the Blessing of Heaven, we began our March, but both *Gito* did not like this new Slavery, and the Servant which *Eumolpus* had hir'd, bearing most of our Baggage, in a little time beginning to be uneasy in his Service, wou'd often rest his Burthen, with ten thousand wry Looks, and as many Curses for our going so fast ; at last he swore he would either leave his Charge, or go quite away with't. 'S death, said he, d'ye think I'm a Pack-horse, or a Dray, that you load me thus ? I was hir'd for a Man, not a Horse ; nor am I less a Gentleman by Birth than any of you all, tho' my Father left me in a mean condition. Not content with reproaches, but, getting before us, he lift up one Leg, and venting his Choler at the wrong end, fill'd our Nostrils with a beastly scent.

Gito mock'd his Humour, and for every crack he gave, return'd the like, that one ill scent might stifle another.

But even here *Eumolpus* returning to his old humour : Young-men, began he, this Poetry deceives many ; for not only every one that is able to give a Verse its numbers, and spin out his feeble Sence in a long train of Words, has the Vanity to think himself inspir'd ; but Pleaders at the Bar, when they would give themselves a loose from Business, apply themselves to Poetry, as an

Entertainment without Trouble, believing it easier
to compile a Poem than maintain a Controversy,
adorn'd with a few florid Sentences : But neither
will a generous Spirit affect the empty sound of
Words ; nor can a Mind, unless enrich'd with
Learning, be deliver'd of a Birth of Poetry ; there
must be the Purity of Language, no vulgar Expression or Meanness, as I may call it, of Words,
is to be admitted, but a Stile perfectly above the
common, and with *Horace*——

Scorn the Illiterate Herd,
And drive 'em from you.

Besides, you must be strictly diligent, that your
Expressions appear of a piece with the body of the
Discourse, and your Colours so laid, that each may
contribute to the Beauty of the whole. *Greece* has
given us a *Homer* and the Lyricks for Example,
Rome a *Virgil* and a *Horace*, the Purity of whose
Language is so happily correct : Others either
never saw the Path that leads to Poetry, or seeing,
were afraid to tread it. To describe the Civil
Wars of *Rome* would be a Masterpiece, the un-
letter'd Head that offers at it, will sink beneath
the weight of so great a Work ; for, to relate past
Actions is not so much the Business of a Poet as
an Historian ; the boundless Genius of a Poet
strikes thro' all Mazes, introduces Gods, and puts
the Invention on the Rack for Poetick Ornaments,
that it may rather seem a Prophetick Fury than a
strict Relation, with Witnesses of meer Truth.

180

As for Example, this Rapture, tho' I have not
given it in the last hand :

Now Rome *reigns Empress o'er the vanquisht Ball*
So far as Earth extends, obey'd by all :
Uneasie, yet with Lust of Power, she's curst ;
And boundless as her Empire *is her Thirst.*
Her daring Sails remotest Worlds explore,
The Baltick *Seas, and happy* Albion's *Shore.*
Her Impious Troops did still the Rich invade,
And either found a Cause for War, or made.
With Seeds of Woe thus Fate the Empire fill'd,
And a Luxurious Soil in Mischiefs till'd.
In Wealth abounding, difficult to please,
The pamper'd City ransacks Earth and Seas :
She scorns the Dye which Tyrian *Altars boast,*
And seeks a nobler on th' Iberian *Coast.*
Her wanton Troops in purple Armour shine,
Deck'd with the Spoil of Gods and things Divine ;
Naked and bare their sacred Wardrobe stands
Too much expos'd to Sacrilegious Hands :
The Indian *Silks, the* Arabs *Species lend,*
And rich Perfumes in hazy Clouds ascend :
O'er Lybian *Fields the painted Leopard flies,*
And for his Skin the gaudy Monster dies :
The warlike Beasts, which on Tarentum's *Plain*
Fabricius *beat, are for their Ivory stain :*
And Punick *Huntsmens mercenary Guilt*
Forgets the Blood their beastial Soldiers spilt.
Yet deeper Crimes foretel her certain Doom,
Calling for Vengeance on Luxurious Rome.

Now motled Tygers, eager to engage,
With bloody Claws growl on th' Imperial Stage,
And whilst their Teeth convicted Wretches try,
The People clap to see their Fellows die.
But, oh! who can without a Blush relate
The vicious Modes of our nefarious State?
When Persian *Customs, into fashion grown,*
Make Nature start, and her best Work disown,
Male Infants now are snatch'd from all that can
By timely progress ripen into Man:
Thus circling Nature, dampt a while, restrains
Her usual Course, and in a pause remains:
The Herd of Fops a Frantick Humour take,
Scarce Men themselves they Manly Modes forsake.
Behold the mighty Luxury of Rome,
From Africk *Slaves and costly Tables come,*
And Carpets wrought in a Numidian *Loom.*
Stupendious Domes our haughty Senate build,
With all the Riches of the Orient fill'd:
The Boar's insipid, tasteless is the Fish,
If Ivory Pards bear not the Silver Dish.
Vast Flocks of Sheep, and Herds of Oxen die,
Whose Price their Lords with foreign Toys supply.
The Soldier's Cask, and pond'rous-hilted Sword,
Turn'd into Plate, grace his voluptuous Board.
Sicilian *Mullets, caught in dangerous Seas,*
First charm our Eyes, and then our Fancies please.
To raise our Gusts with wanton Arts we try,
And with expensive Sauce new Hunger buy.
In our Elections see what Frenzies reign,
Where brib'd Assemblies sell their Votes for Gain;

Their servile Choice obeys the Power of Gold,
For that the People and the Senate's sold:
That awful power which should our Rights defend,
Fawns on the Rich, and for their Int'rest bend:
Merit and Worth, by Gold corrupted, dies,
And trampl'd Majesty beneath it lies.
Cato's Excuse the giddy Rout neglect,
And, as they're paid, their guilty Choice direct.
  'Tis true, he won, ——
But yet the Candidate with Blushes stands
Asham'd of Power he took from worthier hands:
O Manners ruine, and the Peoples shame!
He suffer'd not alone, the Roman Name,
Virtue and Honour, to their period came.
Thus wretched Rome does her own Ruin share;
She sells her self, and is her self the Ware.
All lands are mortgag'd, the whole Empires bound;
And in the Use the Principal is drown'd.
Thus Debt's a Fever, and, like that Disease,
Bred in our Bowels by unfelt degrees,
Will thro' our Vitals every Member seize.
  Fierce Tumults now to Arms for Succour call,
For Want may dare, but never fear a Fall.
Wasted by Riot, Wealth's an Ulcerous Sore
That only Wounds can its lost strength restore.
What Rules of Reason, or soft gentle ways,
Rome from this Lethargy of Vice can raise?
When such mild Arts can no impression make,
Wars, Tumults, Noise, and Fury must awake.
Fortune one Age with three great Chiefs supply'd,
Who by the Sword in various manner dy'd:

On Asia's *Plains the* Parthians Crassus *slew,*
An broke his Troops with their revengeful Yew.
Great Pompey's *Blood the* Egyptian Tyrant *shed ;*
In thankless Rome *the murder'd* Cæsar *bled.*
Thus, as one Soil alone too narrow were
Their glorious Dust and great Remains to bear,
O'er all the Earth their scatter'd Ruin lies,
Which no one World could in it self comprize.
    Betwixt Parthenope *and* Baja's *Tide*
A Cavern lies, most dreadful, deep, and wide.
Here heavy Styx *and dire* Cocytus *Streams*
Emit sulphureous Fogs and hazy Steams ;
Around the fatal Compass of their Breath,
No joyful Springs indulge the fruitful Earth ;
Nothing but black Confusion all around,
Omens of Death, and Birds obscene are found ;
Where lonely Rocks in dismal Quiet mourn,
Which Cypress shade, and gloomy Yews adorn.
Here Pluto *rais'd his Head, and thro' a Cloud*
Of Smoke material, unto Fortune bow'd ;
Then spake,—Great Queen, whose sov'reign Sway
No less than Fate, both Gods and Men obey,
You seldom like what too securely stands ;
Does Rome *not tire your faint supporting Hands ?*
How can you longer bear her sinking Frame ?
Nor Romans *hate, who hate the* Roman *Name.*
See, all around luxurious Trophies lie,
And their decreasing Wealth new Ills supply.
Here Golden Piles the azure Skies invade,
There on the Sea incroaching Moles are made ;
On Palaces here Spicy Groves are seen,

And verdant Woods load Deities marine;
Inverted Nature's injur'd Laws they wrong,
And threaten Realms which do to me belong.
Such mighty Caverns in the Earth they make,
They undermine, and Hell's Foundations shake:
Whilst near the Verge of Night they sink for Stone,
And hollow Rocks beneath their Fury groan;
Proud in Expectance of forbidden Day,
The haughty Ghosts begin to disobey.
   Fortune, be kind; sign this proud City's Doom,
And lay in Dust the glitt'ring Spires of Rome.
No Age *or* Sex, *propitious Goddess, spare,*
But crowd with Spirits the infernal Air.
Infernal Lips no human Victims taste;
For want of Food, Hell's sooty Dæmons waste.
When Sylla's *Sword let out a purple Flood,*
And Roman Gods *were stain'd with* Roman Blood,
Then Hell rejoyc'd.—The Goddess strait replies,
Father, whose Realm beneath our Empire lies,
If dangerous Truths may be with Safety told,
My Thoughts with yours a due Proportion hold.
A Sense of Wrongs my injur'd Breast inspires,
And Rage my Mind with just Resentment fires.
I curse the Blessings which to Rome *I lent,*
And of my Bounty, now abus'd, repent.
Thus the proud Height of Rome's *aspiring Walls,*
By the same God that rais'd her Grandeur, falls.
Methinks I see Pharsalia's *fatal Plain*
Glutted with Blood of noble Romans *slain;*
Congested Piles the mighty Slaughter tell,
And pitying Gods mourn the sad Work of Hell.

Ægyptian *Woes and* Lybian *Groans I hear;*
Their Sun-burnt Dead in ghastly Shapes appear.
At Actium Cæsar's *Naval Force prevails,*
And Cleopatra *flies with purple Sails;*
Forboding Signs a bloody Harvest tell,
Set open all the Avenues of Hell.
Charon *to* Proserpine *can ne'er convey,*
The num'rous Dead shall for their Passage stay;
Furies shall be with the vast Ruin crown'd,
And, fill'd with Blood, remangle ev'ry Wound.
The universal Fabrick of the World,
Rent and divided, to your Empire's hurl'd.

   Scarce had she spoke, ere from a Cloud there flies
A nitrous Flame, and Thunder rent the Skies;
At Jove's *avenging Bolts to lowest Hell,*
Earth closing up, th' affrighted Pluto *fell;*
When soon the angry Gods dire Omens show,
That bode Destruction and approaching Woe;
Astonishment surpriz'd the darken'd Sun,
As if the War already was begun;
The rip'ning Ills presaging Cynthia *knew,*
And conscious, from Impiety withdrew;
With hideous Noise the falling Mountains cleave,
And Streams repuls'd, their usual Courses leave;
Battalions charge and combat in the Air,
And Mars *excites his fiery Sons to War:*
Sicilian *Plains hear dreadful* Ætna *roar,*
And sulph'rous Streams surprize the wond'ring Shore.
Presaging Tombs, and melancholy Urns,
Sad Groans emit, whose Fire no longer burns.
Portending Comets, with long purple Streams,

Affright Mankind, and dart their sanguine Beams.
Jove once descended in a Golden Shower,
Now angry Clouds a bloody Deluge pour,
Warning Great Julius *from* Batavian *Fields,*
To fetch the Crown Rome's *conquer'd Empire yields.*
High on the Alps, where the divided Rock,
Amilcar's Son did with strange force unlock ;
Altars devoted to Alcides *Smoke,*
And Græcian *Pray'rs do* Græcian Gods *invoke.*
The Temple with eternal Ice is crown'd,
Whose milky Top in hazy Clouds is drown'd.
This sacred Dome you'd think't did Heav'n sustain,
And brawny Atlas *eas'd of half his Pain.*
The melted Snow ne'er from its Summits run,
Thaw'd by the Force of a Meridian *Sun.*
Here conqu'ring Julius *leads his joyful Bands,*
And in the midst a while consid'ring stands.
From thence Italian *Plains the Chief surveys,*
And thus to Heav'n with low Submission prays :
   Saturnian Jove, *and* Jove's *Almighty Bride,*
With Aid divine assist the juster Side.
Witness these Arms unwillingly I wear,
Compell'd by Injuries too great to bear :
Proscrib'd and banish'd, whilst I mix'd with Blood
The conquer'd Rhine, *and swell'd its angry Flood.*
The mournful River, as it swiftly runs,
Hugs in its bloody Arms its slaughter'd Sons.
Preparing Gauls, our Empire to invade,
Skulk in the Alps, *of* Cæsar's *Arms afraid.*
Twice thirty *Fields our conqu'ring* Troops *have won,*
As many States have found themselves undone.

The German Troops, *in Fastnesses inclos'd,*
My Legions fought; to unknown Wars expos'd,
Did first the Depth of trembling Marshes sound,
And fix'd their Eagles in unfaithful Ground.
But what Return has Rome's *proud Senate made!*
Conqu'ring Abroad, I am at Home betray'd.
They think my Conquests dang'rous to their Peace,
And as my Glory, so my Crimes increase.
A Mob in Arms against my Fame declare,
And Actions slight, the Gen'rous only dare.
No Asian *Slave shall bind this Arm in Chains,*
And unreveng'd contemn my warlike Pains.
Bold with Success, I'll to new Conquests lead;
Come, my Companions, thus my Cause I'll plead:
Let's boldly fight, alike upon us all
Does equal Guilt and equal Danger call.
With you I did the British Ocean *plow,*
And haughty Nations to our Arms did bow.
Fortune invoke; see, glitt'ring Crowns appear!
With such an Army, who Success can fear?

   Thus Cæsar *spoke: From the propitious Sky*
Descending Eagles, boding Victory,
Drive the slow Winds before 'em as they fly.
From dark Recesses of a Grove proceed
Shrill Cries, and visionary Soldiers bleed.
The Sun-beams with unusual Brightness rise,
Spreading new Glories round the gilded Skies:
Fir'd with the Omens of their vast Success,
The glitt'ring Troops o'er Rocks *and* Mountains *press,*
Where frozen Earth, cover'd with Ice and Snows,
A dreadful Quiet in dull Stiffness shows;

But when the Cuirassiers had broke the Chain,
And soften'd milky Clouds of frozen Rain ;
So quick the melted Snows to Rivers run,
That soon a Deluge from the Mountains sprung ;
When sudden Colds the shudd'ring Currents seize,
Stop their slow Streams, and rising Billows freeze.
The Currents, frozen to an Icy Way,
To sudden Falls both Man and Horse betray.
Now pregnant Clouds a gloomy Horror form,
And breaking, are deliver'd of a Storm.
Cæsar advancing, braves the threatning Skies,
And steddy on his conscious Worth relies.
Alcmena's Son did less securely rush
From the proud Height af rising Caucasus.
With such an Air Jove *on the Giants prest,*
Who scal'd the Skies, and durst his Heav'n molest.
The Mountains Tops now Cæsar's *Armies gain,*
And spread Confusion o'er the troubl'd Plain.
Big with the News, Fame takes her sudden Rise,
Proud of her Toil, and stronger as she flies ;
In dreadful Terms the wanton Goddess tells
Th' approaching Wars, and Truth *to* Falsehood *swells.*

Thrice she proclaims———
A num'rous Fleet is riding o'er the Main,
The melted Alps are hid with Cæsar's *Train ;*
Which wreaking from a German *Conquest come,*
And with alike Destruction threaten Rome.
New Arms, Blood, Death, *and dismal Scenes of War*
Are to each Eye presented from afar ;
With anxious Thoughts of coming Ills possest,

A horrid tumult reigns in ev'ry Breast.
This flies by Land, and this the Deep explores,
Thinking the Sea less dang'rous than the Shores.
The daring Soldier trusts his Sword and Shield,
And boldly runs the Hazard of the Field.
The Priests *and* Women, *pious in Distress,*
For Aid in vain reluctant Heav'n address.
The Flamen's Fears, and Clamours of the Gown,
Add fresh Distraction to the trembling Town.
A various Course the giddy Vulgar steer,
Following the blind Impulses of their Fear :
One takes his children in his pious Arms,
Another keeps his Household gods from Harms :
Their frighted Wives uxorious Husbands bear,
These guard their Parents with a filial Care.
Some their rich Goods to distant Cells convey,
And only for their Foes prepare a Prey.
So in a Storm, when no Sea-Arts prevail,
To guide the Ship with any certain Sail,
Some bind the splitted Mast, some swim to Shore,
And their lost Wealth at ev'ry Stroke deplore.
But why do we of vulgar Fears complain,
When both the Consuls did their Honour stain,
And Rome's *high Towers deserting* Pompey *fled,*
And hid in humble Cottages his Head,
Whose Triumphs o'er the Earth made Jove *afraid*
That Gen'ral next should Heav'n's *high Walls*
      invade.
Yet he, of Empires and of Men the Shame,
Quitting the Lustre of his shining Name,
Meanly at once abandon'd Rome *and* Fame.

Terrestrial Jars to Heavens do Fears impart,
The peaceful Train of quiet Gods depart:
Weary of Crimes, they quit the impious World,
Leaving Mankind in sad Confusion hurl'd.
Fair Peace, *as Leader of the Heav'nly Train,*
Beating her lovely Arms, did first complain;
A Wreath of Olives bound her drooping Head,
And to th' infernal Realms of Night she fled:
Justice *and* Faith *as her Attendance went,*
And mourning Concord *with her Garments rent.*
Sad Proserpine *unbolts her brazen Doors,*
And strait the Furies quit the Stygian *Shores.*
Erinny's *Fraud, Despair, and pannick Fear,*
Troubles, and Death, in horrid shapes appear.
Disorder'd Rage, *from brazen Fetters freed,*
Ascends to Earth with an impetuous Speed.
Her wounded Face a bloody Helmet hides,
And her left Arm a batter'd Target guides;
Red Brands of Fire supported in her right,
The impious World with Flames and Ruin fright.
The Gods descending, leave their bless'd Abode,
And wond'ring Atlas *miss'd his usual Load.*
The embattell'd Powers their saphire Walls forsake,
And ripe in Faction, various Parties take:
For Cæsar *first* Dione *does appear;*
For him Minerva *shakes her pond'rous Spear:*
His mighty Sword the God of Battel draws,
Breathes Death and Woes, and aids the Julian *Cause.*
To the same Side the Moon *her Forces bends,*
And now, uncall'd by magick Power, descends.
Presaging Phœbus, *from his Silver Bow,*

Shoots certain Arrows, and unerring Woe:
The bearded Shafts on Pompey's *Squadrons light,*
And force the wounded Horse to sudden Flight:
The Trumpets sound, and with a dismal Yell
Wild Discord *rises from the Vales of Hell:*
From her swell'd Eyes there ran a briny Flood,
And clotted Gore upon her Visage stood.
Around her Head Serpentine Eff-locks hung,
And Streams of Blood flow'd from her sable Tongue,
Her tatter'd Clothes her yellow Skin betray,
(An Emblem of the Breast on which they lay)
And brandish'd Flames her livid Hand obey.
Thus from Hell's Deep she pass'd, with dire Design,
Up to the Top of noble Appennine,
From whose proud Height *she distant Plains descry'd,*
And glitt'ring Troops, which march'd on ev'ry Side,
When bursting into Passion, thus she cry'd:

   Let murd'rous Rage to Arms the World inspire,
And deadly Feuds set all Mankind on Fire:
The Wise *and* Brave *alike, involv'd in Arms,*
Shall feel the Rage of Rome's *intestine Harms;*
The Seas shall murmur, frighted Nature quake,
And rooted Hills, like bending Oziers, shake.
But why does Cæsar *march so slowly on,*
And not at once pass o'er the Rubicon?
The Gods decree he shall Rome's *Trenches force,*
And to the Forum *lead his* British *Horse.*
If frighted Pompey *dreads th' approaching Foe,*
Let him to fatal Epidamnum *go,*
And fill its Plains with Blood.—Thus Discord *said,*
And impious Earth her black Decrees obey'd.

When *Eumolpus*, with his usual Freedom, had deliver'd himself of these Lines, we arriv'd at *Crotona*, where having refresh'd our selves in a little Inn we took up at, the next Day, desiring an Enlargement of our House and Fortune, we fell into the Company of some flattering Parasites, who immediately enquir'd what we were, and from whence we came ; when, according to our Contrivance, prudently advancing our Characters, we told the credulous Knaves from whence we set out, and the Occasion of our Voyage. Upon which immediately all their Fortunes were at *Eumolpus* Feet ; and each, to ingratiate himself into his Favour, strove to exceed the rest in presenting.

While this Flood of Fortune was for a long Time flowing upon us, *Eumolpus*, 'midst his Happiness, having lost the Memory of his former Condition, so boasted his Interest, that he affirm'd, none in *Crotona* could resist his Desires ; and that whatever Crime any of us should be guilty of, he had Friends potent enough to secure us from Punishment.

But tho' our daily-increasing Riches left my pamper'd Body no Desire unsatisfy'd ; and tho' I flatter'd my self into an Opinion, that ill Fortune had taken her last Leave of me, yet not only the Thoughts of my present Condition, but the Means of getting to it, would often break in upon my Joys, and embitter all the Sweet. And what, said I to my self, if some one wiser than the rest, should dispatch a Messenger for *Afric*, should we not soon be discover'd? What if the Slave *Eumolpus* pick'd up, glutted with his present Happiness, should betray us to his Companions, and maliciously discover the whole Intrigue? We should then be put upon the Stroul again, and be oblig'd with Shame to renew our former Beggary. Heavens! how ill it fares with wicked Livers! that they must ever expect a deserv'd Punishment.

'Going out full of these Thoughts, to divert
'Melancholy, I resolv'd on a Walk, but had
'scarce got into a publick one, ere a pretty Girl
'made up to me; who, calling me *Polyænus*, told
'me her Lady would be proud of an Opportunity
'of speaking with me.

'You're mistaken, Sweet-heart, answer'd I in
'a little Heat, I am but a Servant, of another
'Country too, and not worthy of so great a
'Favour.

No, Sir, said she, I have Commands to you; but because you know what you can do, you're proud; and if a Lady would receive a Favour from you, I see she must purchase it: For to what End are all those Allurements, forsooth, the curl'd Hair, the Complexion advanc'd by Washes, the wanton Roul of your Eyes, the affected Air of your Gate, unless in order to invite a Purchaser? For my part, I am neither Witch nor Conjurer, yet can guess at a Man by his Physiognomy; and when I find a Spark walking, can guess the Meaning. To be short, Sir, if so be

you are one of them that sell their Ware, I'll
procure you a Buyer ; but if you're a courteous
Lender, confer the Benefit.   As for your being a
Servant, and below (as you say) such a Favour, it
increases the Flames of her that's dying for you.
'Tis the foolish Humour of some Women to be
in Love with Filth ; nor can they be rais'd to an
Appetite, but by the Charms forsooth, of some
Slave or Laquey : Some can be pleas'd with
nothing more than the strutting of a Prize-fighter,
with a hack'd Face, and a red Ribbon in his Shirt ;
or an Actor, incited to prostitute himself on the
Stage by the Vanity of shewing his pretty Shapes
there. Of this Sort is my Lady, who indeed,
added she, prefers the paltry Lover of the upper
Gallery, with his dirty Face and Oaken Staff, to all
the fine Gentlemen in the Boxes, with their Patches,
Gunpowder-spots, and Tooth-pickers.

When, pleas'd with the Humour of her Talk, I
beseech you, Child, said I, are you the She that's
so in Love with my Person ? Upon which, the
Maid fell into a fit of Laughter. I would not,
return'd she, have you so extreamly flatter your
self ; I never yet truckled to a Waiter ; nor will
Venus allow I should embrace a Gibbet. You
must address your self to Ladies that kiss the
Ensigns of Slavery. Be assur'd that I, tho' a
Servant, have too fine a Taste to converse
with any below a Knight. I was amaz'd at the
Relation of such unequal Passions, and thought
it miraculous to find a Servant with the scornful

Pride of a Lady, and a Lady with the Humility of a Servant.

Our pleasant Discourse continuing, I desir'd her to bring her Lady. She readily consented, and taking hold of her Petticoats, tript it gently into a Lawrel Labyrinth, that border'd on the Walk. 'Twas not long ere she usher'd her Lady to me; a Beauty excelling even the Flattery of Painters; Words can't express so perfect a Creature: Whatever I should say of her, would fall short of what she was.

Her Hair spread all upon her Shoulders, and seem'd in easy Curls to wanton in the Air. Her Forehead was oval, and naturally inclin'd the Hair to its Advantage. The Shape of her Eye-brows was most correct. Her eyes eclips'd the Glory of the brightest Star. Her Nose had an easy Turn, and her Mouth was such as *Praxiletes* believ'd *Venus* had. Then her Chin, her Neck, her Arms, and Feet gently girt with embroider'd Sandals, to whose Whiteness the *Parian* Marble would serve but as a Foil. 'Twas then I began to despise my old Mistress, *Doris:* And thus broke out in a Rapture.

> *Sure amorous* Jove's *a holy Tale above,*
> *With fancy'd Arts that wait upon his Love;*
> *When we are bless'd with such a Charm as this,*
> *And he no Rival of our Happiness;*
> *How well the* Bull *would now the God become,*
> *Or his grey Hairs to be transform'd to Down?*

Here's Danae's *self, a* Touch *from her would fire,*
And make the God in liquid Joys *expire.*

She was pleas'd, and smil'd with such an Air,
that she seem'd like the Moon in her silver Glories
breaking through a Cloud ; when addressing herself, her pretty Fingers humouring the Turn of
her Voice, If a fine Woman, very lately acquainted
with your Sex, said she, may deserve your Love,
let me commend you to a Mistress.   I am sensible
you have a Friend already, nor have I thought it
below me to enquire into your Circumstances :
But why not a Mistress too ?   I enter the List on
the same Bottom with your Friend, nor do I
desire to engross all your Caresses ; only think me
deserving, and confer them as you please.

Let me beseech you, Madam, return'd I, by all
those *Cupids* in your Face and Mien, to permit a
Stranger in the Number of your Admirers, you'll
find him most religious, if you'll accept his Devotions ;   and to convince you, Madam, that the
Way to this Heaven (like the Paths of Paradise)
is not to be trod *gratis*, I present you with my
Friend.

What ! said she, do you give him, without
whom you could not live, on whose Lips your
very Being depends, whom you love as I do you ?
Her Words were attended with such a Grace at
their Delivery, and the sweet Sound so charm'd
the yielding Air, you would have sworn some
Syren had been breathing Melodies.   Thus wrapt

with every Thing so amazing, and fancying a Glory shin'd in every Part, I ventur'd to enquire what Name the Goddess own'd. My Maid, I perceive, said she, has not inform'd you; I am call'd *Circe;* I would not have you believe, tho' I bear that Name, that I derive my Original from *Apollo;* nor that my Mother, while she lay in the God's Embraces, held the fiery Steeds : Yet I shall know enough of Heaven, if Fate will give you to my Arms. And who can penetrate into the Decrees of Destiny? Therefore come, my Dear, and crown my Wishes. Nor need you fear any malicious Disturber of our Joys, your Companion is far enough from hence.

Upon which, she threw her Downy Arms about me, and led me to a Plat of Ground, the Pride of Nature, deck'd with a gay Variety of every pleasing Object.

On Ida's *Top, when* Jove *his Nymph caress'd,*
And lawless Heat in open View express'd,
His Mother Earth in all her Charms was seen,
The Rose, the Violet, the sweet Jessamin,
And the fair Lilly smiling on the Green.
Such was the Plat on which my Venus *lay;*
Our Love was secret, but the charming Day
Was bright, like her, and as her Temper gay.

Here we prepar'd for Battel, and thro' ten thousand Kisses press'd to a closer Engagement ; but a sudden Weakness robb'd me of my Arms. Thus cheated in her Expectation, she highly re-

senting it, ask'd whether her Lips, her Breath, or
some ill Scent of any Part of her, offended me?
Or if none of those, whether I was afraid of *Gito?*

I was so asham'd of my self, that if there was
any Spark of the Man left in me, I lost it. And
finding every Part of me feeble, and as it were
lifeless, I beseech you, Madam, said I, don't
triumph o'er my Misery: I'm certainly bewitch'd.

'So slight an excuse could not allay her Resent-
'ment; but giving me a disdainful Glance, she
'turn'd to her Maid, And I prithee, *Chrysis*, said
she, be free with me, don't flatter your Mistress,
is there any Thing misbecoming or ungenteel
about me? Or have I us'd Art to hide any
natural Deformity? I can't tell how you've
dress'd me to Day.

Upon which, ere *Chrysis* could make a Return,
she snatch'd a Pocket-Glass from the Maid: and
after she had practis'd all her Looks, to try if any
appear'd less charming than before, she took hold
of her Petticoats, that were a little rumpl'd with
lying on, and immediately ran to a neighbouring
Temple dedicated to *Venus.*

I could not tell what to say or do; but, as if
I had seen a Vision, at last began with Horror
to consider whether I had been robb'd of any
real Joy.

So when a Dream our sleeping Sight betrays,
And to our View some hidden Gold conveys;
Our busy Hands th' inviting Treasure seize,

And short-liv'd Joys our active Fancies please.
But soon we fear, lest any conscious Spy
May find the Secret, and the Theft decry.
And when with Spleen our charming Dreams are o'er,
Our Minds restor'd to what they were before,
Concern'd, we wish the fancy'd Loss regain'd,
And with the Image still are entertain'd.

    ' This Misfortune might make me justly think
' it not only a true Vision, but real Witchcraft ;
' for I was so weak, I could scarce get upon my
' Legs ; my Mind at last a little freed, began by
' Degrees to recover its Vigor ; upon which I
' went to my Lodging, and dissembling a
' Faintness, lay down upon my Bed. A little
' after, *Gito*, being inform'd I was ill, came to
' me much troubl'd ; but to allay his Concern,
' I told him I was only a little weary, and had a
' Mind to repose my self, but not a Word of my
' last Adventure. I talk'd to him about several
' Things ; I was afraid to disclose the Secret,
' because I knew he envy'd every one that appear'd
' agreeable to me ; and to prevent his Suspicion,
' throwing my Arms about him, I endeavour'd to
' give a Proof of my Tenderness ; but being
' disappointed in my Expectation, he arose very
' angry, accusing my Weakness and strange Be-
' haviour to him, told me, that of late he had
' found my chief Favours were bestow'd to Persons
' who did not merit my Kindness.
    ' My Respect for you, *Gito*, said I, has ever

'been the same ; but now my Dancing-days
' submit to Reason.'

Gito fell a laughing, and with a Sort of an ill-
natur'd Railery, reply'd, That he was pleas'd with
my Discretion, but conceiv'd that Friendship was
consistent with Reason ; that the wisest Persons
had always the profoundest Respect for that
venerable Name ; and, that *Socrates* thought it no
Diminution to his Wisdom, to contract a solemn
Friendship with *Alcibiades*, one of the most
agreeable of Men.

Ending these Words, *Gito* went out of the
Room in a Passion, affronted at my Conduct and
Behaviour.

He was hardly gone, ere *Chrysis* enter'd my
Chamber, and gave me a Billet from her Mistress,
wherein I found this written.

*H AD I flatter'd my self with an Expectation
of Pleasure, how had I been deceiv'd ! But
pray, Sir, if I may be so free, I desire to know how you
design to bestow your self, and whether you dare
venture abroad on those Legs, which ten thousand to
one but may sink under you. Let me advise your tender
Years to beware of a Palsy ; I never saw any Body
in so much Danger. On my Conscience, you are just
going ; and should the same Chilness seize you all
over, I might be soon oblig'd to weep at your Funeral.
But, to convince you I am sincerely concern'd for your
Recovery, I shall give you a Prescription for your
Cure ; Eat heartily, drink moderately, and sleep*

three Nights alone. *As to my self, I am not in the least apprehensive of appearing to another less charming than I have to you; I am told neither my Glass nor Report do flatter me. Farewel, if you can.*

When *Chrysis* found I had read the Reproaches of her Mistress, This is the Custom, Sir, said she, and chiefly of this City, where the Women are so potent in magick Charms, even to make the Moon confess their Power; therefore the Recovery of languishing Love becomes their Care. 'Tis only writing some soft Things to my Lady, and you make her happy. For 'tis confess'd, since her Disappointment, she has not been herself. I readily consented, and calling for Paper, thus address'd my self:

'T*IS confess'd, Madam, I have often sinned, for I am not only a Man, but a very young one, yet never left the Field so dishonourably before. You have at your Feet a confessing Criminal, that deserves whatever you can inflict; I've cut a Throat, betray'd my Country, committed Sacrilege; if a Punishment for any of these will serve, I am ready to receive Sentence. If you fancy my Death, I wait you with my Sword; but if a Beating will content you, I fly naked to your Arms. Only remember, that 'twas not the Workman, but his Materials, that fail'd. I was ready to engage, but wanted Arms. Who robb'd me of them, I know not; perhaps my eager Mind out-run my Body; or while with an unhappy Haste I aim'd at*

*all, I was cheated with abortive Joys. I only know
I don't know what I've done. You bid me fear a
Palsy, as if the Disease could do more, that has
already robb'd me of that by which I should have
purchas'd you. All I have to say for my self, is this,
That I will certainly pay with Interest the Arrears
of Love, if you allow me Time to repair my Misfortune.*

Having sent back *Chrysis* with this Answer, to
encourage my jaded Body, after the Bath and
strengthening Oils had a little refresh'd me, I
betook my self to such a Course of Diet, as might
render me strong and vigorous, using Wine very
moderately; upon which, to settle myself, I took
a little Walk, and returning to my Chamber, slept
that Night without Company; so great was my
Care to acquit my self honourably with my Mistress,
that I was afraid of any Temptation which might
have drawn me from my Duty.

The next Day rising without Prejudice either to
my Body or Spirits, I went, tho' I fear'd the Place
was ominous, to the same Walk, and expected
Chrysis to conduct me to her Mistress: I had not
been long there, ere she came to me, and with her
a little old Woman. After she had saluted me,
What, my nice Sir *Courtly*, said she, does your
Stomach begin to come to you?

At what Time the old Woman drawing from
her Bosom a Wreath of many Colours, bound my
Neck; and having mix'd Spittle and Dust, she

dipt her Finger in't, and mark'd my Fore-head,
whether I would or no.

When this Part of the Charm was over, she
made me spit thrice, and as often put into my
Bosom enchanted Stones, that she had wrapt in
Purple ; after which, she began to examine me
very nicely ; when, quick as Thought, she found
all Things to her Satisfaction. She was all Joy ;
And d'ye see, my *Chrysis*, said she, d'ye see what
a Hare *I have started for another to have the
Pleasure of the Chace ?*

Never despair ; Priapus *I invoke,*
To help the Parts that make his Altars smoke.

' After this, the old Woman presented me to
' *Chrysis*, who was very glad she had recover'd
' her Mistress's Treasure ; and therefore hastening
' to her, she conducted me to a most pleasant
' Retreat, deck'd with all that Nature could
' produce to please the Sight.

Where aged Elms cast a refreshing Shade,
And well-trimm'd Pines their shaking Tops dis-
    play'd ;
Where Daphne, *'midst the Cypress, crown'd her*
    Head.
Near these a circling River gently flows,
And rouls the Pebbles as it murmuring goes.
A Place design'd for Love, the Nightingale,
And other Birds, its soft Delights can tell,
Who on each Bush salute the coming Day,
And in their Orgies sing its Hours away.

She was in an Undress, reclining on a flowery Bank, and diverting herself with a Myrtle Branch. As soon as I appear'd, she blush'd, as mindful of her Disappointment. *Chrysis* very prudently withdrew, and when we were left together, I approach'd the Temptation; at what Time she skreen'd my Face with the Myrtle, and as if there had been a Wall between us, becoming more bold; What, my cold Spark, said she, have you brought all your self to Day?

Do you ask, Madam, I return'd, rather than try? and throwing my self to her, who with open Arms was eager to receive me, we kiss'd a little Age away, when giving the Signal to prepare for other Joys, she drew me to a more close Embrace; and now our murmuring Kisses their Sweetness tell, bidding us prepare for greater Pleasures; now our twining Limbs try'd every Fold of Love; now, lock'd in each other's Arms, our Bodies and our Souls are join'd: But even here, alas! even amidst these dear Beginnings, a sudden Chilness press'd upon my Joys, and made me leave 'em all imperfect.

Circe, enrag'd to be so affronted, had Recourse to Revenge, and calling the Grooms that belong'd to the House, made them give me a Warming; nor was she satisfy'd with this, but calling all the Servant-Wenches, even the meanest in the House, she made 'em spit upon me. I hid my head as well as I could; and without begging Pardon, for I knew what I had deserv'd, was turn'd out of doors with a large Retinue of Kicks and Spittle : *Proselenos*, the old Woman, was turn'd out too, and *Chrysis* beaten ; and the whole Family wondering with themselves, enquir'd the Cause of their Lady's Disorder. I hid my Bruises as well as I could, lest my Rival *Eumolpus* might sport with my Shame, or *Gito* be concern'd at it ; therefore, as the only way to disguise my Misfortune, I began to dissemble Sickness ; and having got in Bed, to revenge my self of what had been the Cause of all my Misfortunes, took hold of it, and

With dreadful Steel the Part I would have lopt,
Thrice from my trembling Hand the Razor dropt.
Now, what I might before, I could not do,
For, cold as Ice, the fearful Thing withdrew,
And shrunk behind a wrinkled Canopy,
Hiding his Head from my Revenge and me.
Thus by its fear I'm baulk'd of my Design,
When I in Words more killing vent my Spleen.

At what Time raising my self on the Bed, in this or the like Manner I reproach'd the sullen Impotent ; With what Face can you look up, thou Shame of Heaven and Man, that can'st not be seriously mention'd ? Have I deserv'd from you, when rais'd within Sight of the greatest Joy, to be doom'd to the highest Misfortune ? To have a Scandal fix'd on the very Prime and Vigor of my Years, and to be reduc'd to the Weakness

of an old Man ? I beseech you, Sir, give me an
Epitaph on my departed Vigor; tho' in a great
Heat I had thus said ;

He still continu'd looking on the Ground;
Nor more, at this had rais'd his guilty Head,
Than wither'd Poppies on their tender Stalks.

Nor when I had done, did I less repent of my
ridiculous Passion ; and with a conscious Blush
began to think, how unaccountable it was, that
forgetting all Shame, I should contend with that
Part of me that all Men of Sense reckon not
worth their Thoughts. A little after, relapsing
to my former Humour ; But what's the Crime,
began I, if by a natural Complaint I was eas'd of
my Grief? Or how is it, that we blame our
Stomachs or Bellies, when 'tis our Heads that are
distemper'd? Did not *Ulysses* beat his Breast, as
if that had disturb'd him ? And don't we see the
Actors punish their Eyes, as if they heard the
tragick Scene ? Those that have the Gout in their
Legs, swear at them ; those that have it in their
Fingers, do so by them ; those that have sore
Eyes, are angry with 'em.

Why do the solemn Coxcombs of the Age
At my familiar Lines unjustly rage ?
In Measures loosely plain blunt Satyr flows,
And ev'ry Vice in proper Colours shews.
Love I describe, and all the wanton Joys
Of blushing Matrons, and of am'rous Boys.

There's nothing more deceitful than a ridiculous Opinion, nor more ridiculous than an affected Gravity. After this, I called *Gito* to me ; And tell me, said I, but sincerely, whether *Ascyltos*, when he took you from me, pursu'd the Injury that Night, and treated you in an unhandsome Manner ? The Boy, with his Finger in his Eyes, took a solemn Oath, that he had no Incivility offer'd him by *Ascyltos*.

This drove me to my Wits End ; I was in so much Confusion, I knew not what I said ; but at last I considered to what Purpose I should reflect on Misfortunes which were past and gone, and make my self uneasy with calling them to Mind. At last I did what I could to recover my Vigor ; and being willing to invoke the Assistance of the Gods, I went out to pay my devotions to *Priapus*, and as wretched as I was, did not despair, but kneeling at the Entrance of the Chamber, thus besought him :

My guiltless Hands with Blood I never stain'd,
Or sacrilegiously the Gods prophan'd :
Thus low I bow, restoring Blessings send,
I did not thee with my whole self offend.
Who sins thro' Weakness, is less guilty thought ;
Indulge my Crime, and spare a venial Fault.
On me when Fate shall smiling Gifts bestow,
I'll (not ungrateful) to your God-head bow ;
A sucking Pig I'll offer to thy Shrine,
And sacred Bowls brim-full of gen'rous Wine ;
A destin'd Goat shall on thy Altar lie,
And the horn'd Parent of my Flock shall die ;
Then thrice thy frantick Vot'ries shall around
Thy Temple dance, with smiling Garlands
    crown'd,
And most devoutly drunk, thy Orgies sound.

While I was thus at Prayers, an old Woman, with her Hair about her Ears, and disfigur'd with a mournful Habit, coming in, disturb'd my Devotions ; when taking hold of me, she drew me in a great Surprize out of the Entry ; And what Hag, said she, has devour'd your Manhood? Or what ominous Carcass have you stumbled over in your Nightly Rambles ? You have not acquitted your self like a Man, but, like a washy Jade, have tir'd and founder'd upon the Road : Nor have you been content to sin by your self, but you have also betray'd me into your Crime, and expos'd me as well as your self, to the just Resentment of the Gods ; and do you imagine I will not be reveng'd?

When leading me, submissive to all her Commands, a second Time to the Cell of a neighbouring Priestess of *Priapus*, she threw me upon the Bed, and taking up a Stick that fasten'd the Door, reveng'd herself on me. I with a great deal of Patience receiv'd her Fury ; and at the first Stroke, if the breaking of the Stick had not lessen'd the Force of the Blow, without Doubt she had broke my Head and Arm.

I groan'd, and hiding my Face with my Hand, lean'd upon a Pillow, and burst into a Flood of Tears. The old Woman sate down by me, and wept as bitterly as my self, complaining of the Miseries of Age, 'till the Priestess came in upon us ; And what, said she, do you do in my Chappel, as melancholy as if you came from a Funeral? Don't you consider these are Holidays, in which even the Miserable ought to be merry ?

Alas ! my *Enothea*, said she, this Youth was born under an ill Star ; for not the greatest Beauty can raise him to a perfect Appetite. You ne'er beheld a more unhappy Man : In his Garden the weak *Willow*, not the lusty *Cedar*, grows. In short, you may guess what he is, that could rise unbless'd from *Circe*'s Bed.

Upon this, *Enothea* set herself between us, and moving her Head a while ; I, said she, am the only one that can give a Remedy for that Disease ; and, not to delay it, let him sleep with me to Night, and next Morning examine how vigorous I shall have made him.

All Nature's Works my magick Pow'r obey,
The blooming Earth shall wither and decay,
And, when I please, be verdant, fresh, and gay.
Here, flow'ry Vales shall vernal Beauties know,
There frozen Plains shall hide themselves in Snow.
By magick Charms I'll make a Whirlwind cease,
Contract its Breath, and murmur into Peace.
Tygers and Pards, submissive to my Will,
Obey my Orders, and neglect to kill.
At my Commands, substantial Darkness soon
O'erspreads the Skies, and hides the Silver Moon.
Sol's fiery Carr stopt on th' Ætherial Plain,
And Thetis long expects her Lord in vain.
The Pontick *Bull's emitting Fire and Smoke,*
The Witch Medea *to her Service broke,*
And made their swelling Chests sustain the Yoke.
Refulgent Circe, *Daughter of the Sun,*
Could into Swine Ulysses's *Soldiers turn.*
In woods Silenus, Proteus *in the Seas,*
Conceal the God, and take what Forms they please.
As great's my Skill, as far my Pow'r extends,
The servile World to my Enchantment bends.

I shook with fear at such a Romantick Promise, and began more intentively to view the old Woman: Upon which she cry'd out, O! *Enothea,* be as good as your Word; when, carefully wiping her Hands, she lay down on the Bed, and half smother'd me with Kisses.

Enothea, in the Middle of the Altar, plac'd a Turf-Table, and laid upon it burning Coals, and an old crack'd Cup repair'd with Pitch, in which she us'd to sacrifice. When she had fix'd it to the smoaky Wall from which she took it, putting on her Habit, she plac'd a Kettle by the Fire, and took down a Bag that hung near her, in which a Bean was kept for the Use she now put it to, and a very aged Piece of a Hog's Forehead, with the Print of a hundred Cuts on't ; when opening the Bag, she threw me a Part of the Bean, and bid me carefully strip it. I obey'd her Command, and try'd without daubing my Fingers, to deliver the Grain from its nasty Covering ; but she, blaming my Dullness, snatch'd it from me, and skilfully tearing its Shells with her Teeth, spit the black Morsels from her, which lay like dead Flies on the Ground. *How ingenious is Poverty, and what strange Arts will Hunger teach?* The Priestess seem'd so great a Lover of this Sort of Life, that her Humour appear'd in every Thing about her, and her Hut might be truly term'd, Sacred to Poverty.

> *No flaming Rubies here are set in Gold,*
> *No Marble covers the deluded Mold ;*
> *Void of expensive Art, the rev'rend Shrine*
> *With nat'ral modest Ornaments does shine.*
> *Round* Ceres *Bower the bending Ozier grows ;*
> *Earthen is all the Plate the Priestess knows :*
> *The Jug is Earth, which holds the holy Wine,*
> *Ozier the Dish, sacred to Pow'rs divine.*
> *The Fane can boast————*

No brazen Knobs, nor splendid purple Pride,
Mud mix'd with Dirt the pious Relicts hide ;
Rushes and Reeds the humble Roof adorn,
And Straw depriv'd of its Autumnal Corn.
On an old Shelf a sav'ry Ham is found,
And Service-berries into Garlands bound :
Such a low Cottage Hecale *confin'd,*
Low was her Cottage, but sublime her Mind.
Her bounteous Heart a grateful Praise shall crown,
And Muses make immortal her Renown.

After which, she tasted of the Flesh, and hanging the rest, old as herself, on the Hook again, the rotten Stool on which she was mounted, breaking, threw her into the Fire ; her Fall spilt the Kettle, and what it held, put out the Fire. She burnt her Elbow, and all her Face was hid with the Ashes that her Fall had rais'd.

Thus disturb'd, I arose, and laughing, took her up immediately, lest any Thing should hinder the Offering. She ran for new Fire to the Neighbourhood, and had hardly got to the Door, ere I was set upon by three sacred Geese, that daily, as I conjecture, about that Time were fed by the old Woman. They made a hideous Noise, and, surrounding me, one tears my Coat, another my Shoes, while their furious Captain made a very brisk Attack upon my Legs ; 'till, seeing my self in Danger, I began to be in earnest, and snatching up one of the Feet of our little Table, made the valient Animal feel the Prowess of my Hand ; nor content with a slight Blow or two, I reveng'd my self with its Death.

Such were the Birds Alcides *did subdue,*
That from his conqu'ring Arm to Heav'n withdrew.
Such were the Harpyes, who at Phineus *Board*
Met poys'nous Death, in Silver Dishes stor'd.
Their dreadful Shrieks disturb the trembling Air,
And Pow'rs above the wild Confusion share ;
Horrors disturb the Order of the Sky,
And frighted Stars beyond their Courses fly.

By this Time the other two had eat up the Pieces of the Bean that lay scatter'd on the Floor ; and having lost their Leader, return'd to the Temple. When, glad of the Booty, and my Revenge, I cur'd the slight Wound in my Leg which the Goose had made, with Vinegar. But fearing the old Woman's Anger, I design'd to make off ; and taking up my Cloaths, began my march. I had scarce reach'd the Door, ere I saw *Enothea* bringing in her Hand an Earthen Pot fill'd with Fire ; upon which, I retreated, and throwing down my Cloaths, fix'd my self in the Entry, as if I were impatiently expecting her coming.

Enothea entering, rak'd the Fire together which she had made of broken Sticks ; and putting more Fuel upon it, began to excuse herself for staying so long, telling me, that a Friend of her's would not let her go before she had (against the Laws of Drinking) taken three Healths together ; when

looking about her, What, said she, have you been
doing in my Absence ?   Where's the Bean ?

I, who thought I had behav'd my self very
honourably, told her the whole Fight ; and to
end her Grief for the Loss of the Bean, presented
her the Goose.   When I shew'd the Goose, the
old Woman set up such an Outcry, that you
would have thought the Geese were re-entering
the Place.

Being in all the Confusion imaginable at so
strange a Humour, I ask'd the Meaning of her
Passion, and why she pity'd the Goose, rather
than me.

But wringing her Hands, You wicked wretch,
said she, who d'ye speak to ?   D'ye know what
you've done ?   You've kill'd the Gods Delight,
a Goose the Pleasure of all Matrons ; and, lest
you should think your self innocent, know, if a
Magistrate should hear of it, you'd be hang'd.
You have defil'd with Blood my Cell, that to this
Day has been inviolable.   You have done that, for
which, if any's so malicious, he may expel me
from my Office.

> *She said, and trembling, rends her aged Hairs,*
> *And both her Cheeks with mad Distraction tears.*
> *Sad Murmurs from her troubl'd Breast arise,*
> *And Show'rs of Tears there issu'd from her Eyes.*
> *Two falling Streams her wrinkled Bosom lave,*
> *And drown her Garments in a Briny Wave.*

Upon which, I beseech you, said I, don't grieve ;

I'll recompense the Loss of your Goose with an Ostrich.

Whilst I was speaking, she sat down on the Bed, lamenting her Loss ; at what Time *Proselenas* came in with the Sacrifice, and viewing the murder'd Goose, and enquiring into the Cause, began very earnestly to cry and pity me, as if it had been my Father I had kill'd, and not a Goose. But tir'd with this Stuff, I beseech ye, said I, tell me, tho' it had been a Man I had slain, would not Gold wipe off the Guilt ? See here are two Pieces, with these you may purchase Gods, as well as Geese.

Which when *Enothea* beheld, Pardon me, young Man, said she, I am only concern'd for your Safety, which is an Argument of Love, not Hatred ; therefore we'll take what Care we can to prevent a Discovery. You have nothing to do, but to intreat the Gods to forgive the Sin.

> *The wealthy Lord thro' Storms at Court may sail*
> *Into preferment with a prosp'rous Gale,*
> *On Honour's gilded Pinnacles may stand,*
> *And have the World and Fortune at Command.*
> *He, by the Force of Gold's prevailing Charms,*
> *Can bring a beauteous Goddess to his Arms,*
> *And bribe her Father, tho' a King like* Jove,
> *To hide the Joys of her forbidden Love.*
> *He can be Lord Chief Justice, Chancellor,*
> *Can grace the* Pulpit, *or adorn the* Bar.
> *Surprizing Lines with easy Art he writes,*

And Numbers smooth as Addison's *indites.*
Sure of Applause, the gilded Pages shine,
And dare contend, immortal Garth, *with thine.*
Of wealth possess'd, you do whate'er you please,
The Judge *or* Priest *your awful Nod obeys;*
All straight your Skill and mighty Knowledge own,
And equal you to Holt *or* Littleton.
All Things submit to Gold, and you may have
Whate'er your wanton Thoughts or Wishes crave,
You of all Pow'r and Grandeur are possest,
Have Heav'n and Jove *too lodg'd within your Chest.*

While my Thoughts were engag'd in these odd
Adventures, she plac'd a Cup of Wine under my
Hands, and having cleans'd my prophane extended
Fingers with sacred Leeks and Parsley, she threw
some Hazel-Nuts into the Wine, with an Ejacu-
lation; and as they sunk or swam, gave her
Judgment; but I well knew, without the Help of
a Conjurer, the empty rotten ones would swim,
and those whose Kernels were whole, would
naturally sink to the Bottom.

When applying herself to the Goose, from its
Breast which she had open'd, she drew a lusty
Liver, and then told me my future Fortune.
And that no Mark of the Murder might be left,
she put the dead Goose upon a Spit, which, as
she said, she had fatten'd a little before, as sensible
it was to die.

In the mean Time the Wine went briskly round,
and now the old Women gladly eat up the Goose

they so lately lamented. When they had pick'd
its Bones, *Enothea*, half drunk, turn'd to me ;
And now, said she, I'll finish the Charm that
recovers your Strength. When drawing out a
Leathern Effigies of the Deity she worshipp'd,
she dipt it in a Medley of Oil, small Pepper, and
the bruis'd Seed of Nettles, and began by degrees
to direct its Passage thro' my hinder Parts. With
this Mixture she barbarously sprinkled me all
over ; and with the Juice of *Cresses* and *Suthern-
wood* washing my Breast, she began with a Bunch
of green Nettles to strike gently all the Vale
below. Upon which, jumping from her, to avoid
the Sting, I made off. The old Women, in a
great Rage pursu'd me ; and tho' drunk with
Wine, and their more hot Desires, took the right
Way, and follow'd me thro' two or three Villages,
crying, *Stop Thief* ; but having wounded my Hands
in my precipitate Flight, I got off.

When I came Home, I went to Bed to ease my
weary'd Limbs ; but the Thoughts of my Misfortunes would not let me sleep ; when considering
how unparallell'd a Wretch I was, I cry'd out,
Did my ever cruel Fortune want the Afflictions
of Love to make me more miserable ? O Un-
happiness ! Fortune and Love conspire my Ruin.
Severer Love spares me no Way, or loving, or
belov'd, a Wretch. *Chrysis* adores me, and is
ever giving me Occasion to oblige her. She, that
when she brought me to her Mistress, despis'd me
for my mean Habit, as one beneath her Desires ;

that very *Chrysis*, that so scorn'd my former Fortune, pursues me even to the Hazard of her own ; and swore, when she first discover'd to me the Violence of her Love, that she would be ever true to me. But *Circe*'s in Possession of my Heart, I value none but her ; and indeed who is so charming as she ? Compar'd to her, what was *Ariadne* or *Læda ?* What *Helen*, or even *Venus ? Paris* himself, the Umpire of the wanton Nymphs, if with these Eyes he had seen her contending for the Golden Apple, would have given his *Helen* and the Goddesses for her. If I might be admitted to kiss her sweet Lips again, or once more press her divinely rising Breasts, perhaps my Vigor would revive, which now I believe lies oppress'd by Witchcraft. I should dispense with my Reproaches, I should forget that I was beat, esteem my being turn'd out of Doors a Sport, so I might be again happy in her Favour.

These Thoughts, and the Image of the beautiful *Circe*, so rais'd my Mind, that I oft, as if my Love was in my Arms, with a great deal of fruitless Ardor, hug'd the Bedcloaths, 'till out of Patience with the lasting Affliction, I began to reproach my Impotence ; yet recovering my Presence of Mind, I flew for Comfort to the Misfortunes of ancient Heroes, and thus broke out :

Not I alone have Heav'n's just Anger felt ;
The Gods with others have severely dealt :
By Juno's Rage the Heavens Alcides bore,

And lost fair Hylas *on the* Pontick *Shore.*
Laomedon *did* Jove*'s Resentments feel,*
And Telephus *bled by the fatal Steel.*
Fate's sure Decrees no mortal Pow'r can shun ;
Nor can the swiftest from Heav'n's Vengeance run.

Full of anxious Cares I spent the Night ; and *Gito*, being inform'd I lay at Home, the next Morning enter'd my Chamber by Daybreak ; when having passionately complain'd of my loose Life, he told me the family took much Notice of my Behaviour, that I was seldom in waiting, and that perhaps the Company I kept would be my Ruin.

By this I understood he was inform'd of my Affairs, and that some one had been in Pursuit of me ; upon which I ask'd him whether any Body was to enquire for me ? Not to Day, said he, but Yesterday there came a very pretty Woman, who, when she had tir'd me with a long sifting Discourse, at last told me you deserv'd to be punish'd, and should be us'd as a Slave, if you longer complain'd.

This so sensibly touch'd me, that I began afresh to reproach Fortune ; nor had I done, ere *Chrysis* came in, and wildly throwing her Arms about me, Now, said she, I'll hold my Wish ; you're my Love, my Joy ; nor can you think to quench this Flame, but by closer Embraces.

I was much disturb'd at *Chrysis*'s Wantonness, and gave her fair Language, to get rid of her ;

for I was very apprehensive of the Danger of *Eumolpus*'s hearing it, since his good Fortune had made him so proud. I did therefore what I could to appease her Rage ; I dissembled Love, whisper'd soft Things, and, in short, manag'd it so like a Lover, that she believ'd me one. I made her understand in what Danger we both were, if she should be found with me in that Place, and that our Lord *Eumolpus* punish'd the least Offence. Upon which, she immediately made out, and the more hastily, because she saw *Gito* returning, who had left me a little before she came.

She was scarce out, when on a Sudden one of the Slaves came to me, and told me, that our Lord so highly resented my two Days Absence, that unless, as he advis'd me, I invented a good Excuse to allay his Heat, I should certainly be punish'd.

Gito perceiving how concern'd I was, spoke not a Word of the Woman, but advis'd me to behave my self merrily to *Eumolpus*, rather than serious. I pursu'd the Counsel, and put on so pleasant a Face, that he receiv'd me in Drollery, without the grave stiffness of a Master. He was pleasant on the Success of my Amours, prais'd my Mein and Wit, that was so agreeable to the Ladies ; And I'm no Stranger, said he, to your Intrigue with a very beautiful Lady. But now, *Eumolpus*, consider, your Amours, rightly manag'd, may turn to our Advantage ; therefore do you personate the Lover, I'll continue the Character I've begun.

He was yet speaking, when there enter'd the

Room a very venerable Matron, her name *Philumene*, who, by the well-manag'd Vertues of her Sex, had often got great Booties, and now grown old, and past her blooming Years, had a Mind to thrust her Son and Daughter upon a childless old Man ; and to put her Device in Execution, she comes to *Eumolpus*, and addressing herself to him, commends her Children to his Conduct, affirming, that she committed herself and all her Hopes to his Wisdom ; that he was the only Person in the World she could confide in.   In short, that she would leave her Children there, to hear his Wisdom, which was the only Portion she could give them.   Nor was she worse than her Word ; and leaving a very beautiful Girl, with her little Brother, went out under Pretence of paying Heaven publick Thanks in the Temple for the Favours she had receiv'd.   *Eumolpus* was too quick-sighted not to perceive with what Intent the two young Objects were assign'd to his Care ; and thinking it no Crime to betray a Trust which was founded on Treachery, invited the young Girl to celebrate the Mysteries of Love. The Damsel, tho' young, and seemingly unacquainted with the World, knew her Interest too well to refuse him any Thing, she lost what young Ladies value themselves upon, and feasted *Eumolpus* luxuriously with her Beauties.   For my Part, as soon as I was sensible of the Intrigue, I put in for my Share of the lovely Prize.   She consented to my Wishes, but my adverse Fortune still attended me.

I was not so concern'd at this, as the former ;
for a little after my Strength return'd, and finding
my self more vigorous, I cry'd out, the courteous
Gods are great, that have made me whole again.
For *Mercury*, that conveys and reconveys our
Souls, by his Favours has restor'd what his Anger
had taken away. Now, thought I, my Reputation
shall be as great as that of *Protesilaus*, or any other
of the ancient Heroes.

This great Blessing making us merry, we laugh'd
at *Philumene*'s cunning, and the young Lady's
Compliance, which would profit 'em little with us ;
for to no other End were they left, but to be
Heirs to what we had. When reflecting on this
sordid Manner of deceiving childless Age, I took
Occasion to consider the Condition of our present
Fortune, and told *Eumolpus* that the Deceivers
might be deceiv'd, that therefore all our Actions
should be of a Piece with the Character we bore ;
that *Socrates*, the wisest of Men, us'd to boast he
never saw a Tavern, nor ever had been in the
common Company that frequents such Places ;
that nothing was more convenient than a discreet
Behaviour. All these are Truths ; nor should any
Sort of Men, added I, sooner expect the sudden
Assaults of ill Fortune, than those that covet what's
other Mens. But how should Pick-Pockets live,
unless, by some well-order'd Trick to draw Fools
together, they get Employment ? As Fish are
taken with what they really eat, so Men are to be
cheated with something that's solid, not empty

Hopes. Thus the People of this Country have
hitherto receiv'd us very nobly ; but when they
find the Arrival of no Ship from *Africa*, laden, as
you told 'em, with Riches and your Retinue, the
impatient Deceivers will lessen their Bounty, or I
am mistaken ; for Fortune already begins to repent
her Favours.

I have thought of a Means, said *Eumolpus*, to
make our Deceivers continue their Care of us.
And drawing his Will out of his Pocket, thus read
the last Lines of it.

All that have Legacies in this my last Will and
Testament, my freed Men excepted, receives 'em
on these Conditions, That they divide my Body,
and eat it before the People ; and that they may
not think it an unjust Demand, let them know,
that to this Day 'tis the Custom of many Countries,
that the Relations of the Dead devour their Car-
cases, and for that Reason they often quarrel with
their sick Kindred, because they spoil their Flesh
by lingering in a Disease. I only instance this to
my Friends, that they may not refuse to perform
my Will ; but with the same Sincerity they wish'd
well to my Soul, they might devour my Body.

When he had read the chief Articles, some that
were more intimately acquainted with him, enter'd
the Chamber, and viewing the Will, earnestly
intreated him to impart the Contents of it ; he
readily consented, and read the whole. But when
they heard the Necessity of eating his Carcase,
they seem'd much concern'd at the strange Pro-

posal ; but their insatiate Love of the Money,
made 'em conceal their Surprize, and his Person
was so awful to 'em, they durst not complain ;
Gorgias by Name told him, he was willing to
accept the Conditions, so he might not wait for
the Body.

To this *Eumolpus* reply'd, I'm not in the least
apprehensive of your Performance, nor that your
Stomach will refuse the Task, when to recompence
one distastful Minute, you may promise your self
Ages of Luxury. 'Tis but shutting your Eyes,
and supposing, instead of Man's Flesh, you were
eating an hundred thousand Crowns. Some Sawce
may be added to vary the Taste ; for no Flesh
pleases alone, but is prepar'd by Art to commend
it to the Stomach. If you desire Instances of this
Kind to make ye approve my Advice, the *Sagun-
tines*, when they were besieg'd by *Hannibal*, eat
human Bodies, without the Hopes of an Estate for
doing it. The *Petavii*, reduc'd to the last Extremity, did the like ; nor had they farther Hopes
in this Banquet, than to satisfy Nature. When
Scipio took *Numantia*, Mothers were found with
their Children half eaten in their Arms. But
since the Thoughts only of eating Man's Flesh,
create an Abhorrence, 'tis but resolving, and you
gain the mighty Legacies I leave you.

Eumolpus recounted these shameless Inhumanities
with so much Confusion, that his Parasites began
to suspect him, and more nearly considering our
Words and Actions, their Jealousy increas'd with

their Observation, and they believ'd us perfect
Cheats. Upon which, those who had receiv'd
us most nobly, resolv'd to seize us, and justly
take their Revenge ; but *Chrysis*, privy to all
Stratagems, gave me notice of their Designs ;
the frightful News so struck me, that I made
off with *Gito* immediately, and left *Eumolpus*
to the Mercy of his Enemies ; and in a few
Days we heard the *Crotonians*, angry that that old
Rascal should live so long at such a sumptuous
Rate on the publick Charge, had sacrific'd him the
Massilian Way. Whenever the *Massilians* were
visited with a Plague, some one of the poorest of
the People, for the Sake of being well fed a whole
Year at the publick Charge, would offer himself
a Sacrifice to appease the Gods. He, after his
Year was up, dress'd in holy Wreaths and sacred
Garments, was led about the City with Invocations
on the Gods, that all the Sins of the Nation might
be punish'd in him, and so was thrown from a
Precipice.

The End of the Second Part.

THE
THIRD PART
OF THE
WORKS
OF
Petronius Arbiter,

CONTAINING

Epigrams, Poems, and *Satyrs.*

By several Hands.

EPIGRAMS,

POEMS, and SATYRS.

On a happy Life's consisting in Vertue. A Fragment, beginning, Non est falleris, *etc. By Mr. Tho. Brown.*

YOU're mightily deceiv'd, I swear,
    And mightily, my Friend, you err ;
    Wretched's the State in which you guess
Consists our Life's chief Happiness.
'Tis not your Fingers to behold,
Loaded with Rubies set in Gold ;
Nor, like a Royal Miss, to wear
A Nation's Value in your Ear ;
Nor all the Trifles to receive,
That the *Exchange* or Mint can give ;
With all the shining Toys and Cost
The *Strand* or *Lombard-street* can boast.
Nor is't, like Popes, our selves to please,
With holy Luxury and Ease ;
Nor yet on purple Beds to sleep,

Whilst Centinels your Palace keep ;
Nor yet in mighty Pomp to feast,
Or smell the Odours of the *East.*
Nor is't to have our glitt'ring Board
Uncommon Rarities afford ;
Tall Pyramids of Fowl or Fish,
For which e'en Epicures might wish ;
And whatsoe'er the costliest Feast
Can boast of, when by *Locket* drest.
Nor to possess the Spicy Store,
Which our *East-India* Fleet brings o'er.
But 'tis to have a Conscience
Guarded with spotless Innocence ;
And, with a Courage, to advance
'Gainst all the Shocks of Time and Chance ;
And not, as *Monmouth* did, to go
Amongst the scoundrel Mob, and bow
On both Sides popularly low ;
Nor yet to be with Fears possest,
Tho' naked Swords insult your Breast.
The happy Man, that thus can be
From all these anxious Sorrows free,
May giddy Fortune make his Sport,
And smile at both the Camp and Court.
A Mind so steddy, unconcern'd, and brave,
May force th' imperious Jilt to be his Slave.

A FRAGMENT.

Upon the Levity of Woman.

Beginning, Crede Ratem Ventis, &c.

COmmit your Ship to Sea and Wind,
    But not your Thoughts to Womankind.
    The veering Wind, and faithless Sea,
Have much more faith than any She.
All Maids are treach'rous in their Love ;
Add if, by chance, one constant prove,
I know not how she e'er should be
Made constant by Inconstancy.

EPIGRAM.

IMpubis nupsi valido, nunc firmior annis
    Exsucco & tremulo sum sociata viro.
    Ille fatigavit teneram, hic ætate valentem
Intactam tota nocte jacere Sinet.
Dum nollem licuit, nunc dum volo non licet uti,
    O Hymen aut annos, aut mihi redde virum.

Translated thus.   By Mr. Tho. Brown.

COming a tender Girl from School,
    Marrying, I met a thund'ring Tool :
    But fit for Love's Embraces grown,
I've got a Man that's next to none.

The first with Youth's too vig'rous warmth
    inspir'd'
With Love's untasted Joys, my Weakness tir'd.
My second grunting Spark, cold to Love's Charms,
He fills my Bed, 'tis true, but not my Arms.
  When I'd no Appetite, Love cloy'd me ;
Now I've a Mind to't, 'tis deny'd me.
Oh ! Hymen, Hymen, for my Quiet,
Contract my Stomach, or enlarge my Diet.

On the Power of GOLD.

By Mr. Burnaby.

Beginning, Quisquis habet nummos, *&c,*

WHoe'er has Money, may securely sail ;
    On all things with all mighty gold
      prevail ;
May *Danae* wed, or rival am'rous *Jove,*
And make her Father pandar to his Love ;
May be a Poet, Preacher, Lawyer too ;
And bawling win the Cause he does not know,
And up to *Cato*'s Fame for Wisdom grow.
Wealth without Law will gain at Bar Renown,
Howe'er the Case appears, the Cause is won,
Ev'ry rich Lawyer is a *Littleton.*
In short, of all you wish, you are possest,
All Things prevent the wealthy Man's Request,
For *Jove* himself's the Treasure of his Chest.

That the Dog of Hell was a Lawyer.

By the Author of the London Spy, *beginning,*
Cerberus, forensis erat Causidicus, *&c.*

SUre *Cerberus* a lawyer first must be,
   Whose clam'rous Mouth would open for a
      Fee ;
But, since whene'er he wrangled, still he had
Three specious Reasons for the Noise he made,
To please his Client, to inform the Court,
And to gain Riches for his own Support ;
Therefore he's doom'd in Hell three Heads to bear,
And in his Mouth three howling Tongues to wear,
That the loud Eloquence he once could boast,
To his own Int'rest, but his Client's Cost,
Might now be turn'd to dreadful Howls and Yelps,
The snarling Language of illit'rate Whelps :
And tho' on Earth no other Bribe but Gold
Would make the Pleader for his Client scold,
Yet now in Hell a greasy Sop must be,
Instead of Coin, the growling Puppy's Fee.

233

On a WIFE.

By the same, beginning, Uxor, legitimus debet
quasi Census amari, &c.

A Wife, who as our own by Law we hold,
We ought to value as we do our Gold ;
But even that, which few delight to pay,
On some Accounts we ought to throw away.
    Wiving, like Coining, for our Ease began ;
Both were intended for the Good of Man.
The Coin the Image of the Prince should wear,
The Woman should her Husband's Image bear.
Both from the Pow'r of others should be freed,
And both should serve us at a Time of need :
But if by keeping either Wife or Coin,
We find that neither answers our Design,
Both should be parted with whene'er we please,
And not be kept to interrupt our Ease ;
For when the End propos'd, is once destroy'd,
The Vows that make us wretched, must be void.
    True, we should prize our Money and our Wives,
So long as they add Comfort to our Lives ;
But if the Metal or the Dame proves base,
And bears the Stamp of an adult'rous Face,
As worthless Dross and Counterfeits, they ought
To be despis'd, whene'er we find em naught ;
And as each Plant their Fruits when rotton shed,
So both should be divorc'd from Bag and Bed ;
For Coin that's bad's a Scandal to the Purse,
And a false Woman is a matchless Curse.

By the same beginning, Morbus & Vultu Mulier
quæratur habenda, *&c.*

HE that for Money weds prepost'rous Shapes,
    Is brib'd to get a Brood of monst'rous
        Apes,
Such as may fright their Nurses, shame the Earth,
And be hereafter bound to curse their Birth ;
For female Pigmies must infect their Breed,
And stint the Growth of Man's prolifick Seed.
The wary Farmer scorns to spend his Toil
Upon a hungry and unfruitful Soil.
The prudent Potter breaks and throws away
The faulty Mold, that would deform his Clay.
What upright Mortal would not then disdain
The Womb that should degrade the Shape of Man,
And, by its strange distorted Cells, debase
The heav'nly Image of the God-like Race ?
    Which adds most Comfort to the Husband's Life,
Full Bags with a prepost'rous homely Wife,
Whose plenteous Fortune he may soon exhaust
On some kind Harlot, who has Charms to boast ?
Or she, whose lovely Form is so divine,
That 'tis enough to bless thee, that she's thine ?
What, tho' her Fortune's small, her Beauty's great,
And will delight thee more than an Estate.
She'll make thee happy in a sprightly Brood
Of infant Angels cloath'd in Flesh and Blood ;
Such whose sweet Charms will please you more
    than Gold,

And cause you to be reverenc'd when old.
But the crook'd Arm-full of distorted Bones,
Will turn your nuptial Joys to Sighs and Groans,
And curse you with a Race of monkey Sons.

The Rope-Dancer.

By the same, beginning, Stupea suppositis tenduntur
vincula lignis, *&c.*

Since active Man can in the Air rebound
   Upon a Rope, far distant from the Ground,
   And by unweary'd Practice grow so bold,
To do what others tremble to behold ;
Why should we wonder *Icarus* should fly,
Upon his Father's Wings, so high ?
Old *Dædalus* from Birds deriv'd this Whim,
As Men by croaking Frogs were taught to swim.
To these, Delight and Safety first inclin'd
The active Pains of the industrious Mind ;
But what mysterious Project could induce
Mankind to bring Rope-dancing first in Use ?
(An Art acquir'd with so much Fear and Pains,
And next rewarded with so little Gains.)
'Tis hard to guess, since ev'ry Step they take,
The active Fool's in danger of his Neck ;
And all the Profit to himself he draws,
Is little more than scandalous Applause.

However, by this Art we may discern,
That nothing is too hard for Man to learn ;
Unheard of Wonders human Race might do,

Conquer *Herculean* Labours daily new,
Had we but Courage to pursue with Pains
The vast Conceptions of our teeming Brains.

A Fragment imitated, beginning, Candide sidereis,
&c.

By Tho. Brown.

Divine *Cosmelia* has two burning Eyes,
   From which refulgent Beams and Glories
     rise.
Her Neck with od'rous Sweets of Roses flows ;
Her wanton Hair in golden Ringlets grows.
Her fragrant Lips are charmingly o'erspread,
Like young *Aurora*'s, with a purple Red.
In various Branches each meand'ring Vein,
With azure Hills her lovely Bosom stain.
Beauty it self, Youth smiles, and ev'ry Grace,
Pay all their Tribute to her heav'nly Face ;
A dazzling Goddess's bright Form she bears ;
Not stronger Charms the Queen of Beauty wears.
Your silver Hands will coldest Bosoms warm,
And with a Touch the Old and Pious charm.
Your pretty Foot, despising common Floors,
On Carpets treads, or *Genoa*'s Marble Stores.
Nor shall th' ignoble Pavement of the Street
Hurt or prophane *Cosmelia*'s sacred Feet.
When you amongst the Beds of Lillies stray,
Their Leaves drop down, as proud to strew your
     way,

237

Whilst, like *Camilla*, over them you pass,
Leaving no Print upon the Flowers or Grass.
Let meaner Beauties with successless Care
Purchase rich Pearls, and glitt'ring Gems prepare
T'' adorn their Necks, or grace their lovely Hair.
Cosmelia only can attract my Eyes,
Rich in herself, when stript of Vanities.
Not flattery, nor yet poetick Fire,
Can do her Justice, or enough admire.
The Muses and the Syrens cease their Song,
Pleas'd with the Musick of your charming Tongue.
From which increasing Sweets do ever flow,
And my poor panting Soul you ravish so,
That to your humble Slave you cruel prove,
And dart at him a thousand Shafts of Love ;
A raging Flame feeds on my wounded Heart,
No Herbs can cure me, nor the Surgeon's Art.
One Kiss from you will all my Cares remove,
And make me smile like the young God of Love.
This healing Med'cine can my Grief controul,
And cure the wild Disorders of my Soul.
Let not your face such killing Fairness wear ;
Ah ! do not thus my Nerves in Pieces tear :
Nor let my Tomb, when I am dead, complain,
That I was by my Dear's Unkindness slain.
But if you think this Boon too great to grant
To me your Slave, and humble Supplicant ;
Yet grant me this, that when I breathless lie,
Kill'd with the murd'ring Ligh'ning of your Eye,
In mournful Arms you would the Dead embrace ;
I'll soon revive, touch'd by that lovely Face.

A Fragment of Petronius *paraphras'd by another* Hand, beginning, Naufragius ejecta natus rate, *&c.*

FRom mutual Wounds the Wretched find
      Relief,
    And social Woes calm or direct their Grief.
The Merchant, ruin'd by the faithless Main,
Seeks a known Partner of his Ship-wreck'd Pain,
On whose kind Breast he may his Loss bemoan,
Inclin'd to pity Sorrows by its own.
When poys'nous Blights wings the infectious Air,
And noxious Winds beguile the Tiller's Care,
Reluctant Furrows twice the Corn entomb,
And faded Poppies lose their purple Bloom ;
In barren Fields no teeming Seeds appear,
Lost are the hopeful Blossoms of the Year.
To some low Vale the frighted Farmers fly,
And mourn the Ruins of the angry Sky.
Their various Wrongs the sad Convention show,
And in the publick lose their private Woe.
Funerals the Sad in mutual Friendship bind,
And childless Parents Consolation find ;
Each of the others Pain assumes a Part,
Divides his Sorrows, but unites his Heart.

WHoe'er would with ambitious just Desire,
    To Mast'ry in so fine an Art aspire,
    Must all Extreams first diligently shun,
And in a settled Course of Vertue run.
Let him not Fortune with stiff Greatness climb,
Nor, Courtier-like, with Cringes undermine ;
Nor all the Brother Blockheads of the Pot
Ever perswade him to become a Sot ;
Nor flatter Poets, to acquire the Fame
Of, I protest, *a pretty Gentleman.*
But whether in the War he would be great,
Or in the gentler Arts that rule a State ;
Or else his am'rous Breast he would improve
Well to receive the youthful Cares of Love,
In his first Years to Poetry inclin'd,
Let *Homer*'s Spring bedew his fruitful Mind ;
His manlier Years to manlier Studies brought,
Philosophy must next employ his Thought.
Then let his boundless Soul new Glories fire,
And to the great *Demosthenes* aspire,
When round in Throngs the list'ning People come,
T'admire what sprung in *Greece* so slow at Home.
Rais'd to this Height, your leisure Hours engage
In something just, and worthy of the Stage ;
Your Choice of Words from *Cicero* derive,
And in your Poems you design should live ;

The Joys of Feasts, and Terrors of a War, ⎫
More pleasing those, and these more frightful are, ⎬
When told by you, than in their acting were. ⎭
And thus, enrich'd with such a golden Store,
You're truly fit to be an Orator.

Tryphæna's Speech for Peace, on Board the Ship of
    Lycas, *beginning,* Quis furor exclamat, Pacem
    convertit, *&c.*

WHat Fury did these sudden Broils engage ?
        How have these guiltless Hands de-
        serv'd the Rage ?
No *Paris* a stoll'n Dame to *Troy* conveys,
No Witch *Medea* here her Brother stays :
But slighted Love must needs resenting be ;
And 'midst the Waves, who is the raging he,
Now robb'd of Arms, that can attempt my Fate ?
By whom is simple Death so little thought ?
Let not your murd'rous Rage out-storm the Seas,
And Dangers of the angry Waves increase.

On the Misery of Mankind, beginning, Heu, Heu,
        nos Miseros, *&c.*

UNhappy Mortals, on how fine a Thread
        Our Lives depend ! How like this Puppet
        Man
Shall we, alas, be all, when we are dead !
    Therefore let's live merrily while we can.

In Defence of Satyr, beginning, Quid me constricta
spectatis fronte, *&c.*

WHY do the strict-liv'd *Cato's* of the Age
　　At my familiar Lines so gravely rage?
　　In Measures loosely plain blunt Satyr
　　　flows,
Which all the People so sincerely shows.
For who's a Stranger to the Joys of Love?
Who can't the Thoughts of such soft Pleasures
　　move?
Such *Epicurus* own'd the chiefest Bliss,
And such Lives the Gods themselves possess.

An Epigram on Tantalus, *beginning,* Nec bibit
inter aquas, *&c.*

UNhappy *Tantalus*, amidst the Flood,
　　Where floating Apples on the Surface
　　　stood,
Ever pursu'd them with a longing Eye,
Yet could not Thirst nor Hunger satisfy.
Such is the Miser's Fate, who curs'd with Wealth,
In midst of endless Treasures starves himself.

By Capt. Ayloffe.

FRom slavish Fear the dreadful Gods arose,
    Who still on tim'rous Fools strange Laws
      impose.
When from the burning Sky fierce Thunder came,
And Walls are tumbled down with the impetuous
    Flame ;
And lofty *Athos* shook with blasting Fires,
Fill'd mortal Breasts with pannick Dread and fond
    Desires ;
Then *Phœbus* mounting up the *Eastern* Skies,
From prostrate Man receiv'd his Sacrifice.
Then to the waining Moon strange Rites were paid,
And to the growing Honours on her Head.
Hence sprung the Mob of Idols, Brass and Stone,
And humbler Wood, th' imagin'd Gods t' atone,
And the divided Year, by changing Months,
    was known.
This Crew the Projects of degen'rate Vice
Supported, and promoted still by Lies.
Vain Error first the Husband-man compell'd
To give the Autumn Honours of the Field
To yellow *Ceres; Bacchus,* hence divine,
Had his Head crown'd with the full cluster'd Vine
Misled by *Error*'s powerful Command,
Pales grew glad from the dull Shepherd's Hand.
Blue *Neptune* roul'd thro' all the rolling Waves,
And *Pallas* challeng'd all the gloomy Caves.

The perjur'd Wretch, a Traytor, now combine
To purge their Guilt by forming Gods divine ;
And ev'ry one, with Avarice and Lies,
Contend to multiply the Brood of spurious Deities.

Upon the Vanity of our Taste, beginning, Nolo
quod Cupio, *&c.*

WHat's soon obtain'd, we nauseously receive,
All hate the Victory that's got with
Leave.
We scorn whate'er from our own Isle proceeds,
And follow Fops our neighb'ring Climate breeds.
The Mullets which *Sicilian* Nets betray,
Exceed not those which in the *Tyber* play.
But these are cheaply taken, those come far,
With Difficulty got, and cost us dear.
Thus the kind She abroad we admire above
Th' insipid Lump, at Home, of lawful Love ;
Yet once enjoy'd, we strait anew desire,
And absent Pleasures only do admire.

Hymn to Priapus, *beginning*, Nympharum Bacchique
comes, *&c.*

B*Acchus* and Nymphs Delight, O mighty God !
  Whom *Cynthia* gave to rule the blooming
  Wood.
Lesbos and verdant *Thasos* thee adore,
And *Lydians* in loose flowing Dress implore,
And raise devoted Temples to thy Pow'r.
Thou *Dryad*'s Joy, and *Bacchus*'s Guardian, hear
My conscious Prayer with attentive Ear.
My Hands with guiltless Blood I never stain'd,
Nor yet the Temples of the Gods prophan'd.
Restore my Strength, and lusty Vigor send,
My trembling Nerves like pliant Oziers bend.
Who sins thro' Weakness, is not guilty thought,
No equal Pow'r can punish such a Fault.
A wanton Goat shall on your Altars die,
And spicy Smoak in Curls ascend the Sky.
A Pig thy Floors with sacred Blood shall stain,
And round the awful Fire and holy Flame,
Thrice shall thy Priests, with Youth and Garlands
    crown'd,
In pious Drunkenness thy Orgies sound.

THE
ORACLE.

A Fragment, paraphras'd, and adapted to the modern
Times, beginning, Linque tuas sedes Juvenis, *&c.*

Hast, gen'rous Youth, a foreign World explore,
    And quit this cruel, this ungrateful Shore;
    The rapid *Rhine*, and *Ister*'s foaming Wave,
Expect a Chief so resolute and brave.
Upon their Banks you shall the War decide,
And routed Troops shall swell the purple Tide.
In vain the *French* uncertain Saints invoke,
Dunkirk once more shall feel the *British* Yoke;
Ipres our Troops, our Arms shall *Lisle* subdue,
And storm *Namur*, when reinforc'd by you.
But prudently of future Wrongs afraid,
If you deny, ungrateful Squadrons aid,
Charge with the *Prussian* Foot, or *Danish* Horse,
And Lines defended by the Household Force.
Or if your Thoughts on bolder Hazards run,
Fir'd by the Rays of a *West-Indian* Sun,
O'er unknown Ways your daring Fleet shall go
Far to the *South* of burning *Mexico*:
No more in Gems their Pagan Gods shall shine,
But all the Treasures of the *West* be thine.
Ulysses bury'd in his barren Isle,
Illustrious *Greece*, by Banishment and Toil,
His adverse Fate did but his Worth approve,
And fighting Goddesses pursu'd his Love.

CHloe, you write to me for Coin,
   And in Return I send you Wine,
   Like Wealth, its Pow'r is equally divine.
E'en stick to that, 'twill make you merry,
For mine or others Absence chear ye ;
That softens ev'ry Nymph that's cruel,
For mellow *Venus* is a Jewel.
So *Ariadne*, when her Wanderer,
False *Theseus*, left her, wash'd off Grief and Care,
Enjoy'd God *Bacchus*, and became a Star.

TH' Almighty's Image, of his Shape afraid, \
And hide the noblest Part e'er Nature made, \
Which God alone succeeds in his creating \
    Trade. \
The Fall this *Fig-leav'd* Modesty began, \
To punish Woman, by obscuring Man ; \
Before, where'er his stately Cedar mov'd, \
She saw, ador'd, and kiss'd the Thing she lov'd. \
Why do the Gods their sev'ral Signs disclose, \
Almighty *Jove* his Thunder-bolt expose, \
Neptune his Trident, *Mars* his Buckler shew, \
Pallas her Spear to each Beholder's View, \
And poor *Priapus* be alone confind \
T'obscure the Womens God, and Parent of Man- \
    kind ? \
Since free-born Brutes their Liberty obtain, \
Long hast thou* Journey-work'd for Souls in vain. \
Storm the *Pantheon*, and demand thy Right, \
For on this Weapon 'tis depends the Fight.

Anima ex Traduce.

Cupid *crucify'd*. *Written in* Latin *by* Ausonius.
Aeris in Campis, memorat quos Musa Maronis,
&c.

Ithin the Aerial Fields by *Maro* sung,
   That to the gloomy State of *Dis* belong,
   Where Myrtle Groves the frantick
    Lovers shade,
The HEROINES kept their Orgies in the Glade.
Each in her Hand the fatal Weapon bore,
That sent her bleeding to the *Stygian* Shore,
In pathless Woods, in Desarts waste and wide,
By a malignant Light they wand'ring glide,
Thro' drowsy Poppies, and thro' sedgy Brakes,
O'er silent Brooks, and smooth unruffled Lakes,
Around whose rueful Banks were thinly spread
The drooping Flow'rs of various Heroes dead ;
Uncheer'd by any Sun, they languid lay,
And scarce distinguish'd by the sickly Ray.
The self-belov'd *Narcissus* there was found,
And *Hyacinthus* slain by foreign Wound.
The golden Saffron, and the purple Flow'r,
Dy'd with the Blood of *Venus* Paramour.
All that could make their Sorrows yet survive,
And keep the Memory of Pain alive ;
In spight of Death the *Heroines* compel
To feel below the Woes by which they fell,
Recal their fatal Scenes of hap'less Love,
That rag'd within their tender Hearts above ;
The Loss of Life no Loss of Grief obtain'd,
For e'en in Death their fond Desires remain'd.

Poor *Semele*, lost by *Juno*'s curs'd Deceit,
Deplores, in empty Tears, her dreadful Fate ;
The Midwife-Thunder still renews her Pain,
And she laments her blasted Joys again ;
While the dissembled Light'ning's idle Flame
She waves around, she feels the mimick Wounds
    the same.
Cænis with Rage upbraids her Lover God,
That rules the wat'ry Kingdoms with his Nod,
That with fallacious Gifts he but betray'd
An injur'd, yet a fond believing Maid,
When in a fleeting Manhood he deny'd
The Sum of all her Wishes and her Pride ;
Since forc'd to her old Figure to return,
She here must still her ravish'd Honour mourn.
Still *Procris* stenching of her blood is found,
Yet blessing still the Hand that gave the Wound ;
Fond of the Hand that sent the fatal Dart,
Her *Cephalus* still fills her love-sick Heart.
The *Sestian* Maid down to the fatal Shore,
Where here belov'd *Leander* lay before,
The smoaky Taper head-long with her bore.
The manly *Sappho*, without Fear or Dread,
Threatens to leap from off the cloudy Head
Of lofty *Leucade*, a Med'cine sure,
And by the Gods, for Love, a promis'd Cure.
The sad *Eriphyle* does still refuse
Harmonia dang'rous Ornaments to use.
Here all the Stories of the Aerial *Crete*,
In dusky Images appear compleat.
Pasiphae does the snowy Bull pursue,

And *Ariadne* bears the fatal Clew.
The love-sick *Phædra* with dispairing Eyes,
Her Suit rejected with her Letters spies ;
This bears the Noose, her wretched End to own,
And that the Shadow of her empty Crown.
Here Laodamia *still renews her Pains,*
And of her disappointed Love complains,
Hoping her Lord from Trojan *Wars in vain.*
He first of Grecians *fell upon that Coast,*
She first of Grecians *there a Husband lost ;*
A Husband dearer to her, than her Life,
So fierce a Lover she, so fond a Wife !
The Fates in pity of her wild despair,
Gave him again to her impetuous Pray'r ;
But oh ! the fleeting Gift is of one Night,
For with the dawn he takes eternal flight,
And she thro' Shades pursues his gloomy way,
Resolv'd no more to view the hostile Day.
Sorrow, or Rage appear'd in every Face,
And e'ry Hand a naked Sword did grace.
Thisbe *and* Canace ; *the* Sidonian *Queen,*
With mournful Eyes and armed Hands were seen.
This bore her Husband's Sword, her Father's that,
And this her Guest's, the Causes of their Fate
Unhappy Dido *wanders through these Groves,*
To seek the Faithless Fugitive she loves.
Thus horn'd Diana *with her starry Crown,*
And her pale Torch, in duskie Night, alone,
Through Latmian *Hills her secret Steps convey'd,*
With strange desires, to the dear conscious Shade,
Where her Endymion *in kind Sleep was laid,*

To feed her odd fantastick Love with Bliss,
That reach'd no farther than an empty Kiss.
A thousand more about dejected rove,
Repeating still the Wounds of ancient Love,
With sweet, yet sad Complaints their Pains renew,
Pleas'd yet to suffer for their being true.
   Amidst this mournful Train, for want of Eyes,
Uncautious Love with sounding Pinnions flies;
His flaming Torch, with hostile Light dispels,
The native darkness of those dismal Cells.
All knew the fatal Boy, one common smart,
His presence gave to e'ry love-sick Heart.
Tho' humid Clouds obscure his shining Belt,
And his gay Quiver now but faintly shone,
Yet to the conscious Troop the guilty God was known.
They rouze their empty Vigour by consent,
All, to revenge their ancient Ills, are bent:
Their common Foe had ta'en a devious Flight
Beyond his Empire, to the Realms of Night.
So thronging close into a Crowd, they press
Upon the trembling God; who in distress,
In vain designs to make a swift Retreat;
All thoughts of safety came, alas! too late.
Into the middle of this furious Throng,
The captive Deity is dragg'd along,
   A well-known Myrtle in this dismal Grove,
Is chose to execute the God of Love;
A Tree invidious to the Gods of yore,
For on this Tree Adonis hung before.
The God they fix upon the loftiest Bough,
His Hands behind him ty'd, his Feet below;
Their Threats no bounds, no moderation know.

And LOVE accus'd, without a Judge or Crime,
Is guilty made in that infernal Clime.
Each would her self of proper Faults absolve,
And on the suffering God their Guilt devolve,
And each with furious exprobating Breath,
Prepares the cruel Instrument of Death.
This is their Glory, their malignant Joy,
Their sweet Revenge upon the captive Boy,
To punish him with the same Weapon here,
By which above she fell in her Despair.
This holds the Noose on high with eager Hand;
And this the Dagger with her Gore distain'd.
This brings the Image of the hollow Stream,
And this the lofty Rock, and this the Flame.
Some, as relenting, only seem to play,
And with a gay Insult but mock their Prey:
While subtil Points of airy Weapons draw
Nectareous Blood from out some little flaw.
From the nectareous Blood springs up the Rose,
That does its Parent, in its Blush, disclose.

   Amid these wild Debates and Tumults loud,
Bright Venus *safely penetrates the Crowd;*
Obnoxious as her Son to their Decree,
Yet, by th' Injustice of the Sex, *is free.*
She brings no Joy to drooping Cupid's *Grief,*
She gives no Help, she offers no Relief;
But doubling, with contracted Brow, his Pain,
The pausing Furies she provokes again:
Upbraids him loudly with her own Disgrace,
How oft he made her d at on M rta! Race.
That he expos'd her, as a publick View,

In Vulcan's *Net, to all the heavenly Crew.*
But not content with angry Words, she chose
A Rod made up of many a new-born Rose,
And gave the weeping Boy a thousand Blows.
The frequent Blows by repetition drew
From his bruis'd Flesh a sweet and purple Dew.
The purple Dew a nobler Red supplies,
And the faint Rose with double Blushes dies.
Mov'd with the Sufferings of the lovely Boy,
Their furious Threats no more his Ears annoy,
Accusing Venus *of excess of Rage,*
The Heroins strive her anger to asswage.
And each ascribes her Death to cruel Fate,
And not to Cupid's *Fury or his Hate.*
The pious Mother thanks the gentle Dames
For quitting of her Son, his Darts and Flames.
The Crowd disperse each to her several Care,
Alone to groan, eternally despair;
And Cupid *upward took his speedy flight,*
Resolv'd no more to seek the Realms of Night.

THE
FABLE
OF
PASIPHAE.

Beginning, Filia Solis, &c.

By Mr. Tho. Brown.

THE Daughter of the glorious Sun
    Wanders to her self unknown ;
Burning with new and monstrous Fires,
Raving Pangs, and impotent Desires ;
Roving o'er the Lawns and Meads,
Among the horned Herd her frantick Life she leads.
    The decent Honours of her Nuptial Bed,
    The Royal Dignity, nor Name,
      Nor care of her great Husband's Fame
      Aw her with a modest Shame ;
The care of Honour, Fame, and Modesty is fled.
    Her charms, that Women ever prize,
    The force of her victorious Eyes,
    The ruddy Beauties of her Face,

In which the Sex their greatest Glories place,
With indignation, she does now despise,
Since the white Bull insensible remains
Of all their Darts, and all their amorous Chains.
    The Cow's more happy Figure she admires,
    The Cow's more happy Figure she desires,
    Proportion'd more to her unhappy Fires.
She Prætus *wand'ring Daughters happy deems,*
  Doom'd by the angry Wife of Jove
To range with Herds, the Forest and the Grove.
  Jo *to her most blessed seems*
  Not for the Honours of Jove's Bed,
    Or for the nobler Fame
Which she obtain'd in Isis *sacred Name ;*
But for the Horny Honours of her Head.
  When Fortune smiles upon her Fires,
    And gratifies her wild desires,
About his sinewy Neck she'll throw
Her Arms, more white than driven Snow ;
  His Horns she'll deck with all the Flow'rs
  That spring from April's *pregnant Showers.*
Her balmy Lips she to the Bull will join,
    To ease the rigour of her Pain.
    Th' outragious force of Cupid's *Darts,*
  Fires with daring boldness Female Hearts.
  Unlawful Arts she now imploys
  To reap the foul detested Joys.
For by Dædalian *Skill she pregnant grows,*
And does a double Nature soon disclose ;
Which the Cecropian Theseus *slew,*
Conducted to his Fate by Ariadne's *Clew.*

The End of Petronius Arbiter.

256